High Battle Cry

By

David Falash

This one is for my son, Avery

No Man's Sky
Memoirs Book 5

The last chapters of my previous book (No Man's Sky) recounted the death of the Red Baron, Manfred von Richthofen, and my subsequent adventure aboard a training flight of the new super zeppelin L-70. Having encountered gas leaks and engine trouble, the giant airship was coming down for repairs over the German town of Freiburg when it was attacked by four French Nieuport 28's. I was dropped from the zeppelin in a Pfalz D.III to help give the ship cover while it climbed to escape. During the dogfight with the Nieuports, I was forced to flee westward deep into enemy territory. Having managed to escape my pursuers - but cutoff from returning to any friendly confines - I decided to fly on for the Seine River near Troyes. I was incredibly fortunate not to be harassed by Allied planes during the journey. After landing the Pfalz in a secluded area, I headed on foot for the nearby Seine. A river taxi operator offered me an expensive ride all the way to Paris but then tried to steal my money clip at gunpoint. The robbery attempt ended badly for the pirate. I took his motorboat to the city of light, and from there I hailed a taxi and rode twelve miles to Versailles and the Chateau de Guerintaux. A gleeful Maurice the butler was there to greet me and announced that my beloved Michelle was at home.

Mick Gallagher
Dublin
January, 1971

1
Balearic Getaway

The 1.5 carat diamond engagement ring fit snuggly above the second knuckle of my right little finger. Before making our way to the beach, I'd concealed the ring in the front pocket of my black swimming trunks and inconspicuously slipped it on just before Michelle and I entered the clear, turquoise colored water of Menorca's Saint Tomas beach. I rotated the diamond under my finger lest my wife-to-be catch a glimpse of the sparkling gem. Unless she suddenly grabbed hold of my hand, there'd be no way for her to discover the instrument of my proposal before I was ready.

My original plan was to 'hide' the ring either inside or underneath an eye-catching shell of some kind while we explored the rocky shallows. It would then be easy for me to strategically guide Michelle back to the selected shell and wait for her eruption of joy.

However, the plan would radically change after meeting a 60-something beanpole of a man who caught our attention while stretching his overly tanned arms and legs on shore a few yards from us.

"*Halo cómo estás,*" said the waving, skimpily-trunked stranger.

"Hi ya," I replied.

"Oh - hello there. I should have guessed you are not Spanish."

"No, far from it. Easy to tell where I'm from, yeah?"

The man laughed heartily. "One of my very best friends is Irish like you. My name is Miguel Serrano."

"I'm . . . Mick, Mick Coburn - and this here is my girlfriend, Michelle." Using my real last name was still too dangerous out in public.

"*Bonjour* Miguel," greeted Michelle.

"And *bonjour* to you," Miguel returned with a slight bow of his head. "My, my, my . . . You are the prettiest young lady I have ever seen on this island."

"Try all of Europe," I playfully corrected. "But it doesn't matter what we or anyone else says Miguel. She thinks she's only average in looks."

Michelle elbowed me in the ribs. "Would you stop? I don't always think that."

"Yes you do."

The tall and thin Spaniard frowned as he stepped forward into the watery sand. "My dear, all the flattery in the world cannot equal what you deserve. And Mick, you remind her of that every day, all right?"

"I do, sir, and I always will."

"Good man. - After you're finished looking for shells, you might want to swim out to the shipwreck. That's where I'm going now."

"What shipwreck?" I asked.

Miguel pointed behind me. "Fifty yards out . . . you see that big rock sticking out of the water?"

"Yeah."

"Now look left . . . Do you see that triangle-shaped object twenty yards from the rock?"

"I see it," Michelle said.

"Me, too," I answered. "It looks like the edge of a wooden crate or something."

"That's no wooden crate," Miguel stated. "It's the rusty bow of the *Estrela Vento* – which means 'Star Wind' in English – a Portuguese merchant ship that sunk in 1877. It ran aground on the hidden rocks during a bad storm. The water isn't too deep out there - sixty feet at the wreck site, but from the beach the water gets over your head quickly. Are you a good swimmer?"

"Oh, I can keep from drowning I guess. Michelle here is the Olympic swimmer - and I'm not foolin' ya."

This time Michelle left my ribs alone and smiled modestly. "I'd like to go see it. Don't you want to, Mick?"

"Yeah, sure. Your folks and Claudette will still be able to see us when they get here."

"*Magnifico!*" Miguel enthused. "Let me put on my diving belt and I will take you to the wreck."

Maybe I can put the ring on the rock someplace? I thought. *That would be grand!*

* * * * *

The late June sun beat down on us as we swam toward the 10-foot wide jutting rock. Miguel was a fast swimmer, and he was determined to be the first one there. Michelle could have easily outmatched him (and I might have been able to keep up with him), but she stayed at my leisurely pace right beside. The idyllic water was coolly refreshing on a day that pushed the thermometer near 90 degrees. Silver gulls and Balearic shearwaters, the most common birds of the Balearic Islands, soared over our heads, circling and swooping as they squawked. I could easily see the seaweed-strewn bottom through my diving goggles. The Mediterranean Sea was alive with a variety of fish, mollusks, and starfish.

When we reached the slippery rock, Miguel was completely out of the water sitting on a large flat section. There was plenty of room for all of us. I climbed up first, then helped Michelle sit down.

"That wasn't too bad," I said.

"You both are excellent swimmers," Miguel commented. "You can really see the ship now. It's leaning against the rock formation that caused it to sink. When you run out of breath you can latch onto the bow instead of swimming back to the rock."

Michelle jiggled her shoulders and swept back her long brunette hair. "This is exciting. Maybe we can find a treasure."

Miguel shook his head. "Every millimeter of this wreck has been searched. There is nothing of value to be found."

"Rats," Michelle replied. "But wouldn't it be amazing if we did find something buried in the ocean floor near the ship?"

"There's only one way to find out," I said, looking down at my side at a slightly recessed part of the rock that would make an ideal spot for the ring.

There we go . . . perfect.

I slipped off the ring and set the diamond near my hip.

"Both ready?" asked Miguel.

"Let's go," I said.

Miguel checked the knife on his diving belt and adjusted his goggles. "We may see some moray eels, and they can get angry if you mess with them. There will be triggerfish, too. If you get near their eggs they might bite."

"What about sharks?" asked Michelle.

"If we see any they'll be blues. They'll leave you alone if you mind your business. If they start getting too aggressive we'll get out of there – but I've never had a problem. Nothing to worry about, my dear. We have the best possible diving conditions today. - Follow me!"

Gerard Guerintaux started flipping his birthday celebration on its head when he was in his late teens. Instead of accepting presents from others, he'd buy gifts for family and close friends instead. This year, his 61st birthday, was no exception; however his family all received the same gift: a fortnight holiday trip to anywhere reasonable given the current state of the war. The travelers would be Gerard and Marci, Beau and his fiancé Christine Larango, Cousin Claudette, and Michelle and me. Michelle's older sister Gabrielle and her husband Vincent were also invited to come along, but they had already made travel plans of their own in Switzerland and northern Italy.

So where would we be going?

After a half hour of friendly debate, the only thing we could agree on was that the trip should be to somewhere in the western Mediterranean - not too far away but not too close either. Marci voted for Sicily, Michelle picked Sardinia (so I did, too), Beau was passionate about Corsica, Christine and Claudette were happy to be going anywhere. Gerard had to finally put his foot down and make an executive decision. His choice surprised us all, though it proved to be unanimously popular: the Balearic Islands.

"The islands have spectacular beaches, breathtaking scenery, unique shopping opportunities, savory cuisine to die for, and not an overwhelming number of holiday seekers," Gerard said at his June 3rd birthday dinner, a little over a month since I'd adventurously returned from the Flying Circus via zeppelin, airplane, motor boat, and Paris taxi.

* * * * *

I'd spent the weeks of respite basking in leisurely pleasures with Michelle and the Guerintaux family. Of course I played a ton of golf, and it was especially fun because Michelle tagged along most of the time. She really took to the game. Her day-to-day improvement was nothing short of remarkable.

"If I keep improving at this rate, I might have to enter a local tournament," she joyfully commented while walking off the 18th green after sinking a seven-foot putt to save par.

"Don't get *too* good," I said. "If you get better than me then our relationship will suffer a double bogey."

* * * * *

I hadn't seen my good friend Paul Coburn since December when he'd surprised me with a visit for my 16th birthday. It was now my turn to go see him, but the only surprise in my four-day visit was the telephone call announcing it. I knew that he and his family had moved to Bordeaux in March.

My bleach-blond hair, tweed cap, and sunglasses hid all traces of my Emerald Ace identity while we were out in public. Even without the hat and sunglasses I didn't raise any eyebrows joining Paul's second place rugby league team as a temporary player: 'Connor Coburn' - Paul's visiting American cousin. I played in two pivotal games and was a key factor in both wins. The coach, elated that his team was back in first place, was mightily impressed with my performances. And mightily bummed that I couldn't stay.

"Next time we'll play some hurling and golf," I said to Paul as I stepped aboard the departing train.

"Yeah, I owe you one."

"See ya soon sometime."

"Say hi to Michelle for me. Don't you be marrying her without me there."

"Impossible."

The day after I got back was Gerard's birthday.

* * * * *

"I think the Balearics are a wonderful choice," Michelle confirmed.

"Glad to have your approval," said Gerard. "In fact, I considered taking all of us there for your birthday a couple of weeks ago, but business matters precluded that. As it turned out, the weather wasn't very good."

"That's all right, Father," Michelle said, casting a warm smile at me. "Having Mick here for my birthday was the best present possible."

"Awww . . ." I muttered.

Gesturing at me, Gerard said, "The Balearics have plentiful remnants of a long, rich history that I know you will find fascinating. We will need to be back no later than the first of July in order to prepare for Beau's wedding on the 14th. I've prepared a basic itinerary that will enable us to visit the four main islands - Mallorca, Menorca, Ibiza, and Formentera - allowing for plenty of flexible time to either reduce or extend our various stays. And to answer the question that I know Beau is thinking right now . . ."

Everyone at the table - including Maurice, who abruptly stopped filling Gerard's coffee cup - snapped a look at Beau, who had uneasily stiffened straight in his seat.

"Question, Father?" Beau said slyly. "And what might that be?"

Gerard grinned and held out his coffee cup for Maurice to top-off. "You're wondering about my diving accident, aren't you?"

"Why would he be thinking of that?" asked a dumbfounded Marci.

"Mother," Beau said, "don't tell me you've forgotten where the accident occurred?"

Marci's eyes lit up. "Goodness! Oh of course! It happened in the Balearics . . . on Menorca, right dear?"

"How can I forget?" Gerard replied with a nostalgic half-frown. "The 7th of August, 1878. I was 21, with a full head of the blackest hair back then."

"Hair or no hair," Marci interjected with a loving smile, "you are as handsome as ever, dear."

Gerard graciously nodded and kissed his wife of thirty-five years on her cheek. "I'd taken a ferry steamer from Barcelona and arrived in Menorca to participate in the Iberian Cliff Diving Championship. The competition was held at the cliffs of Arenal D'en Castell on Menorca's northern coast. I had some trouble making my way there and missed the entry deadline by twenty minutes. Fortunately, a nice registration official bent the rules and let me into the contest." Gerard shook his head blankly and took a long sip of coffee. "From a height of 26 meters, my first dive was close to perfect. After the opening round I had the top score out of eight competitors. It was my second dive that went disastrously wrong. The wind had gathered strength and was blowing across the cliff in powerful gusts. In hindsight the contest should have been postponed until the winds died down. Anyway, at the start of the dive, right as my feet left the rock, a gust caught me and threw off my front tuck. Stupidly I tried to keep it going. My body hit the water at a crazy angle - almost sideways. It felt like I had fallen onto concrete. They had to rescue me or I would have drowned. I could hardly move."

"How bad was your neck?" I asked.

"Not good. I was put onto a ferry and taken to a Barcelona hospital. They had a brand new X-ray machine and took pictures of my neck. The pictures showed partial fractures in two of the upper vertebrae. A complete fracture would have either killed me of left me paralyzed from the neck down. - So, thus ended my diving career."

"How awful!" cried Michelle. "You had never told me the details of the accident."

"Forgive me. It's not my favorite topic of discussion."

"Have you been back to Menorca since?" asked Christine, herself a practicing nurse.

"Not to Menorca, but I did visit Mallorca and Ibiza in the mid-90's."

"Will we be going back to the scene of your accident?" Michelle inquired.

"I would like to - if time allows for it."

"We'll make time, Father," Beau insisted. "In your honor I will jump - *not dive* - from the exact point you did."

"And I will jump with you," Gerard said triumphantly. "My neck has calcified plenty for me to do that."

"If you don't mind, I'd like to join you guys," I said.

"Of course," Gerard replied. "Anyone else care to jump with us?"

* * * * *

We left Paris by train on the 16th of June and traveled southwest with stops in the cities of Toulouse and Perpignan before crossing into neutral Spain. Gerard had a fictitious identity professionally prepared for me. The flawless passport and other travel documents carried the name Michael Fitzpatrick.

After spending a relaxing night in Barcelona (where the evening was topped-off with an outrageously expensive meal of hot egg and cheese *tapas* and deliciously sweet Iberian pork), we boarded a newly refurbished 300-passenger steamship and sailed for Ibiza, the most distant Balearic island. Gerard thought that it would be better to work our way northeast from Ibiza to Mallorca and sail back to Barcelona from Menorca, that way we could do the nostalgic cliff jump on our final day before departing the islands.

The relaxing 10-hour boat journey through the calm Mediterranean waters was a delightful experience, the longest time I'd spent at sea in my brief 16-year-old life. Our ship made port in Eivissa, Ibiza's largest and most beautiful city.

After a busy day of strolling through Eivissa's vibrant hilltop streets, the seven of us spent the next two days exploring many of the island's sites relating to its prehistoric and ancient Carthaginian past. We also squeezed in a four-hour excursion to the small island of Formentera (32 sq. miles) and enjoyed a lazy afternoon at Platja Migjorn beach. Michelle taught me the basics of snorkeling and we kicked around an unclaimed rubber ball with Beau, Christine, and Claudette.

The gorgeous sunny weather followed us over to Mallorca, the biggest and most populous island. We spent a full day in the capital city of Palma wandering around the shops of Placa Major Square and the wide corner avenue of Passeig d'es Born. The next morning, we took the "Red Arrow" electric train to Soller to visit the lush Moorish gardens of Jardines de Alfabia and three of Mallorca's nearly 200 limestone caves. One of these enormous caves contained an underground lake on which a flatboat carried a quintet of musicians. Taking advantage of the excellent acoustic qualities afforded by the cave, the floating band joyfully played their instruments to the delight of the two dozen visitors.

An entire day at Cala Millor was followed by a sightseeing drive around Mallorca's southern coast to Cala Major. Along the way we trekked to the top of Puig de Randa hill for some stunning views of the entire island.

The last leg of our holiday was Menorca, the second largest Balearic island. Less crowded than both Mallorca and Ibiza, Menorca offered us more isolation, a quieter atmosphere, and ground dotted with many 3,000 year-old monuments. It was in Mao, the island's largest city, that I sneaked away long enough to pop into a small jewelry shop and purchased Michelle's engagement ring. The selection wasn't great and I didn't have a lot of time, but the lady who helped me picked out a nice diamond that fit my price range of 80 pounds.

Saint Tomas beach was our main stop the next day, an ideal location to make a formal marriage proposal. It was here during the mid-afternoon when Michelle and I encountered Miguel Serrano.

2
Blood Diamond

The hull of the *Estrela Vento* loomed before us in the crystalline water, a ghostly, brownish leviathan of moss-covered steel. An abundance of colorful sea-life streamed about the artificial coral reef, scattering every which way as we approached. I hadn't a clue as to what triggerfish were, but I knew what a moray eel was. The pictures I'd seen of them looked pretty menacing. What about blue sharks? I'd never heard of them before. The only shark names I knew were 'tiger' and 'hammerhead,' and this was because of a story I remember reading in primary school.

No sense worrying about eels and sharks, I thought. *Miguel knows what he's doing. Just enjoy the dive.*

Michelle followed close beside me as we tailed Miguel down along the side of the vessel. We passed a cluster of golden starfish and a watermelon-sized orange octopus clinging tensely to a porthole. I was anxious to go inside the ship and explore the labyrinth of corridors and rooms, but already I was feeling my lungs beginning to strain. At that moment Michelle tapped my shoulder and pointed to the surface. Up she went. I wasn't far behind her.

We reached the surface and swam to the jutting bow. Once there it took us a short while to catch our wind. Before I could say anything, Michelle planted a kiss on my lips.

A long kiss.

"Wow!" I said, lifting my goggles. "Didn't expect that."

"I love you, Mick. During the dive I was suddenly overcome with elation. My whole body began to twinge! I'm so happy!"

I gave her a short return kiss. "Me, too. Maybe we'll both be overcome with elation every time we go down there. If that happens, we could be kissing all afternoon."

Michelle twinkled her eyes at me. Looking about, she said, "Miguel should be showing soon."

"The man might have grown gills with all the diving he's done."

"Oh, there he is."

* * * * *

"You'll be able to stay down longer each time," Miguel said, jiggling a finger in his ear to get some water out. "Your lungs will adjust and your body will learn to relax. You will double, or possibly triple the length of your breaths."

"Is there a quick way to get inside the ship?" I asked.

"Yes, there is. We'll go on the port side of the ship this time. There's an open hatch on the deck. From where we are now it's only twenty-five feet away."

"Grand. Anything we need to know before going in?"

"It's dark, and you can easily get lost. If you panic, you will probably drown. The mercury-vapor lamp that I put inside last week quit working yesterday, so we'll only have sunlight. I'll retrieve the lamp on this dive. I could have it working again by later today."

"I'm going to stay glued to your side," Michelle said, clutching my arm.

"Very wise," Miguel replied. "Always know where the hatch is. Keep it in your view. We'll never get anymore sun shining down there than we have this afternoon."

"Probably a dumb question," I said, "but Michelle's not going to see any crewmen bones or anything, right?"

"No. No one died in the storm. All of the crew evacuated safely before the vessel went down."

"And what about blue sharks and eels? All good there?"

"Didn't see them. – Got your lungs back?"

"We do. We're ready to go."

* * * * *

It only took a few seconds to get to the meter-wide open hatch. Without any hesitation, Michelle followed Miguel inside the *Estrela Vento* with me trailing at her heels. To my left, Miguel was holding onto a fixed ladder that led deeper into the ship. Showing us our exploratory options, he pointed down to the next level and then straight ahead into a spooky-looking corridor. It didn't matter to me where we went, so I brushed my hand at him to indicate it was his call.

I was pleased at how my lungs seemed to be holding more air this time. Being more relaxed sure made a difference. Doubling my dive time would be a cinch. I hoped Michelle was feeling the same.

Miguel set off down the corridor. Michelle and I followed him side by side with me slightly ahead. The natural light faded quickly, and soon I could barely see the white soles of Miguel's feet. Suddenly Miguel stopped swimming, causing me to bump into him. He reached out for a football-sized glass and metal object hanging from a hook – what I assumed to be the out-of-order mercury-vapor lamp. It didn't come off the hook easily, and Miguel began trying to shake it loose. Moments later his right hand shot back as if he'd been bitten.

He must have cut himself, I thought.

A thin trail of blood started leaking away from his body, confirming my inference. Miguel pointed at the lamp and shook his head, indicating its dysfunction. Then he pointed farther down the corridor.

Must be another lamp down there.

Miguel twisted around and swam off like a human torpedo. There was no way I could follow him. My air was running out. I tugged on Michelle's arm and bobbed my head up. We made for the surface.

* * * * *

"Can we go over to the rock for a minute?" Michelle asked upon reaching the bow. "I'm feeling a little light-headed."

"Yeah, me, too. Probably normal. Our bodies are trying to adjust."

The perfect time for her to find the ring! I thought.

Once we reached the rock, I helped Michelle out of the water at a section where I'd knew she'd see the diamond. It didn't take her long to find it.

"Mick . . . what - what is this? - Oh my heavens!"

I pulled my legs onto the rock and scooted next to Michelle wearing the biggest smile of my life.

"Mick . . . I . . . I love it! When did you . . ." She slipped on the ring. "It's beautiful! And it fits perfectly!"

"Yeah, so you see . . . I was wondering if maybe we might like to keep each other company for the next, oh I don't know, seventy years or so."

Michelle threw her arms around me. "You silly Irishman! I was wondering when we would make it official."

"So are you saying *yes*?"

Michelle kissed my cheek. "Yes. - *Oui, oui, oui, oui, yes.*"

"Oh grand, what a relief," I playfully replied.

"Sure you're relieved - because we've only known we were going to be married since the day we met!"

"There you are," Miguel called out from the bow. "Taking a rest are you?"

"Something like that," I said. "How's your hand - all right, yeah?"

"It's stinging, but the bleeding has subsided. The other lamp is working and the light is good. Are you coming down for another dive?"

"We will here in a minute. We're doing a bit of celebrating at the moment."

Michelle wiggled her ring finger in the air. "Mick and I are engaged."

"You don't say? How fabulous! Congratulations to you!"

"Thanks," I said.

Miguel's shoulders suddenly jerked around right . . . then left. He bobbed his face in the water. Pulling himself higher up the bow, he drew his diving knife and began thrashing it wildly about.

"What's wrong?" I shouted.

"Something touched my feet . . . I think it's a - *ahhh!*"

Miguel vanished.

A huge scythe of gray shot out of the water and splashed down.

* * * * *

"Jaysus!" I cried. "A shark!"

Michelle screamed.

I froze.

For a few seconds the image of the shark's tail was all I could see. The shocking scene hung in the air like a surreal three-dimensional painting. Staring out to sea, I sat paralyzed while my thoughts were thrown into a mental blender.

Then I snapped out of it.

I gotta do something!

But what? Was Miguel Serrano already dead? Could he escape the shark? Could he be rescued?

Michelle's fingernails dug into my arm as she screamed again.

Think!

And at that moment, Miguel reappeared. Minus his goggles and snorkel, he broke the surface just in front of the bow and began swimming frantically for the rock.

"Swim Miguel!" I shouted. "Swim man!"

"The shark!" Michelle hollered, pointing off to Miguel's right. About twenty-five yards adjacent to him an enormous dorsal fin was slicing through the glistening blue water. The tip of the shark's crescent tail glided rhythmically six-feet behind.

"Keep swimming!" I yelled. "You're gunna make it!"

I gauged the distance between Miguel, the shark, and the rock. Miguel had a chance, but the race was going to be very close.

With Michelle crouched next to me, I extended my body from the rock and reached out my arm. "You're almost there! Come on man! Don't look back, just swim!" To Michelle, I said, "Hold tight to my legs. Get some leverage!"

"All right - be careful Mick! Don't go in!"

The huge shark, easily fifteen feet from head to tail, was gaining on him, rapidly cutting the distance as Miguel slowed. By this point he was almost exhausted. His left arm wasn't doing much; he could barely get it out of the water. Miguel was close enough now that I could see the pool of blood trailing him. It was attached to his back like a liquid cape.

I strained my arm out another inch or two. "Don't stop! Keep going!"

Five feet . . . four . . . three . . .

"Got ya!"

The grip wasn't great, but it held firm to allow me to haul Miguel forward enough so I could latch on with both hands. "There we go!" I pulled as hard as I could. "Keep ahold Michelle! Pull my legs back!"

As Miguel's torso lifted from the water, I saw the gaping bite that had been taken out of his side. One of the shark's teeth was stuck into the shredded, sinewy flesh. Miguel was losing a lot of blood. He let out a guttural moan as he gasped to catch his breath.

The shark kept coming, now only several yards away. Its snout rode above the water's surface, exposing massive jaws filled with rows of white triangular teeth.

"Almost - almost!" I hollered. "Get your legs up!"

Miguel's right knee lifted from the water. He slipped once, and then found a foothold on the rock. Now for the other leg.

Only there wasn't another leg. It had been bitten off at mid-thigh.

Instantly nauseated, I heaved with all my might in an attempt to throw Miguel forward. But it was a second too late. Rising out of the ocean, the great white shark blocked out the hazy sun behind Miguel and chomped onto his left hip. The power of the fish was incredible. Miguel was snatched away in a flash.

And me along with him.

* * * * *

I plunged into the water feeling like my right arm had been pulled out of its socket. Despite the searing pain, my first thought was for Michelle. Her grip around my calves had given way, so I didn't think she'd followed me in. I surfaced quickly to discover the rock was only five yards away. Michelle, horrified but safe, was sprawled flat on her stomach with both arms extended. With my right arm out of commission, keeping my head above water wasn't easy.

"Hold out your hand!" Michelle cried. "I can lift you!"

I scissor-kicked my legs for all their worth and made long strokes with my left arm. "Do you see him?" I garbled out, spitting salty water from my mouth.

"No, he's gone. Hurry!"

A few more strokes and I'd be at the rock.

Come on . . . big kicks, long strokes . . .

My peripheral vision caught on to something.

It was a bloodied, battered, and lifeless Miguel. He'd poked above the surface and was dangling from the shark's mouth like a play toy.

And Miguel was coming straight for me!

He looked like an aquatic zombie hell-bent on eating me. His entire lower body had been bitten off. I couldn't see much of the shark.

"Go Mick!" yelled Michelle.

It was another race, this time with me as a contestant.

Two yards to go.

One yard.

I thrust my left arm out for Michelle's hand, but it was too late. Miguel's body rammed into my back and slammed me off the edge of the rock. As the shark passed, it clipped my side with its long pectoral fin. The grazing blow didn't hurt much, but it did draw some blood. I then saw the black handle of Miguel's diving knife. The blade was stuck deep into the shark, between the pelvic fin and the tail. With my good arm I instinctively made a grab for the handle. Only my thumb and index finger latched on, but I had just enough grip to yank the knife out.

After a last shake of its dead prey, the shark let go of Miguel and dove out of view. Michelle had scrambled around the rock to get herself closer to me. I was about three yards away.

"Hurry, Mick! Hurry!"

At last some life was coming back to my right arm - not a lot, but at this point any bit helped.

"Can you see the shark?"

"I don't see it," Michelle answered.

Good. Bugger off you devil!

All it took was another couple of kicks and I reached the rock. Holding the knife in my mouth, I grabbed hold of Michelle's hand. It only took one pull for me to realize that further efforts would be futile. There was no way she could haul me out of the water on this side of the rock. It was too steep and too slick with moss, and there was no place to get any leverage. My injured right arm didn't help matters either.

"Other side," I said, moving the knife enough to talk. "This way's impossible."

"Ok, go - go!"

I edged around to the rock's lower side. While doing so the mutilated half-body of Miguel Serrano suddenly floated into my path. His wide-open, blood-shot eyes stared back at me, imprinted with the torturous moments of being eaten alive. I pushed his face away and made my way around a jagged corner.

"We got it now," I said, my words barely decipherable.

"Oh my god! Here it comes!"

I pushed at the side of the rock and lunged for Michelle's outstretched hand. Her fingertips slipped from my grasp, so I tried again. This time the grip held.

"Got you!"

Michelle then tapped into a reserve of strength that would have made the Greek god Hercules proud. I rose steadily out of the water.

But where was the shark?

I looked left, then right.

Jaysus!

The great white was there - twenty feet away, swimming slowly, but dead-on for me. There wasn't time to get fully onto the rock. The shark would take me the same way it had taken Miguel.

So I let go of Michelle's hand and readied the knife.

Ok you dungfish, let's go!

The shark maintained its curiously slow speed, giving me time to mentally play out my course of action.

Don't let it get close. Stick it first.

Six feet away.

"Mick!" Michelle screamed. "Mick!"

Five . . . four . . .

Now!

Using every ounce of my strength, I pushed off the rock with my hurt arm and launched for the side of the shark's head. The knife rammed home near its right eye as I dodged the gaping jaws. I maneuvered to the side of the shark and plunged the knife repeatedly into its eye. Beginning to slip off, I stabbed the blade two times deep into its gills. The shark swam out of view, around the other side of the rock.

I was now ten yards away from Michelle.

"Swim!" Michelle shouted, frantically motioning her arms.

Ignoring the pain in my shoulder, I stroked like mad for the rock.

* * * * *

We never saw the shark again.

Michelle and I sat there on that rock, arm in arm, for another fifteen minutes until a local fisherman motored out to rescue us. Gerard, Marci, and Claudette were waiting for us on the beach.

I didn't know it was a great white at the time. The shark got caught up in a net a few days later and drowned in the shallows. From snout to tail it measured 14 feet 9 inches. If it had been a full-grown adult instead of a juvenile, I wouldn't have stood a chance. Great whites can grow to over twenty feet in length. They are responsible for more attacks on humans than any other type of shark.

Poor Miguel . . .

3
Beyond Repair

Michelle and I tried our best not to let what happened that day dampen the joy of our engagement - but it was almost impossible to do. Quite the emotional rollercoaster to say the least! The shark incident was shockingly terrifying and profoundly sad. For heaven sakes, Michelle saw a man bitten in two right in front of her! As for me, handicapped with an injured shoulder and armed with only a small diving knife, I went one-on-one against a beastly great white! And won the fight!

Janey mack! A great white shark!

The graphic images of the experience still give me the willies to this day.

* * * * *

We checked out of our St. Tomas hotel early the next morning. By private bus, we headed 13 miles northeast to the small coastal town of Arenal D'en Castell, where Gerard's cliff diving accident occurred back in the summer of 1878. Our spacious holiday villa along the spectacular sea inlet was within easy walking distance of the diving site.

"This area has hardly changed," Gerard said from the sundeck overlooking the circular beach. "There are a few more villas around than forty years ago, but that is all." Holding Marci's hand, he pointed to the towering dark cliffs. "The spot is by that stone hut near the top, see? We can walk up there after lunch."

Marci nodded uneasily. "Are you sure you want to go through with this?"

"A ridiculous question, my dear. I am not going to *dive* again - that would be insane. I am going to jump feet first, straight down. There's hardly any wind. The weather is ideal today."

"Will we jump together or separately?" I asked.

"It doesn't matter to me. Whatever you would prefer."

"Together would be fun," Beau said. "Mick?"

"Sure, grand idea."

"So be it. That's what we will do," Gerard stated. "Afterwards you two can jump as many times as you wish."

* * * * *

It was a scenic ten-minute walk up the winding ridge to the diving site. When we got there Gerard took out his new Kodak Autographic Jr. camera and asked a passerby to take several photographs of the family. Beau's fiancé, Christine Larango, was deathly afraid of heights, so we kept a prudent distance from the edge of the cliff. Next, Marci assumed camera duties and took a couple pictures of Gerard posing on the narrow jump point in his black swim trunks. Gerard then insisted that Beau and I stand alongside him for another photo. We also were wearing black swim trunks.

"I think we're ready to go," said Gerard, looking down at the still sea. "This view is giving me a strange sensation. Old memories are coming back that are as clear to me as what I was doing a minute ago. The scenery around here, the feel of this rock on my feet . . . it's as though I've been transported back in time."

"This sure looks higher than 26 meters," I commented with a tinge of apprehension in my voice.

"I'd have guessed 35 to 40," Beau agreed.

"No, it's 26 exactly," Gerard confirmed. "We never went higher than 28 meters in competition."

"Well I'm going to do a front double with a back half twist," I joked.

"*Sure* you are," Gerard said with a sardonic smirk. "When we go, both of you jump out a ways from me. We don't want to be crashing into each other when we hit the water."

"That wouldn't be good," Beau said, tying his eye-patch band around his wrist.

The three of us made a final wave at the others. With the exception of Christine, they all had an excellent view.

"You men be careful!" hollered Michelle. "No trick dives or anything like that!"

Gerard laughed. "Not to worry. See you all down below."

* * * * *

"Toes on the edge," Gerard commanded. "Relax and take an easy, deep breath. Jump with both feet, and try to stay perfectly vertical. No leaning."

"Right," I said, my mind suddenly flashing back to the leap from Seve Manon's burning lighthouse.

No worries this time. Just gravity and water. Nothing but fun.

"Let's do it!" Beau roared.

"On the count of three," Gerard said. "Ready? - *Un, due, trois!"*

We jumped from the cliff.

For a long, unsettling moment it felt like I'd leaped from an airplane. The bright azure water rushed toward me at astonishing speed. I kept my eyes open until the last moment.

Splash!

The impact wasn't as hard as I'd expected, but the depth of the plunge caused me some anxiety. Down, down, down, I went. What had I jumped into, a giant water vacuum or something?

Good god, when am I gunna go up?

When I finally began to rise, the surface seemed a mile away, and it felt like forever before I reached air. An ecstatic Gerard was right in front of me, his fist raised out of the water in triumph. Beau was there, too, partially blocked by Gerard. He was laughing up a storm.

"We did it!" I hollered. "Man alive, that was fun!"

"I'm going to jump again," Beau said. "How about you, Father?"

"No, no, once was enough," Gerard replied. "You can jump all afternoon if you want to."

I began swimming lazily to shore, and while doing so I happened to look up at the jump site.

Japers! What's she . . . what's she doing?

Michelle was standing there, with her arms extended like angel wings.

"What are you doing?" I yelled.

"Joining you, silly! You can't have all the fun! Here I come! Look out below!"

"Michelle, don't!"

"No Michelle!" Beau shouted.

She jumped.

My fiancé's arms and legs fluttered birdlike all the way down. The summer dress she had on flew up indecently, almost to her neck. Michelle made a big splash, but surfaced quickly beaming a jubilant smile.

"You wild French girl!" I cried, swimming toward her. "Nice jump!"

"Spur of the moment," she said after spotting me. "An urge came over me and I had to do it!"

"It was too dangerous for a girl!" Beau snapped.

"Oh be quiet!" Michelle fired back.

"Are you all right?" Gerard asked, also swimming closer.

"I'm perfectly fine, Father."

"Loved the view from down here!" I said. "Who says a girl needs a swimming suit?"

Beau and I jumped three more times. Michelle and Claudette (both in modest pink bathing suits) joined me for the last one - despite Beau's protest.

* * * * *

Tanned and refreshed, we left the Balearic Islands on Saturday, June 29. But not all of us were happy, namely Christine Larango. She and Beau had gotten along fine during the first part of the trip, chatting a'plenty, holding hands, and the like. However, somewhere along the way a rift developed between them. I didn't really notice anything until Michelle mentioned it one evening during a stroll along the beach at Calla Millor.

"They've been getting quiet around each other lately," she said. "One word responses, nods and shrugs. There's no spark."

"Hmm . . . I guess so. You're pretty good at detecting that sort of thing."

"Mother senses it, too. We've talked about it." Michelle suddenly tugged me toward the onrush of tide. The cool water splashed up to our knees. "Something's gone wrong," she continued, shaking her head. "It's not right. Two people who are in love and a few weeks from marrying shouldn't be acting this way."

"Ah, rough patches happen. They'll work things out. It's probably something trivial that's blown out of proportion. Try not to worry too much about it." I kissed her hand. "Not every couple can be like us ya know."

* * * * *

By the time we left for Menorca, Beau and Christine seemed to be getting along better. At least I thought so. Michelle wasn't so sure. At an opportune moment she asked her brother if anything was wrong. I wasn't privy to the short conversation.

"There's no crisis," Michelle informed me afterwards. "He said everything is fine. They've been going through some stress with the wedding coming up, that's all."

"There you go - see? It was normal stuff, nothing to worry about."

"You were right. It's just that Beau has a history of things falling apart on him. Usually it's his temper that causes the problem."

"That's not going to happen this time," I said. "He's found the right girl, and won't do anything foolish that would jeopardize the relationship. They'll be walking down the aisle in two weeks. We'll be throwing rice and roses."

"Yes, I'm so happy for them. It's going to be a lovely wedding."

* * * * *

But something traumatic happened a quarter way through the ferry journey back to Barcelona. All seemed ok when the two of them went outside to take in the view. Minutes later, Gerard and Marci saw them in a heated argument.

"You don't want to go out there right now," Gerard advised. "It's ugly. Beau's yelling and Christine is crying."

Eventually Beau came storming inside, leaving Christine on the upper deck. Without making eye contact with us, he plunked down in a far corner seat, head buried in his hand.

"That's odd - he's not raging," Michelle whispered to me. "Oh, Mick, he's upset. I've never seen him so sad, not even when he lost his brothers."

"Jaysus wept. This isn't good. Do you think I should go over there and try to talk to him?"

Michelle considered my question for a few seconds, her worried eyes glued on Beau. "Not right now," she replied. "Give him some time to settle his emotions. I'll do the same with Christine."

I lounged back in the coffee stained cushioned seat holding a wrinkled copy of *The Times*. "We can't stress about it. Your parents are pretty good counselors. This will all blow over in an hour."

* * * * *

I couldn't have been more wrong.

The storm didn't blow over. In fact, it got worse - a lot worse. Beau angrily refused to speak to anyone and didn't budge from that seat for over two hours. Most of that time he appeared to be sleeping, but I doubt he slept a wink. When Beau finally arose he skedaddled downstairs with Gerard hot on his heels.

Christine didn't show her face the entire time. Marci and Michelle tried to talk with her outside, but their repeated attempts were bluntly rejected.

"I don't know what's wrong with her," Michelle said, distraught and frustrated. "Christine's acting so strangely. I don't understand what's going on. She keeps telling us to go away and that her and Beau are through. *'It's over,'* she kept saying, again and again."

"That's all? Nothing else?"

"We couldn't get close enough to have a real conversation. Christine would yell at us and walk away. She's behaving like a bitter child. I didn't know this side of her existed. Mick, it's like she's turned into another person."

I shook my head. "Let's go get something cool to drink. All we can do is wait until things simmer down. Gerard is still with Beau. Maybe we'll find out what happened."

* * * * *

Only Gerard came over to our cafeteria table when he and Beau emerged forty minutes later. Beau made a B-line for the nearest exit door and headed determinedly outside into a drizzly rain.

"I'm afraid to ask," Marci said skittishly.

His face ashen, Gerard pulled over a chair as we made room for him to sit down. He sullenly poured himself some ice water and refilled two empty glasses before speaking. "Are you ready to hear this?"

"Of course we are," snapped Marci.

"There's not going to be a wedding. Christine has left Beau."

"What?" Marci gasped.

"Huh?" I said.

"Why would she do that?" asked Michelle.

Gerard took a long drink, then answered, "There's another man."

"Oh my god," cried Marci. "Someone else? - How could she do this to Beau?"

"That's what I'm wondering, but she has. Beau said it's an old flame from her university days. Evidently he reentered the picture last month after a long absence. He'd been away finishing medical school in the United States."

"How did Beau find out about him?" I asked.

"While we were in Ibiza, Beau discovered a very - shall I say, *friendly* - letter from this fellow on the floor of her hotel room. Christine downplayed it. She said it was just a letter from an ex-boyfriend who didn't know she was engaged to be married. Beau believed her, but that's when all the tension began between them. A few hours ago Christine told Beau the truth."

"That she's in love with this guy?" I speculated.

"Yes," Gerard answered. "Deeply in love."

Marci hissed a French obscenity. I'd never heard her swear before. There was incredulous silence for a while until Claudette asked, "So what happens now?"

Gerard fiddled with his pocket watch and shook his head dejectedly. "I don't know."

* * * * *

The thought of Michelle leaving me for another guy hadn't ever crossed my mind in a serious way until now. Just thinking about her pulling a Christine on me made my insides wobble.

During a walk around the crowded passenger lounge, I said to her, "This isn't something I should be worried about with you, is it?"

Michelle gave me one of her smirky glares. Then she pinched my arm. "You deserved that for asking such a ridiculous question."

"I'm sorry, but with all the time I've been away with the Flying Circus . . ."

"Stop it. Don't even think it. I love you, Mick. We will be married someday soon."

"Yes, I know - and I love you, too. But you've got to admit that the opportunity was there for you to have left me. Jaysus Michelle, I was gone a lot. I could have been killed so many times!"

"And yet I kept believing that we'd be together. I had faith in us - and look at us now." Michelle kissed my cheek. "I am yours forever."

* * * * *

It was about fifteen minutes later when a surprisingly calm Beau stood before us at our table. His black hair was matted from the rain. His clothes were soaked. Shivering slightly, he looked tired and emotionally spent. He didn't launch into his typical tirade of cursing, throwing glasses, and kicking chairs. Sitting rather slumped, he displayed the demeanor of a man who'd just had his heart ripped out by the girl he loved; a girl who, in two short weeks, would have become his wife.

I felt god-awful for him.

Beau Guerintaux forced a strained smile at his parents. "I'm sorry for what's happened. I apologize to you for my earlier behavior."

"You don't need to apologize, Son," Gerard replied. "This wasn't your fault."

"It's her loss," Marci said. "You don't want to be with someone who isn't fully committed to the relationship. Can you imagine if this had happened six months from now? Your marriage would have turned into a disaster."

"I've thought about that," Beau mumbled, staring at his napkin. "I should have known she was lying when I found that letter. What a naive fool I was."

"You were in love with her," Michelle said. "That letter came out of nowhere. Considering how close to your wedding day it was, her story made sense. I would have believed it, too."

"Chin-up man," I said. "There's a silver lining in this somewhere. I bet you ten to one their relationship goes down the tubes. She's a wench."

"Mick!" exclaimed Michelle.

"What? That's how I feel."

"That's all right," Beau said, showing a hint of a grin. "I called her some other names outside."

"Is she going to stay outside in the rain for the rest of the crossing?" asked Gerard.

"I think so. She told me that when the ship gets to Barcelona she will arrange her own way back to Paris."

"I wouldn't want to be around her anyway," I said bitterly. "Let her new lover boy come and get her."

"That's right," Claudette piped in. "You should wash your hands of her. Start anew."

"I'm going to do that," Beau said with an air of confidence. "It won't be easy, but I have to do that. Anything else would drive me mad."

Michelle circled around and hugged her brother. Marci and Claudette did the same. Gerard gave him a manly pat on the arm.

* * * * *

I only caught a few distant glimpses of Christine during the remaining two hours of the ferry crossing. When we arrived in Barcelona she kept ahead of us in the exit line and bolted for the nearest taxi upon entering the port station. Beau talked himself out of pursuing her. What good would it have done? He wasn't going to beg for her to reconsider. "If she wants that man over me, then so be it," Beau said.

"I bet you anything she comes crying back to you in a month," I told him while walking to catch our train. "If that happens, would the wedding be on again?"

Beau looked disgusted. "We're beyond repair. She cast me aside like a piece of rubbish. I won't marry a girl who did that to me."

"Yeah, I wouldn't either. - Hey, at least you know she wasn't after you for your money. This new guy's gotta be in the poorhouse compared to you."

Beau chuckled. "On the contrary. His father is also exceptionally wealthy. Christine will not be missing any luxuries."

* * * * *

I was spot on with my prediction: Christine Larango did come crying back to Beau in late October. She telephoned first, but Beau refused to take her call. An hour later she showed up at the chateau woefully distraught, sobbing uncontrollably. Beau told her, as kindly as he could, that the relationship was finished and that it would be best for her to get back into the taxi and move on with her life. It seems Christine's new man gave her a taste of her own medicine by dumping her for someone else.

Michelle and I weren't present to witness the incident.

Why not?

The next chapter will explain.

4
Homeland

Though Michelle and I were now formally engaged, we knew a wedding date was still a long way out. We talked about it in the dining car during the train ride from Barcelona to Paris. "Even with this ring on my finger, I'm in no hurry," Michelle said. "We are only sixteen. That's young to be getting married."

I turned my head away and quickly stuck a long piece of napkin up my nose. "Yes, but we're a *mature* sixteen."

"Oh, Mick! That's disgusting." Michelle yanked the napkin out, looking around to see if anyone had noticed. "I'm being serious. Don't you think we should wait? I'd feel better about seventeen. To me it sounds a lot older than sixteen."

"All right - seventeen. But why not wait until we're eighteen?"

"Eighteen?"

"Or how about nineteen?"

"Huh?"

"No . . . I say twenty."

"Mick, stop. You're not taking this seriously."

"Ok, ok. How about we get married around this time next year? We'll be seventeen and the war will probably be over by then. It better be. - What do you say?"

Michelle smiled. "I like it. But what date?"

"Geez, I don't care. You choose. I'll go with anything."

"Well, I like August."

"Sounds grand."

Michelle dug out a tiny calendar from her purse and flipped through it. "Saturdays are always good. So how about . . . August 9th?"

I smacked the table. "It's settled. August 9th, 1919 it is."

* * * * *

The day after we returned from the Balearics, Michelle came dashing up to me while I was cooling down after a late afternoon jog.

"I have an important question for you," she said anxiously.

"Ask away."

"I know that we're intending to start the summer session of school soon."

"Right, it begins on the 11th."

Michelle nodded. "What if you and I skipped this session and waited to begin school in the fall?"

"Why would we do that? Beau's wedding is off. We've already gone on holiday. Why not get started now?"

Michelle Guerintaux turned all giddy and sat down next to me.

"What are you up to?" I asked, rubbing shoulders with her.

"You're going to love this. Father just informed me that a business opportunity has arisen in a place you would find most appealing. He's going there next week and asked if we'd like to come along."

"Hmm . . . really? And where might this be? I find most places appealing."

"Here's an easy clue: you were born there."

My mouth dropped. "No kidding? *Ireland?*"

"Yes! Father has to spend most of his time in Dublin, but you, Mother, and me have free reign. Ten days - perhaps more!"

"Holy schmykees!" I roared, pumping my fists. "This is amazing! But what about Beau? Is he going with us?"

"No. He can't take any more leave from his flight instructor job. He's going to have a very busy July."

"With no more Christine, that's a good thing," I said. "Hey, remember that day in the library last fall? We talked about you coming to Dublin and meeting me on the O'Connell Bridge."

"Yes I remember. How could I forget?" Michelle's happy face suddenly faded. "The only thing I'm worried about is you being recognized by British soldiers there. You're a wanted man, Mick."

"*Baahh* - no worries. All I gotta do is put on a disguise again - color my hair, dark glasses, and a hat. The usual. No one's going to know it's me. I'm sure Gerard can get the necessary travel documents?"

"He will take care of that, just like in the Balearics. You won't have any trouble. Just be extremely cautious while you're there."

"You got it. I'll be a *native* tourist."

"School in the fall doesn't sound so bad now does it?"

"Geez, let's push it to the spring," I kidded. "It's been over two years since my father sent me to France - right before the Easter Rising. I've missed Ireland terribly. You're going to love it. After we explore

Dublin we can go to Cork, then drive around the Ring of Kerry. We can watch a hurling match. You can to kiss the Blarney Stone!"

Michelle wrapped her arms around me and planted a sweet kiss. "I can't wait. Until then, you can be my Blarney Stone."

* * * * *

On July 8th, with me again posing as Michael Fitzpatrick and sporting sandy blond hair, an inconspicuous hat, and sunglasses, the four of us took an early morning train to the port city of Le Havre. There we boarded the 1000 passenger steamship *Andre Lebon* and departed on time at 15:00. Only a couple of years old, the twin smokestack liner was sailing for New York City via a quick stop in Queenstown (called Cobh today). Though the Germans were still practicing unrestricted submarine warfare, the threat of a surprise u-boat attack was small. Three years before, in May of 1915, a German submarine torpedoed the *R.M.S. Lusitania* (at the time the world's largest passenger ship) off the coast of southern Ireland. 1,198 people lost their lives in the tragedy. The sinking outraged the civilized world and turned into a public relations nightmare for Germany. The last thing they needed was a similar event. Since the *Lusitania* sinking, Germany had torpedoed mainly merchant vessels and troopships sailing eastward. Identified large passenger ships sailing westward were generally left alone.

Naval mines presented more of a problem. There were many of them in the main shipping lanes between France, Britain, and Ireland. The *Andre Lebon's* captain took extra care to avoid any encounters with these nasty contact bombs, but the tradeoff made for a slow journey - about 21 hours. We didn't arrive in Queenstown until noon the next day.

Clearing customs was a breeze. Gerard happened to know one of the officials, which enabled us to be literally waived through. After a fish and chips lunch, Gerard bid adieu and caught the first train to Dublin. The plan was for us to rendezvous with him on the 17th at the Gresham Hotel, located in the heart of the city on Sackville Street (renamed O'Connell Street in 1924). Gerard hadn't been to Ireland in over twenty years. Following his business dealings, he was eager to get in what sightseeing he could.

In the days leading up to the trip, I'd used a map of the country's extensive railroad network (2,175 miles worth!) to put together an efficient 11-day itinerary: four days would be spent in the southern and western regions, two days in the Midlands, two in the north, and the last three days in the capital city of Dublin and its surroundings. Truth be known, there were some stops on the itinerary that I hadn't visited - mainly in the west and a part of the north - but I knew a lot about these areas from books and school. "It's an exhausting schedule," I warned Michelle and Marci, "but it's the only way to see the major bits of Ireland in the amount of time we have."

"That's all right with us," Marci said. "I haven't been to Ireland since I was eight years-old. We can always come back to the country later for a more leisurely stay."

Michelle agreed. "You're our tour leader. Show us as much as you can."

* * * * *

And they're off!

Our hectic schedule sure seemed like a horse race! From sun up to sundown we maximized every minute of the day. Until we arrived in Dublin eight days later, we zipped about my homeland like politicians on a whirlwind campaign tour. I was amazed at how smoothly things ran. The only minor hiccups were a thirty-minute train delay and an overheated radiator in one of our touring cars. Considering how often we ventured off the beaten tourist track, it's a wonder we never got lost on some of those backcountry roads. The weather cooperated with us too, with lots of sunshine, not too much wind, and only a few spells of rain.

Having an unlimited supply of money provided us the best of everything. We stayed at the finest hotels available, ate the best food, enjoyed first-class train tickets, utilized private transportation at specific sightseeing regions, and bought anything we wanted.

Marci, who had the biggest heart in the world, donated generously to local charities and hospitals along the way. On several occasions she purchased clothes, food, and other necessities for needy families.

With one particular family she outdid herself.

* * * * *

     Late in the afternoon of day 4, while taking an elongated scenic route back to the city of Galway, we stopped for a water break in the small market town of Foxford in County Mayo. Marci stayed in the car to rest her aching feet while Michelle and I set off to do some quick exploring. We were walking down a barren outskirt street when two waifish-looking children, no more than seven or eight years-old, appeared from nowhere and scuttled up to us. The obvious brother and sister were each holding a bundle of long yellow dandelions.

     "Please accept these flowers," the pony-tailed girl said, her smile as bright as her offering.

     "Thank you very much," Michelle replied, kneeling down to accept them. "These are so pretty - aren't they Mick?"

     "They are indeed. The loveliest flowers I've ever seen."

     "We pick them every day and give them to people who pass near our house," said the boy. "You look like tourists."

     "That we are," I said. "What are your names?"

     "My name's Erin."

     "And my name's Kevin. What are you names?"

     "I'm Mick."

     "And I'm Michelle."

     "I like those names," Erin said. "I know two other girls named Michelle."

     "Do you want to know our last names?" asked Kevin.

     "Why certainly," I said.

     "It's McGrath. My full name is Kevin Braden Michael McGrath."

     "And my full name is Erin Neala McGrath."

     "We are very pleased to meet you," Michelle said delightedly.

     "Do you need a place to stay for the night?" asked Erin.

     Michelle and I traded tickled-pink glances.

     "You can stay at our house!" exclaimed Kevin, enthusiastically tugging at my hand. "It's close by."

     "My mom can feed you supper, too!" added Erin. "She is a good cook! You should taste her potato soup!"

     "Tell you what," I said, "while we think over your generous offer, how about you show us your house? We can say 'hello' to your mother and father."

"We don't have a father," Kevin replied with a sad shake of his buzz-cut head. "He fell off a horse and broke his neck."

"Oh my!" shrieked Michelle. "That's terrible!"

"It happened when we were little," Erin said. "We don't remember him too much."

"Come on," Kevin said, tugging my arm. "Our mom is fixing the fence. The ox knocked it over."

* * * * *

So poor, so in need, and yet so selflessly giving, Aileen McGrath welcomed Michelle and I into her ramshackle, two room house and insisted that we stay for dinner. We couldn't refuse her kindness, so I went and fetched Marci and the driver and explained the sudden change of plans.

"Aileen said both of you are also welcome to come to dinner."

"How generous of her," Marci replied, already slipping on her shoes. "We'll follow you."

Just as Michelle and I had been, Marci was instantly besotted by the twenty-eight-year-old widow and her five adorable children (ages 8, 7, 6, 5, and 4). It was amazing to see how happy such a destitute family could be. Our stay with them lasted three unforgettable hours. We departed with more bundles of dandelions and stomachs full of delicious potato soup.

And Aileen Katherine McGrath, blessed angel of a mother, never had to fix another fence or do any obligatory manual labor again.

Marci Guerintaux made sure of that.

Immediately following multiple rounds of goodbye hugs, Marci took Aileen aside and changed her life. "Tomorrow I am going to the best bank in Galway and deposit a substantial amount of money in an account for you. This money will provide you the means to live anywhere you want, in a big house with bedrooms for all your children. Your family will never be in want of food. Your children will be able to receive the finest education. To ensure the stability of the fund, I will see to it that the account is looked after by a trusted financial advisor."

Aileen was overcome with a flood of joyful tears. She began to tremble, and could barely stay on her feet. It came as no surprise when, after finally coming to grips with the reality of the windfall,

Aileen announced she intended to use a large portion of the money to help other impoverished community families put food on the table and clean clothes their backs. "It would be deplorably selfish to use the money only for my family," she told Marci. "The financial freedom you've so generously bestowed will not change the fundamental values that we McGraths hold dear in our hearts. I promise you."

She kept her word.

Marci stayed in close touch with Aileen for the rest of her life. She moved to Killarney that summer, had a nice, modestly-sized house built in the countryside, got remarried in 1920 to a loving factory worker, and grew to be independently wealthy from wise investments. Four of her children blossomed into healthy, successful adults (one died of tuberculosis in his early teens). Her dedicated philanthropic efforts helped hundreds of poverty-stricken families.

Family at her bedside, Aileen McGrath died in 1946 from breast cancer.

* * * * *

A 20-page travelogue here would bog down the narrative. Below instead is a list of the major sights we visited during days 1 through 8. If you would like to learn more about these wonderful places, all you need to do is pick up a first-rate Ireland travel book, preferably one with lots of pictures!

- Cork

- The lakes of Killarney

- Kinsale

- The Ring of Kerry

- Blarney Castle

- The Burren region

- The Cliffs of Moher

- Bunratty Castle

- The Rock of Cashel

- The Connemara National Park
- Galway
- The Inishowen Peninsula
- Clonmacnoise
- Midland Bogs
- Belfast
- Giant's Causeway
- The Lower Lough Erne

* * * * *

On the morning of day 9, we took the train from Belfast to Dublin and arrived at Amiens Street Station (named Connolly Station today) a little before 10:00.

5
An Evening Walk Along the Liffey

The Easter Rising of 1916 left central Dublin looking like a section of bombed out Berlin at the end of World War II. Take a look at some of the photographs and you'll see what I mean. The area around the General Post Office (GPO) on Sackville Street lay in ruins after six days of bombardment from British artillery.

"There's still much rebuilding yet to be done," Michelle commented as we strolled over O'Connell Bridge for the first time. "It had to be terrible for the citizens to see their beautiful city being destroyed."

Nodding blankly, I stopped at the halfway point and gazed out at the River Liffey toward the Ha'penny Bridge. The weather was gorgeous, sunny and warm, perfect to enjoy a walking tour of Dublin. I turned and pointed ahead at the bombed out shell of the General Post Office. "My father died up there in the GPO - on the last day of the fighting. It was Saturday, April 29th. He fought to the end knowing the Rising had no chance of military success."

"Seamus sacrificed himself for an Irish Republic," Marci said.

"He did, along with many other patriots. What they did that week wasn't understood by the majority of the public at first. Now that's changing. Their sacrifice is beginning to pay off, and passions are running high."

Michelle took my hand. "They certainly are in you."

"Yeah . . . I'm getting all stirred up here. But I'm right. Just looking around I can tell things are getting ready to boil over. See the British soldiers over there? They're nervous - you can see it in their faces. That one guy can hardly light his cigarette. And over there, too - see? Look at'em. They know we want them out."

"Don't let the soldiers get a close look at you," Michelle said. "They would love to arrest the Emerald Ace."

"Ah - there's no way they can recognize me. Sheesh, I can barely recognize me in this get-up. - Hey, did you know that the O'Connell Bridge is wider than it is long? It's the only bridge in Europe like that. Up ahead is the Daniel O'Connell Monument and Nelson's Column. The Gresham Hotel is just ahead on the right."

* * * * *

Gerard was standing in the Gresham Hotel's luxurious lobby sipping coffee when we walked in. "We meet again!" he greeted exuberantly, loud enough to distract the line of guests at the check-in desk. "It's been a year to me!"

"The time went faster for us," Marci replied, embracing her stylishly dressed husband so as not to spill his cup. "But I missed you too!"

"Mick took good care of us," Michelle said, hugging her father and pinching my cheek at the same time.

Gerard shook my hand with both of his. "Of course he did. Thank you for showing them around your country. I wish I could have been with you. Eight days in Dublin and I still haven't properly seen the city."

"A grand time it was," I said. "We covered a lot of ground, bottom to top."

"There are four rolls of film to develop!" Michelle trumpeted, tapping the bulky camera case hanging about her shoulder. "I can't wait to see the picture of Mick holding my legs while I'm kissing the Blarney Stone."

* * * * *

We decided to squeeze in some sightseeing before lunch. Heading back across the Liffey, the four of us entered illustrious Trinity College to have a look at Ireland's greatest national treasure - the world renowned *Book of Kells*.

"Exceptional calligraphy, yeah?" I said as we circled around the ornately illuminated manuscript of the four gospels.

"The scribes were incredibly talented and patient," Michelle commented. "When was it made?"

"Around 800 A.D., when the Vikings were busy plundering, ravaging, killing, and setting towns on fire."

"What a shame if they had destroyed this," Marci said.

* * * * *

"Grafton Street dead ahead," I said after we exited Trinity. "It's a pedestrian street with lots of shops and eateries. After lunch at

Bewley's we'll visit the National Museum, the National Gallery, St. Stephen's Green, and then swing over to St. Patrick's Cathedral - that's where you can 'chance your arm' through the *Door of Reconciliation*. We can also go by the Guinness brewery and see where I used to live. Christ Church Cathedral is a must-see as we make our way back to -"

Gerard cut me off with a laugh. "I'm out of breath already. Was this the pace of sightseeing during the past week?"

"Yes, Father," Michelle replied proudly. "Will you be able to keep up with us?"

Gerard pursed his lips. "Shush! I'm not *that* old!"

* * * * *

I don't remember the house I was born in. It was located north of the Liffey close to the edge of Phoenix Park (the largest park in Europe). When my mother died of pneumonia in January 1904, my father immediately sold the old but spacious three-bedroom house and we moved to a newer and smaller one in the St. James Gate area. My birth home is no more. It was torn down in 1913 to make room for an expanded access road.

St. James Gate in southwest Dublin is synonymous with one thing: *Guinness*. Arthur Guinness founded the beer company in 1759, and leased a brewery there for 9,000 years at an annual cost of 45 pounds! Our house was located 150 yards from the brewery's main entrance. Growing up, I got to know many of the workers as they made their way back and forth to work. Seamus got in good with a big-wig at *Guinness* who was always giving him free bottles. My father drank a lot of Guinness (and *Jameson* whiskey, too). He really loved the stuff, but seeing him passed out on the floor one too many times must have turned me into a semi-teetotaler.

Standing in the middle of the narrow, tree-lined street, I said, "Well, it's been painted a different shade of brown, but there she is."

"The house is lovely," commented Michelle. "Simple, compact, and cute. I wonder who is living there now?"

"Beats me," I said. "I don't really want to find out. It feels like I'm going home after school. Weird. - Let's keep going."

* * * * *

Christ Church Cathedral was our last sightseeing stop of the day. Hungry for dinner, we found a particularly inviting restaurant on Dame Street near Dublin Castle. In a lively atmosphere of traditional folk music, we enjoyed the house specialty of cottage pie with apple cake for dessert. Gerard's feet were aching, so after the meal he and Marci took a taxi back to the Gresham. Michelle and I decided to take a stroll along the Liffey and soak in the gorgeous sunset.

"The Ha'Penny Bridge is coming up," I said. "There should be enough light for a photo. We can have someone take the picture – that is if we can find somebody. There aren't many people out tonight."

"I have three exposures left," Michelle replied, peeking into her camera case. "Tomorrow I'm going to get some more film."

Directly ahead, two strapping British soldiers turned out of an alley. They took their half out of the middle of the pavement as they ambled toward us. Both men were armed with Enfield rifles and holstered pistols. They weren't talking, they weren't smiling; nothing about them was remotely friendly. As I led Michelle a few steps right to make passing room, the inside soldier veered with us.

You bugger!

So I made more room.

The soldier veered again, this time followed by his buddy.

Ok – this isn't good.

If Michelle hadn't been with me I'd have stood my ground. But not wanting to cause trouble, I tugged at Michelle's hand and we stopped with our backs against a brick wall. The bullying soldiers continued to angle toward us, trying to look all tough-like with their spiteful sneers.

"We're too fat for you to pass?" I said with a snicker. "Man, we gotta lose some weight."

"What was that?" replied the leading soldier. "I didn't quite hear you. Did you just call me fat?"

"He did," said the other Brit. "Clear as day."

I took a half-step forward. "That's some pitiful lying. You heard what I said. Are you trying to pick a fight or something?"

"Mick let's go," Michelle said.

"*Mick let's go*," the first soldier mocked in a whiny voice.

"And where might you be going to?" asked the second soldier.

"That's none of your business," I fired back.

"It is too our business," replied the first soldier. "You might be a Republican Brotherhood swine heading to a secret meeting."

I pretended to laugh. "Jaysus mate, that's it! How on earth did you know? We're having a big IRB meeting in Temple Bar tonight. Why don't you two come along? You guys'll love it!"

Neither Brit was amused.

"Irish pig," the first soldier said, leaning forward to bump into me.

You gobshite!

Michelle saved the schmuck from one of my patented head-butts.

"Excuse me," she interjected politely. "My boyfriend is obviously joking with you. All we want to do is get our picture taken on the Ha'Penny Bridge. Please let us pass. There's no reason to have this confrontation."

"Brody and I love to make French girls like you happy," the second soldier said. "Let me take your photo. I'm an expert with cameras." He suddenly snatched hold of the camera case strap. Michelle pulled back, but the soldier didn't let go. Michelle stumbled forward as the camera was jerked from her shoulder. I lunged for the soldier, but the other guy charged into me with his rifle slung sideways across my throat. The back of my head hit the brick wall hard enough to bring on stars. Through a painful wave of dizziness, I saw the soldier twirl the camera case like a lasso and hurl it into the Liffey. Michelle cried out, running in vain toward the river.

"Oops, sorry about that," the fleshy-faced soldier said. "The bloody thing slipped from my hand. Too bad!"

The Brit named Brody had me pinned on the brick. I couldn't budge an inch with my head in a fog.

Wait a bit - it'll pass. Get your head clear. Stall them.

"That . . . that wasn't very nice," I mumbled out.

"It was an *ac-ci-dent*," Brody slowly articulated underneath his thin mustache. "He's not at fault. Could've happened to anyone."

I spat to the side. "All right, that's it. You wankers have crossed the line. I have no choice but to lay the hurt on ya."

Brody was incredulous. "Ha! Did you hear that, Simon? This Fenian rat turd said he's gunna hurt me. Can you believe that?" He pressed the rifle harder, stressing the limits of my collarbone. "Be my guest. Go ahead and try."

I took some deep, controlled breaths. My head was clearing.

"Come on," repeated the soldier. "Try and hurt me."

"Gimme a moment," I said.

"What? Chickening out already?"

"No, not at all - but you gotta give me some room here. Geez oh Pete - two against one, and you guys have multiple guns? Not fair is it?"

"Sure it's fair."

"Let him go!" screamed a crying Michelle. "I will get the police!"

"We *are* the police, missy," Simon said, coming closer. "It looks like we're going to have to make an arrest."

"Off to the Castle with this one," Brody said. "They'll give him the treatment." He eased off his rifle and took a small step back.

And that's all the room I needed.

At mongoose-speed I grabbed onto the Enfield rifle and viciously head-butted Brody's nose. The Brit let go of his weapon as he wobbled back with blood spurting over his face. In one continuous motion I slammed the butt of the rifle into the side of his head and then spin-rolled at a slow-to-react Simon. He'd barely gotten his Enfield off his shoulder when I crashed into his legs, knocking him down. I sprung to my feet. As Simon was rising to his knee, I caught him with a bone shattering rifle butt uppercut to his jaw. Teeth exploded from his mouth and flew across the pavement.

The fight was over.

Brody lay there unconscious - or dead for all I knew - in a pool of blood. Simon was on the pavement writhing in agony, hands on his face. After locating my hat, I picked up the Lee Enfield rifles and flung them into the Liffey. The soldiers were also packing Webley revolvers and knives. Taking no chances, I pulled the pistols and knives off their belts and tossed them into the Liffey as well.

Michelle ran over to me. "Oh Mick!"

"We're all right," I said, holding her tight. Her tears wetted the side of my face. "They were the bad guys and they lost. - We can't stick around. Come on."

We dashed away.

* * * * *

Back in my 3rd floor room at the Gresham, a bitterly distressed Marci gave me an ice bag for my sore head. "The nerve of those brutes! How could they act that way? You are lucky they didn't shoot you."

"They weren't fast enough to do that, Mother," Michelle said. "Mick was amazing! He knocked out those soldiers before they knew what was happening."

"They're the lucky ones, Marci," I said, adjusting the ice bag while sitting at the edge of the bed. "The camera-thrower guy was at least. He just lost some teeth. The other Brit might be dead. I bashed him pretty good."

"Who else could identify you besides the soldiers?" Gerard asked, sitting in a sofa chair across from me.

"I don't think anyone could. Maybe someone saw the action from a distance, or from a window - but I can't be sure. The soldiers wouldn't have accosted us if there had been people around. All the way back to the hotel I kept checking to see if we were being followed. We made it here without a peep of commotion."

"Did anyone come upon the soldiers?"

"We saw one person before getting out of view," Michelle answered. "It was an older man, and he didn't seem too interested. He only stopped for a few moments to look at them and then moved on."

"No one likes the Brits," I said. "If some people saw what happened, they most likely cheered."

"What are you thinking, Father?" asked Michelle.

Gerard stood up in his Chinese-made blue silk pajamas. "Dublin is too dangerous. We must leave for Queenstown first thing in the morning. I will book us on the first ship available. - Mick, you will need a different disguise."

"A different hat for sure. The sunglasses will still work. I wasn't wearing them with the soldiers."

"What about me?" Michelle asked. "I can wear my hair up."

"You can also wear my red bonnet," Marci suggested.

"There is a 'lost and found' in the lobby," Gerard said to me. "I saw several suitable hats on the rack. Now everyone get to bed. I want to be out of here by 0600."

* * * * *

Donning a pristine gray flat cap, I stepped out of the taxi the next morning and heard the news blaring. Outside the main entrance to Amiens Street Station a newspaper vendor was hollering, *"Read all about it! Two British soldiers attacked in central Dublin! One dies; the other suffers severe facial injuries."*

Gerard bought a copy of *The Irish Times*, skimmed a section of the story, and then tucked the paper under his arm.

"Good thing we're leaving," I said as he approached.

"We can read this on the train," Gerard replied, handing the newspaper to me.

"You can't stay out of the front pages for long," Michelle kidded, looking glamorous in Marci's red bonnet.

"Yeah, let's hope nothing comes of this. The sooner we get back to France the better."

"Does part of you wish the other soldier had died, too?" Michelle asked me in a whispery tone.

I nodded. "It would have made things easier. But we'll be all right. They can't find us if they can't recognize us."

"I don't feel the least bit sorry for the dead man."

"You shouldn't. He tangled with the wrong guy."

* * * * *

Once aboard the train, with Michelle and I seated behind Marci and Gerard, I quickly scanned the article. "He was Corporal Brody J. Davenport, aged 26. Died from massive head trauma."

"May he *not* rest in peace," Michelle huffed.

"He won't." I skimmed more of the article and turned the page. "The other guy is Corporal Simon Cosgrove. It says he gave a good description of his assailant and the girl he was with."

"I'm surprised he could talk."

"He probably had to mumble." After reading a few more paragraphs I shook my head in disgust. "What a bunch of rubbish. The story is full of blatant lies."

"Like what?"

Gerard and Marci had heard us. They turned around to hear more. "Your voices are getting too loud."

"Oh, sorry. - This Simon is saying that his attacker was armed and that he and Brody were attacked from behind."

Michelle tried to read over my shoulder. "Of course he's going to say that. How else to explain two stout, well-armed soldiers being overpowered by one man?"

"Yeah, that's true," I replied, puffing out my chest like I was king of the world. "I am a one-man army."

"I've believed that for many months now," Marci complimented.

* * * * *

The sparsely filled train departed at 07:10 sharp. A long three hours and fifteen minutes later we pulled into Queenstown Railway Station.

6
Q the Wolf

There was some time to kill.

Due to stormy weather off Ireland's southern coast, all ferry departures were delayed. Assuming the accuracy of the latest forecast, the earliest we could get out of Queenstown would be 15:30.

"We could go walk around the city again," I suggested.

"It's impossible to tire of the scenery," Michelle said. "I want to get another camera and retake pictures of the colorful stepped houses and St. Colman's Cathedral. And the port, too. It's such a beautiful setting. You said the Titanic's last stop was here?"

"Yeah. It picked up 123 people right from the pier. 79 of them died. It's also where many Irish left for America because of the Potato Famine. This is one of the largest natural harbors in the world. – Let's go find you a camera."

Without a word, Michelle darted after Gerard who was talking to a man at the dock.

* * * * *

In a nearby tourist shop, Michelle purchased a No. 1 Seneca Jr. It was smaller than the Kodak and easier to manage. We then set about retracing our steps from the previous week and took twice as many pictures. Upon returning to the pier Gerard wanted to have a word with us. "If you haven't heard yet, the delay has been extended. We won't be able to leave until early evening."

"So why are you smiling?" asked Michelle curiously.

"Because we have another option."

"Pray tell," I said.

Gerard turned and pointed in the distance toward a nondescript, single smokestack merchant ship that had seen better days. "We can ride in that ship to Calais. I spoke with the captain and offered to pay him for the transport. He agreed. His ship is not restricted by the weather. The captain said there are some small rooms on board that can accommodate us. No frills, of course. Basic transportation only."

"When does it leave?" I asked.

"In thirty minutes. I estimate we'd be back home by dinner time tomorrow. - Or we could wait for the ferry and get back home the day *after* tomorrow in the middle of the night."

"I vote for taking this ship," Marci declared.

"Me, too," I said.

Michelle frowned at me. "I'd rather wait for the ferry."

"Huh? Really?"

She laughed. "I'm just kidding."

* * * * *

Captain Lucas Voclain of the *SS Nanterre* was not there to greet us as we boarded the ship via the cargo loading ramp. In his place was a twenty-something crewman who barely cracked five feet in height. "Welcome aboard the *Nanterre*," he said in a nasally Limerick accent. "I'm first mate Cathal Connors, the only Irishman on this boat. I should be on the *Castlebar* next to us. It's an Irish ship. Ya do speak English I hope, yeah?"

"Aye, that we do Cathal," I said, mimicking the accent to a tee. "These three can speak French."

"So you be from county Limerick, too?"

"No, I'm a Dubliner," I replied, switching back to my normal accent.

Cathal laughed. "You Jackeen! My father used to do that with the accents. There are so many. - Pleased to meet you all. I'm not good with names so we needn't bother with introductions here. By the time we get to Calais I might know what letter they start with. The captain is on the bridge huddled over his maps, making sure we avoid the brunt of the storm. Did you all meet him at the pier?"

"Only me," Gerard said.

"Then you'll know he doesn't speak a lick of English. I know enough French to follow his orders and that's about it. It's a wonder we don't make more mistakes with the cargo. If you would, please follow me to the bridge."

* * * * *

Wearing a filthy captain's hat and an abused black leather coat that was two sizes too big, Lucas Voclain reminded me of one of those old salty dog pirates you see in the movies. He was only 46, but his wrinkly, wind-battered, face tacked on another twenty years. Small in stature like his first mate, he stood five-foot-five in thick-soled boots. The gruff-toned captain used Gerard as a translator to welcome us aboard and exchange some friendly pleasantries. He then informed us that the first half of the voyage would be a rough ride along the edge of a gnarly storm. Once we rounded England's southern coast the waters would smooth out. Expected travel time to Calais was 22 hours. Voclain also mentioned that the *SS Nanterre* would be sailing in tandem with the *SS Castlebar,* a British merchant ship of similar size and appearance. Both vessels were a shade over 200 feet long and in the 1700 tonnage range. They also were filled with the same cargo of machinery parts and fertilizer.

"Including the captain, there's a crew of seven on board," Cathal Connors said as he showed us to our quarters. "The boatswain speaks some English, but none of the other men do. You can help yourself to the galley. There's not a lot to choose from, but make what you can. Your rooms are on the left down there. They've each got two foldaway bunks, a sink, and a small closet - and I do mean small. It may have some trouble storing your luggage. You could always throw it under the bottom bunk. - We'll be sailing here in a few minutes, so I've got to be going. If you need anything, just walk about the ship shouting my name. See ya around."

* * * * *

Huddled together on deck midships, trying to find our sea-legs, Michelle and I watched the gray tower of St. Coleman's Cathedral slowly disappear into the matching gray skies over Queenstown. The wind was blowing a strong gale, but the rain had sealed inside the clouds. Paralleling fifty yards out, flying the Red Ensign of the Merchant Navy, the *SS Castlebar* maintained a full ship-length lead as we reached a maximum cruising speed of 14.8 knots. I expected the ships would soon begin the standard tactic of zig-zagging.

"This could be a fun voyage," Michelle said worriedly, clutching her stomach. "The waves are already making me feel queasy."

"And these are the dinky ones. The captain said it's going to get like a rollercoaster soon. If you're feeling sick you should go to your room and lie down."

Michelle nodded. "Yes, that's what I'm going to do. You may not see me for a long time."

"Pay me no mind," I replied, leading her back inside. "Keep a bucket by your bed."

* * * * *

The big waves hit an hour later.

Talk about a rollercoaster! Gigantic waves crashed down with incredible fury, trying to crush the ship. The sea rocked us high, low, and side-to-side. Janey mack it was a wild ride! I kept thinking that the *Nanterre* was eventually going to dip so deep into the water that it would plunge straight to the bottom!

I'd have bet a million pounds that all the topsy-turvy maneuvering I'd done as a pilot would've totally immunized me from motion sickness. But no, I came mighty close to losing my lunch a couple times. Why so? The only thing I could think of was that when I'm flying I'm the one in control of the twisting and turning. Nothing surprises me in the air. I know what's coming next and my body prepares. Not so on board a ship. The water is in control - and you're at its mercy.

Michelle and Marci were turned pea soup green by the angry sea. Gerard was affected too, though not nearly as bad as the girls. He threw-up once, but after that he kept to his feet and tended to Marci while I did what I could for Michelle.

"We should have taken the ferry," Michelle said deliriously, her head hanging over a messy mop bucket.

"Yeah, we would've had to spend the night in Queenstown to do that," I said, stroking her hand. "I heard from Cathal that all ferries were canceled until tomorrow morning. - Oh well, doesn't matter now. The worst of it is over. Try and get some sleep, then you'll feel better. The second half of the trip will be smooth sailing."

"I hope so. This is miserable."

* * * * *

After making myself a honey sandwich in the galley and exploring every nook and cranny of the ship, I kept to my room for most of the next four hours while Michelle slept. I tried to catch a few zzzz's as well, but that came to no avail. The only thing to do was read *The Irish Times* - multiple times: every story, every advertisement, every word.

When Michelle awoke around 7:00 p.m. she was feeling much better. So was Marci. They both wanted to get out of their cramped sickbay rooms and walk around a bit, so Gerard and I escorted them outside to get some fresh air. The weather had morphed from ghastly to gorgeous, with clear skies and a warm evening sun. The ocean was beautifully serene, making the deck-walk easy on the stomach.

A half hour later, while we were sitting atop a long storage bin watching the sun begin to set, Cathal Conners saw us from above and hollered over the railing, "I see ya survived! That sickness is a bummer. Do ya need anything?"

"Feeling better now," I said. "Had a rough go there for a while, but we're doing all right."

"That's good to hear. I'll let the captain know." Cathal raised his binoculars and scanned out in the direction of the *SS Castlebar*. I squinted into the twilight and noticed the ship was turning hard to port. Crew members were scattering about as if they were in a panic.

"What's going on over there?" I asked Cathal.

But Cathal was gone.

Then the alarm sounded.

* * * * *

I grabbed Michelle's hand. "Come on!"

Gerard and Marci followed us as we scrambled for the nearest lifeboat. If the ship was in trouble, I wanted to be able to vacate as quickly as possible.

"What's happening?" Michelle shouted over the blaring whine of the alarm.

Before I could reply, a deafening explosion rocked the stern of the *Nanterre*. The four of us were jolted violently forward to within arms-reach of the lifeboat.

"Torpedo!" I yelled. "In the boat now! I'll lower us down. Go, go!"

Dead in the water, the powerless (and stern-less!) *Nanterre* was already listing heavily to starboard. Her bow began to rise like the bascules of Tower Bridge as the cold Atlantic Ocean flooded into her. Farther astern, I saw some other crew members madly assemble around the other lifeboat. None of the three men showed the slightest interest in our safety. It was every man for himself.

"This ship's going down fast," I said. "Bleedin' Sub!"

"When will you get in the boat?" cried Michelle.

"I'll get you down first, then jump in."

My biggest fear was that the ship could blow apart at any second. The *Nanterre* was loaded with tons of fertilizer containing ammonium nitrate, making it a sinking time bomb. There was also the possibility that the boiler might rupture. I had to get the lifeboat away fast - but geez oh Pete, the stupid crank handle wasn't cooperating! It was sticky with rust and proving a beasty to turn. By the time I got the boat halfway lowered, the other lifeboat was already in the water heading for the *Castlebar*.

"Let me help you Mick," Gerard offered, standing up precariously in the boat.

"No no, you're too far down."

"How about me?"

It was Cathal.

"Japers man, I was wondering where you were," I said. "Where's the captain?"

"Still on the bridge. He was supposed to be right behind me."

We both looked back at the bridge - just in time to see Lucas Voclain jump awkwardly to the smoke-filled deck 10 feet below, which by now was tilted drastically at about 45 degrees. While Cathal and I cranked on the handle, the captain stumbled toward us like a proverbial drunken sailor, holding on to whatever he could to keep his balance. "*Sauter*," he shouted. "*Sauter Maintenant! Je vis le fair!*"

"He said 'Jump!'" Cathal interpreted. "He'll finish lowering."

"Say no more. Let's go!"

* * * * *

The bow of the lifeboat had already touched the water by the time we leaped from the sinking *Nanterre*. The frigid water felt like a thousand little knives stabbing into my body. I surfaced a couple of yards from the boat and swam toward it with Cathal dog paddling alongside slightly ahead.

Gerard leaned out his hand and helped Cathal climb in. Michelle and Marci quickly abandoned their attempt to assist me because there was now too much weight on one side of the boat. "Get back!" I hollered. "You'll tip over!"

I treaded water until Gerard could haul me aboard. The *Nanterre* was so close it seemed like it might fall over on top of us. The creaking, hissing, scraping cries of a dying ship blistered my ear drums.

"*Sauter*!" yelled Cathal, directing his brave captain to jump.

"Jump!" I shouted, twisting around on the plank seat. "Come on Captain, jump!"

Lucas Voclain adjusted his feet on the railing, which was now almost parallel with the water line. There wasn't much of a jump left, perhaps six feet at most. At that moment an explosion boomed from somewhere deep within the bowels of the ship. The captain was jolted sideways off his feet, and when he came down his left foot slipped between the narrow railing bars. He fell through all the way up to his knee and then whipsawed forward. With his leg immovably stuck, something had to give. I cringed when his thigh bone shattered. The jagged, bloody white ends of the bone ripped through his trousers and stuck out straight to the sky. Voclain didn't scream for long. His head smacked hard against the hull of the ship and he was knocked out instantly.

I covered Michelle's eyes.

* * * * *

The *SS Nanterre* creakily slid below the churning waves as we rowed like mad for the full-stopped *Castlebar*. The other lifeboat, slightly bigger than ours, was twenty yards ahead of us. Chaos was still reigning onboard the *Castlebar* as several crew members were carrying yellow rubber rafts.

They must be abandoning ship, I thought.

"Riopelle and Truchon didn't make it," Cathal said, surveying the other lifeboat. "They were probably in the stern when the torpedo hit. What a shame . . . the two youngest and the two nicest guys."

"Look there!" bawled Gerard, pointing ahead. "Do you see? It's the U-boat! It's coming up!"

"There she blows!" I bellowed.

Approximately 100 yards adjacent from the bow of the *Castlebar*, the German submarine's gray conning tower was emerging from the depths like a metallic leviathan.

"Holy japers would you look at that," I said. "If it isn't Nemo's *Nautalus*."

"What's going to happen now?" asked Michelle, holding tight to my jacket.

"The *Castlebar*'s going to surrender," Cathal answered. "It has to. The crew's already got the rafts. When they've all evacuated, the sub will unleash its deck gun and sink her."

"Leaving us stranded out here," Marci said despondently.

Cathal winced. "Yeah, but we're not too far from the English coast. I imagine a rescue vessel will be out looking for us before too long."

"How about we row away from the scene?" I suggested. "We don't want to get hit with any debris."

"Good idea," Cathal said.

* * * * *

Now fully surfaced, the intimidating German submarine impressed me with its proportions. It wasn't battleship-size by any measure, but it was as long as the *Castlebar* at over 200 feet.

"They sure look a lot smaller in photographs," I said. "But that's a big boat."

"I know my U-boats, and that's a type 93," Castle informed. "They're probably the best diesel powered attack subs in the German fleet. She's got 4 bow and 2 stern tubes. On top is a 105mm, a bonafide cruiser sinker." Cathal glanced back at the *Castlebar*. "The sub's keeping her distance, isn't she? Normally they surface closer to their target. It's still in range to blow the *Castlebar* to pieces."

"It almost doesn't seem fair," Michelle said as we rowed in the opposite direction. "Where is the honor in hiding under the water? It's so cowardly to attack your enemy that way."

"Welcome to the 20th Century," Gerard remarked. "Rules of war and the code of chivalry are becoming things of the past."

"I can't disagree with that," I said. "Even for some fighter pilots" - My head suddenly jerked up at the *Castlebar*. "Jaysus sakes! What the devil's going on?"

"Mother Mary, I knew it!" Cathal exclaimed. "It's a Q-ship! A Q-ship!"

Panels all along the *SS Castlebar* were dropping in rapid succession to reveal an array of deck guns. At the same time a rush of crewmen sprouted out of the ship to man the weapons. The Red Ensign was lowered and the White Ensign of the Royal Navy replaced it. The ship steamed ahead at full speed to avoid a torpedo strike.

"Sucker play!" I hollered, laughing with delight.

"Oh my goodness," gasped Michelle. "It's a disguised warship!"

* * * * *

Michelle's description was spot-on.

Q-ships (sometimes called Special Service ships or Mystery ships) were designed to lure enemy vessels close and then destroy them with their guns hidden behind collapsible deck structures. Q-ship crews would go to elaborate lengths to simulate panic and give the lured enemy every indication that a surrender was imminent. By this point in the war, however, German submarines had become leery of giving small merchant ships and trawlers the opportunity to surrender. Using precious torpedoes on small vessels was also becoming less frequent - which made the attack on the *Nanterre* and the surfacing by the *Castlebar* doubly out of the norm.

So what was the German U-boat captain thinking? Maybe he'd launched the attack under the correct assumption that, at most, only one of the two vessels would be armed. If so, he'd grossly mistaken that the *Nanterre* was the Q-ship and not the *Castlebar*. Keeping at 100 yards was his only precaution - though not a guaranteed safeguard. The U-boat's alarm siren was blaring as it prepared to crash dive. With no one on deck, its 105mm gun was useless.

"Keep rowing!" commanded Cathal. "Work together! Use the legs!"

Boom! Boom! Boom! Rat-a-tat-tat! Rat-a-tat-tat!

The *Castlebar*'s guns erupted in a barrage of shell fire. Heavy machine guns opened up, riddling the U-boat's hull with bullet holes as it began to slowly sink into the gentle waves.

"Blast that thing!" I cried.

Caught in the line of fire, the three *Nanterre* crew members lay flat in their lifeboat.

When the submarine was halfway submerged, it took a partial hit below the conning tower from a 3-pounder/47mm shell. Another two shells exploded off the stern and near midships.

Cathal slapped the wooden seat. "They gotta hurry! She's slipping away!"

More machine gun fire.

More near-miss shells splashed the ocean around the submarine.

"Keeping that distance is saving her," Cathal said angrily. "She's going down too fast."

"The gunners missed their chance," Gerard said. "That conning tower hit should have been the one."

"Maybe it was enough?" I questioned, watching the last traces of the submarine vanish into the depths.

Shaking his head, Cathal said, "No, but the sub's gunna leak like a sieve back to her base. She's gotta get home quick. Other British warships could show up at any time."

"Will the *Castlebar* go after her?"

"It may try and track her for a while before coming back to pick us up." Cathal signaled to the other lifeboat and chuckled. "They'll be sure to stick with us now."

"They would have let us drown," snarled Marci.

* * * * *

We were adrift on the still, pitch black Atlantic for over thirty tense minutes before the *Castlebar* returned to rescue us. Our clothes dried quickly from the heat of the furnace boiler and we were given a hot meal of red bean stew. Two and a half hours later, at 01:45, we steamed into the small port town of Penzance, located on the Cornwall peninsula. Along with Cathal, we spent the rest of a restless night in a complimentary hotel - though Gerard paid full price anyway plus a generous gratuity to the affable hotel owner. Late in the morning we said goodbye to Cathal and caught a ferry to Calais via Portsmouth without further incident. From there we boarded the first train to Paris.

It wasn't until dinnertime that we finally arrived at the chateau by taxi. Beau wasn't at home, but Maurice certainly was. In no time at all, the invaluable butler threw together a soup and sandwich meal that any five-star restaurant would have been proud to serve.

"When will we be sailing on a merchant ship again, Father?" Michelle kidded over her vanilla pudding dessert.

Gerard gave her a friendly scowl. "When France has a king again."

7
La Grippe

I awoke the next morning feeling downright lousy. My head felt like it was in a pressure cooker and I ached all over. Whimpering at the edge of my pillow, Sinn Fein knew something was wrong. I weakly scratched him behind his ears as he snuggled close. "Hey there boy - you might have to help me up."

It was a struggle mustering the energy to get out of bed, and once on my feet I wobbled around for a few seconds like I was three sheets to the wind. A long hot shower revived me somewhat, but the pick-me-up wore off by the time I'd dressed.

"You look terrible," Michelle said to me when I groggily sat down to a scrambled eggs and cinnamon toast breakfast.

"Yeah, a bad cold's got me for sure. Maybe I picked up something from bobbing around in the Atlantic."

Maurice poured me some orange juice. "Here, drink some of this. Can I get you an aspirin tablet?"

"Yes, please. The eggs look grand, Maurice, but I have no appetite. The funny thing is I feel hungry, but I don't feel like eating. - Sheesh, this reminds me of last fall when most of *Jasta 11* got sick. We blamed it on Hermann Göring."

Michelle put her hand on my forehead. "You *are* warm - my goodness."

I nodded weakly. "It came on pretty sudden. I went to bed feeling all right, and I slept ok until about four."

"It couldn't have been the dinner you ate," Marci said, crossing around the table. "We'd all be feeling ill. You should probably go back to bed and get some rest."

"I was wanting to go for a run."

"Not until you feel better." Marci felt my forehead in a couple of places. Nodding, she said, "If this isn't a fever then I don't know what one is."

I took the aspirin from Maurice and swallowed it down with the orange juice. To Michelle I said, "After you've finished eating, do you want to go outside and sit in the garden for a while? Maybe it will help me."

"We can go now. I'll bring an apple. If you get worse, it's straight to bed."

* * * * *

Sitting in the rose garden didn't make me feel any better so Michelle ordered me to bed. "You took care of me on the boat," she said as we walked back inside. "Now it's my turn to take care of you."

"Thank you nurse. It's probably just a case of the Black Death. No need to worry."

"You shouldn't joke about that. People still get the plague and die from it. My guess is you have influenza."

* * * * *

By the middle of the afternoon I was coughing like crazy. It was a thick, deep cough; not the dry, hacking type. My lungs felt like they weighed twenty pounds. I had Siberian chills, a runny nose, body aches, and my fever was getting worse. There were also these weird looking brown spots on my face.

"I've never seen anything like that before," Michelle said quietly, rubbing her temple and looking a bit tired. She wiped my brow with a wet cloth.

"Then it's not the Black Death. I must have the Brown Death."

As bad as I felt, I was still trying to keep my sense of humor. But Michelle didn't laugh. She didn't even crack a hint of a smile. Her eyes slowly closed and she swayed slightly, side to side.

"Jaysus sakes, are *you* ok? You're woozy."

Michelle opened her droopy eyes, blinking rapidly as she steadied herself. "I'm just a little run down, that's all. Maybe I need some more sleep."

"You don't need to hang around me anymore," I said after another coughing fit. "I'm spewing germs all over the room. You should be wearing one of those masks."

There came a knock at the door and Marci entered the room carrying a pitcher of ice water. "Feeling any better?"

"No - and you need to get Michelle out of here," I said. "Now she's not feeling well."

Marci set the pitcher down on the nightstand and felt her daughter's forehead. "Yes," she said, nodding with a worried frown. "You're getting warm."

"I'm all right, Mother."

"No you're not! You look like Mick did this morning. - Come on, it's off to bed you go. I'll tend to both of you."

"I don't want to go to my bedroom," Michelle protested. "I'll lie down for a while, but I want to lie down in here with Mick."

Marci let out an exasperated sigh and thought about it for a moment. "Ok, as you wish. You and Michelle can be sick together. I'll have Maurice bring in the rollaway bed."

"Thank you, Mother."

Marci took hold of Michelle's hand and led her to a cushioned chair by the open window. "The breeze will feel good. Stay off your feet until we get the bed in here. I will bring you some aspirin."

* * * * *

Fighting a losing battle to stay awake, Michelle sat listlessly with her head leaned back against the sill. "Mick, I really don't feel well."

"I know you don't. You've got what I have. Sorry about that."

"You're forgiven. - It's getting hard to . . . talk. My energy is so low."

"Don't try. Just rest. Maurice will be bringing in the bed."

I barely finished the sentence when Maurice arrived with the rollaway. He set it up across from me so that Michelle and I could look straight at each other. I remember Marci helping Michelle into the bed, but then nothing until I awoke later in the evening. Gerard was standing over me. "You and Michelle need to see a doctor," he said tersely.

"I'll go telephone Dr. Brodeur now," Beau said, standing next to Michelle.

"Tell him to get here as soon as possible. I don't like the looks of this."

"Could one of you let Sinn Fein in here?" I requested. "He likes to sleep on my bed."

* * * * *

The long trusted family doctor was on holiday in, of all places, the Balearic Islands. Extraordinarily fortunate for us, he was due back into Paris late that night. Gerard predicted he would head to the chateau immediately upon receiving the message.

He arrived sometime after midnight.

Dr. Brodeur was an older gentleman, small framed, with a bushy white beard that was trying to escape the surgical mask coving his mouth and nose. He spoke very little English. Brodeur examined Michelle first, but I was too weak and tired to closely follow what he was doing. When he got to me, I remember coughing all over him as he ran me through the basic tests. I can recall the doctor putting away his stethoscope as he spoke quietly with Marci and Gerard. He shook his head uneasily several times, and kept saying the words '*bleu*' and '*mort.*'

I knew what those words meant: blue and death.

* * * * *

It was pushing six in the morning when I awoke to the sounds of gurgled coughing and the calling of my name.

"Mick."

At first I thought the coughs were a part of the dream I was having: I was in a hospital walking aimlessly through its low ceiling halls. There was a cluster of babies crawling around at my feet. Bombs were going off outside but I couldn't hear the explosions. An old Chinese nurse came up to me and asked if I was hungry. She handed me a tray full of mashed potatoes and a bowl of tomato soup. Then I heard coughing and -

"Mick."

Who's calling my name? Where am I?

The flapping of curtains from the stiff breeze and my god-awful physical discomfort stirred me to reality.

"Mick . . . are you awake?"

"Michelle?"

She coughed again.

And again.

"It's hard to breath. My head and throat hurt." Michelle's voice was raspy and barely audible.

"Same with me. It feels like I got run over by a herd of elephants."

"Me, too. I'm so thirsty."

"Marci will be back soon with water. - I didn't make out what Dr. Brodeur was saying to your parents."

"I heard most of it. We have the flu, Mick - *la grippe*." Michelle coughed extremely hard, and then said, "It's a really bad flu. He said it can be fatal. When victims start turning blue that means death is coming."

"Really? - Jaysus. We're not blue, are we?"

"No, not yet. He said there is very little he can do. Fluids and lots of bed rest. Aspirin for fever. Our bodies are on their own."

"Blue means no oxygen," I said. "That's weird."

"Mick, I'm . . . afraid. I don't want to die."

"You're not gunna die. I'm not gunna die. You hear me? We're too strong. We just gotta ride this out."

"I hope we can." She coughed some more, then said, "Mother is afraid for us. I could tell. The doctor said this particular strain of flu is killing young, healthy people like us. He didn't have an explanation."

I coughed.

Michelle, too.

"Don't be afraid," I said. "Stay positive. Stay strong. We'll make it through this."

"I'm trying."

* * * * *

Long hours.
Coughing.
Hazy sleep.
Marci taking care of us.
Sinn Fein licking my face.

* * * * *

A few moments after Marci exited the room, Michelle struggled to say, "Mick, are you awake?"

"Yeah - barely."

"I feel worse. - I think that we . . . that we . . ."

"Yeah, you think - what?"

"I think . . . we should get married now."

"Huh? Married *now*?"

"Yes. I want to get married now - as soon as possible. If I die, I want to die knowing I was your wife."

"You're not gunna die, Michelle. I told you."

"You can't know that."

"But I do. You're going to recover. Believe me."

More coughing. It took Michelle a few extended moments before she could reply. "Mick, I don't want to take the risk."

"But what about the elaborate plan you envisioned for our wedding on August 9th? You had it all worked out."

"That doesn't matter to me. Just getting married to you in Notre Dame is enough."

"What about walking down the aisle together? We're in no condition to do that. Maybe we should wait until we can."

"What if we never can? We're so sick."

Suddenly a corner light came on. Squinting, I turned my head to see Marci step lightly into the room.

"Hi ya," I greeted feebly.

"I thought both of you were asleep."

"We were," I said.

"Mother, we're thirsty. - I'm burning up."

"I have ice water and a cold cloth."

* * * * *

Four more torturous hours of sleeping off and on. My fever and coughing didn't improve, but it didn't get any worse, so I took that as a positive sign. Michelle's condition was all over the place. She seemed worse one minute, then better, then worse, then somewhere in between. I tried to convince myself that she was holding steady like me. At my insistence, Marci spent 95% of her time at Michelle's bedside. I kept asking Marci how she was doing, and her general response was, "She's fighting it. It's going to take time."

Gerard and Beau were in and out all day, like recurring characters in a bizarre dream. They didn't say much, but I could tell they were extremely worried. Maurice maintained a stoic countenance when he was present. Forty years back he'd lost his wife Yvette to a ruptured appendix after only six months of marriage. He never married again. In fact, he never got anywhere near serious with a woman again.

While foggily awake, all I could think about was Michelle's condition and her suggestion that we should immediately get married. I didn't hear her mention the emergency wedding idea to Marci or Gerard. During a rare occurrence when Michelle was awake with no one else in the room, I finally said to her, "Have you given more thought to your wedding idea?"

"Yes. I still want to. As soon as possible."

"How are you feeling?"

"My ears hurt now. Everything hurts."

"You haven't mentioned the wedding to your parents, have you?"

"No. I was waiting for you to say yes."

"Ok, good . . . because I'm saying yes."

There was a long pause. Coughing and tears of joy came on together. I raised my head and focused my eyes on her always beautiful face. The bedroom was dimly lit with curtain-blocked sunlight, so I couldn't tell the exact color of her skin.

I looked at my own skin. My arms were pale for sure. But were they blue?

I didn't think so, but . . .

"Mick," Michelle said, lifting her head slightly. "I love you."

"And I love you."

"When Mother comes back in I'll tell her we're getting married. We can be taken to Notre Dame. That's where -" more coughing - "that's where I've always pictured us."

"Ok," I said. "Maybe we'll have enough strength to walk down the aisle."

"I . . . hope so."

"We're gunna pull through this," I declared. "We'll get married, and after we're fully recovered we can have a proper blowout celebration. - Right? Michelle, are you with me? Right?"

"Right."

She vomited.

* * * * *

We mostly slept.

Hours of suffering passed.

* * * * *

Marci returned with a pushcart containing a large bowl, two drinking glasses, and pitcher full of ice water.

Half asleep, Michelle said, "Mother - I have to tell you and Father something important. Beau and Maurice should hear, too."

Marci gritted her teeth. "What is it?"

"Let's wait . . . for the others."

"All right, but Beau is not here. Father is outside with Dr. Brodeur."

Michelle coughed, and then said with her eyes closed, "We'll have to tell Beau later."

Marci wrung out a cool cloth and called for Maurice through the open bedroom door.

* * * * *

Michelle nodded off before Gerard and Maurice got there.

"Are you going to wake her?" I asked woozily.

"I don't think we should," Marci said. "She needs all the rest she can get. Do you know what she was going to tell us?"

After a pause, I replied, "Yes, but she wanted to tell you." I looked over at Michelle. "How is her skin color?"

Marci shook her head. "I don't think there's any difference. Still pale, but not blue. You, too."

I lifted a weak fist. "Good."

We're going to make it! I'm not going to lose you!

"Mick," Gerard said, "Marci and I would very much appreciate it if you would tell us what Michelle has to say."

I took another long gaze at Michelle again, flooding my mind with happy thoughts. Positive thoughts.

Don't get upset, Michelle. They're your parents.

"Ok . . . I'll tell you. Michelle wants to get married today - at Notre Dame."

Marci's face froze as she turned to Gerard.

A long fit of coughing struck me. When I could speak again, I said, "I told her there was no need to panic and rush things. We're both going to get better. But she's worried . . . worried that - you know."

Wearing a faint, pained smile, Gerard knelt at Michelle's bedside and gently kissed her hand. "My precious little girl," he said, stroking her hair. "If your wish is to be married today then we will make it happen." Gerard checked his gold pocket watch. "It's 4 a.m. - Maurice, would you please telephone for an ambulance. Have it arrive at 7."

"At once."

Marci broke into tears and embraced her husband. A few moments later she cried out, "Tell me it won't be the same as when Pierre died. Please, Gerard. The doctors told us he was getting better, then suddenly he was gone. I don't want to go through that again."

Not what I wanted to hear, I thought. *My bullets ended Pierre's life.*

"It won't be like that," Gerard said comfortingly, gently patting her back. "Michelle has not been wounded. This is an illness most people recover from. Michelle and Mick are strong kids. They will recover, too."

"That's right," I asserted. "We're not going to die from the stupid flu!" Raising my voice caused me to cough. When I could speak again, I asked Gerard, "Dr. Brodeur's been on the level with you about our illness hasn't he?"

"What do you mean?"

"I want him to be telling us the truth. If we're doomed, he should say so. He shouldn't be giving out false hopes. If he honestly thinks we'll recover, or if he thinks there's a fifty-fifty chance or whatever the odds, he should say so as well. What I'm saying is, I don't want anyone – not you, Marci, me, Michelle - being kept in the dark."

Marci rose to her feet and came forward. "The doctor has not been giving out false hope - that I can assure you."

"Brodeur leans pessimistic about everything - even a stubbed toe," Gerard added. "It's his way, and has been for twenty years. No one is being kept in the dark. You and Michelle have a serious illness, but the odds are in your favor. I'm telling you the truth."

"Ok . . . thanks. I appreciate the honesty."

Gerard grasped my hand. "You'll be a married man in a few hours."

"Yeah - hard to believe."

"It's the 14th, too - Bastille Day."

"Geez . . . that was supposed to be for Beau."

"Now it's *your* day. - Get some more rest. You're going to need it."

I didn't think it would work, but the warm glass of milk Marci gave me brought on an easy sleep.

* * * * *

The next thing I knew I was awake inside a fast moving ambulance, trying to make sense of my senses. Blurred vision took a moment to focus, and when it did I saw Marci hovering over me.

"He's awake," she said.

Cottonmouth prevented my first attempt at speaking. My second attempt sounded like babble. "Ut - is - appening?"

"Nothing too important," Marci replied in tearful jest. "You're only going to your wedding."

That's right! Yes!

I turned my head left, but too fast. It made me dizzy for a few seconds.

There you are!

Michelle's beautifully tired face was a foot away. "Chelle," I said.

"Hi my love. We're here."

"How are you?"

"Tired . . . weak. Breathing is hard. I don't think I'm getting better."

"Yes you are," I said, waiting for her coughs to stop. "The worst has to be over."

Michelle tried to nod. "I'm going to be your wife."

"Very soon."

"We need to stay awake."

"Yeah - or how could we say our vows?"

The ambulance door opened. Gerard and Beau were there, both dapperly dressed in tailor-fitted black tuxedos. Above them I could see the 68-meter twin towers of Notre Dame Cathedral scraping a sunny blue sky.

Nice day for a wedding.

8
Mrs. Gallagher

The uneven cobblestone was too bumpy to be wheeled across, so our gurneys were carried to the entrance. Awaiting us outside the left portal, underneath the intriguing statue of St. Denis holding his own decapitated head, was a roly-poly priest, decked out in ornate green, white, and gold priestly garb. Standing beside him were two red-clad altar assistants, one elderly and the other not yet in his teens.

Until this very moment, I hadn't given an iota of thought about how religion was going to play into this. In all honesty, God, the Church, heaven, hell, eternal life, and so on was no longer making sense to me. It was the same for Michelle. We'd had several in depth discussions on religious matters, and our atheistic views were nearly in lockstep.

"Good morning to you Mr. Gallagher," the priest greeted in excellent English. "I am Father Mainard."

"Hi ya, Father," I replied. "Good day for a wedding, yeah?"

Mainard gazed at the sky. "A more beautiful day we could not ask for."

"Hey Father, you don't have to make this too religious, ok? I've been doing a lot of thinking about that stuff - and I'm not buying it anymore."

"I'm in agreement, Father," Michelle said, her voice a gurgling crackle. "Sorry, but we're not believers. We just want to be married in this beautiful cathedral."

Father Mainard cleared his throat, obviously caught off guard by our blasphemous comments. He glanced uneasily at his older assistant.

Gerard came up to the priest. "Excuse me Father, may I have a word with you?"

* * * * *

Lying on that gurney with my head slightly propped, the interior of Notre Dame mesmerized me with its immensity. The vaulted ceiling seemed a mile high. Three massive rose windows, grandiosely decorated with vibrant stained glass, filtered an exquisite light that seeped into every corner of the transepts.

I reached out and touched Michelle's hand, feeling the diamond ring I gave her in the Balearics. "Wish we could walk."

Michelle opened her eyes. "Me too."

"Hey, don't you be fallin' asleep on me."

She began to cough.

I starred at her gaunt cheeks. There something about her color . . .

Is she blue?

* * * * *

Since walking was impossible, even with assistance, Michelle and I were positioned so that we could hold hands while being wheeled down the aisle. There weren't many people about yet but, with it being a Sunday, the cathedral would soon be full of worshipers for 9 o'clock mass.

"I had an interesting conversation with Father Mainard," Gerard said to us. "He is a most understanding priest. I didn't have to twist his arm to get him to wed you in a secular manner."

"Grand," I said. "Thought we were out of luck there for a while."

Michelle suddenly erupted into another coughing fit, this one the most intense I'd seen from her. It sounded like there was a gallon of water in her lungs. There was blood trickling out of her nose. Dr. Brodeur dashed to her gurney with his stethoscope drawn. He listened in three places while directing a crying Marci to tend to Michelle's bleeding nose.

Brodeur's dispassionate expression turned grim.

"*Nous devons nous dépêcher*," he said. "*La cyanose est présenté.*"

"What's that mean?" I anxiously asked Beau, who was standing near me.

"He wants us to hurry. Cyanosis is present."

"What's cyanosis?"

"I don't know."

* * * * *

For the first time since the illness began I was scared for Michelle.

Really scared.

And really angry.

Why isn't she getting better? I thought. *This is crazy! We have the flu! People get it all the time!*

Was Michelle going to die?

Was I?

Raging inside, I came within a hair of unleashing a slew of curses that would have permanently stained the cathedral's limestone columns.

Steady on . . . keep it together . . .

"Marry us fast, Father," I said, taking hold of Michelle's hand - which seemed to magically stop her coughing. "We're ready."

"I love you," Michelle said in a whisper.

"I love you, too. Here we go."

* * * * *

I'm willing to bet that our wedding ceremony was the shortest ever in the history of Notre Dame. Father Mainard got to the "Do you take Michelle to be your lawful wedded wife" bit in a flash. We didn't have any rings, so Gerard and Marci let us use their wedding rings as a symbolic substitute. The fit was fairly close.

We were pronounced man and wife at 8:28 on the morning of July 14, 1918.

With the help of Marci and Gerard, Michelle and I were rolled to our side so we could kiss.

"Mrs. Gallagher," I said.

"My husband."

"Now for the honeymoon. Where should we go?"

Michelle's eyes closed again.

The bluish tint in her skin was clearly evident.

Please don't die . . .

* * * * *

When we got outside, Beau and Maurice stopped for a moment to throw some celebratory pink rice at the foot of our gurneys.

"Congratulations," Beau said. "You married the best girl in the world."

"You bet I did. - Pretty lucky, yeah?"

Michelle gave a faint smile. "Best guy," she struggled to say as her coughs started again.

We were carried quickly through a scattering of curious onlookers on their way to mass. Behind me I could hear Gerard trying to comfort Marci, who was crying happy tears out of one eye and tears of sorrow from the other.

The ambulance's motor was running.

Our gurneys were loaded and the doors slammed shut.

We sped off for the chateau at high speed with the siren blaring. Doctors in a hospital couldn't effectually do anything more for Michelle than we could do in the ambulance, so there was no reason for the driver to race through the winding streets of Paris.

"*Ralentir!*" Gerard shouted. "*Vous obtiendrez tous nous tuer!*"

The youthful driver obeyed the commands and slowed down.

* * * * *

This cannot be happening! I thought. *It's gotta be a bad dream. Why can't I wake up from it? Wake up, you! Wake up now!*

But I was awake, living through the worst dream imaginable. For a flashing moment I thought about praying for Michelle. But seriously, what good would it do? Over the past year my opinion about religion had undergone a dramatic change. What was happening to Michelle was the final straw. I no longer bought into the idea of an all-powerful, all-loving, supernatural higher power called *God*. If there was such an entity, and if he decided to answer my prayer by miraculously curing Michelle, then that would mean this higher power picks and chooses who gets help. He plays favorites with his limitless power. I'm sorry, but any god worthy of intelligent worship can't play favorites. Think of all the countless good people who've been prayed for by loves ones but still died? Did God not hear these prayers? Did he not have the power to answer the prayers?

Did he not care?

Or was he *non-existent*?

Growing up I heard that everything happens for a reason and that God has a *master plan*. Oh really? So it's part of God's master plan to allow Michelle to get deathly sick? His master plan had my mother die young? My father, too? His master plan called for my aunt Patti to be gunned down by British soldiers? His master plan condemned millions of innocent men, women, children and babies to die horrible deaths over thousands of years?

Yeah right - tell that to the families of these people. Try saying this to a grieving mother whose baby daughter was swept away in a flood. "Your baby's death was all part of God's master plan. He could have saved her, but he had to let her die." Praying makes even less sense if that were true because if the act of praying influenced God to intervene, then his master plan could be altered. And don't tell me the standard line "God works in mysterious ways." That's a copout. God's supposed to be my best friend, but if I don't believe in him he'll burn me in hell forever. Now that's a good friend for ya!

I had to quit thinking about it.

It's all bollocks! God is a security belief for weak-minded people. Let them pray to their imaginary friend.

* * * * *

Michelle's coughs were incessant, each one causing blood to spray from her nose and mouth. She could hardly take a breath with her lungs so full of fluid. It sounded like she was drowning. Her skin color bore no resemblance to the flawless, radiant olive tone of two days before. It was changing before my eyes, turning a sickly, reddish purple. All I could do was hold her hand and watch her suffer. I lay there beside her and silently cried. Marci and Gerard cried with me as they sat on their knees next to her gurney.

* * * * *

Back at the chateau.

I insisted that Michelle be put in my bed. Holding my own physically, I shunned the rollaway for a comfy chair that Maurice brought into the room. I sat as close as possible to Michelle, Sinn Fein beside me, and never took my eyes off her. Over the course of the next three hours she was in and out of consciousness. During that time she called out my name thrice; she said she loved me twice; she said, "I'm Mrs. Gallagher" once.

I tried everything I could to stay awake: pinching myself, holding my eyelids open, humming, shaking my hands and feet . . .

* * * * *

I awoke in a panic.

Sinn Fein jumped down.

"Michelle!" I blurted.

I couldn't see her. Gerard and Beau had wedged themselves in front of the comfy chair. Marci was sobbing hysterically from the other side of her bed. "No . . . no . . . no," she wailed. "Oh my sweet girl!"

When I tried to rise from the chair my legs buckled and I dizzily toppled back.

"Marci!" I hollered. "Gerard! - How is she?"

Beau turned around and fell to his knees at my side. "Mick . . . I'm sorry. I'm so sorry."

A second attempt at rising barely got my rear end off the chair before I collapsed again. "Help me up! I want to see her!"

Beau and Gerard pulled at my arms and propped me against Michelle's bed.

"Michelle!" I cried, nudging her shoulders. "Michelle! Michelle, wake up!"

You can't go! You can't leave me!

"She's gone, Mick," Beau said. "There's nothing you can do. She's gone."

"No . . . Michelle! It's me! Michelle!"

You can't be gone! It should be me!

My legs gave way.

I passed out.

9
The Dark Light

Sinn Fein licked my face. My eyes opened, but I couldn't see anything.

Huh? What in the world? Must be the middle of the night.

Sinn Fein licked me again.

"Hey boy - it is you. Holy schmykees! Where have I been?" I popped my head up.

"Jaysus, it was dream. A dream! Michelle's alive!"

Wait a minute . . . was it a dream? Janey mack, I don't know.

"Hello?" I hollered. "Is anyone out there? Hey! Michelle? Beau? Anyone? I need to talk to somebody!"

Stiff, weak, and sore, I climbed out of bed and gingerly felt my way through the darkness.

A door opened and the light came on.

Gerard and Marci were there.

I stared at them.

Was it a dream? Please make it a dream.

Marci rushed to hold me. "Mick!"

"Marci, tell me it was a dream. Tell me Michelle's alive. Please!"

Gerard approached. "Mick, you've been asleep for two days."

"Two days?"

"Yes. You've pulled through."

"I have? - But what about . . . oh no . . ." My legs began to falter.

Gerard and Marci stabilized me. "I wish it was a dream, Mick," Marci said, beginning to cry. "I wish it was."

A hot wave of dizziness struck me.

"Stay awake, Mick," Gerard said. "Don't pass out again. - Let us sit you down."

They led me a few wobbly steps to the comfy chair.

"No . . . no . . . no," I said lifelessly. "I need to be left alone."

"You need some water," Marci insisted. "You're dehydrated."

"Leave a pitcher."

"Are you hungry?"

"No. Please - just leave me be."

"All right," Gerard said. "We'll go. If you need anything, just call out. Someone will hear you."

"I need Michelle."

"Yes. - Don't we all."

"Where's my dog?" I asked.

"I'll get him for you. Would you like the light on or off?"

"Off."

If there had been a pistol lying nearby I probably would have grabbed it and put a bullet in my brain. Michelle was my world. And now my world was gone. How could I go on from this? Words can't describe how I felt. Inconsolable, I stayed in my room for the better part of three days.

* * * * *

"Knock, knock."

Startled, I opened my eyes to see a dimly lit Gerard standing in the doorway. He was holding a tray containing a pot of sweet smelling tea. "This is an exotic variety. I thought you might like to try it."

"Maybe later."

Gerard flipped on the light switch with the edge of the tray. The brightness poked into my eyeballs.

"Jaysus man, could you turn that off?"

"No I won't," Gerard replied. "You've been in here long enough. We need to get you moving around. You and I can talk."

"I don't feel like talking."

Undeterred, Gerard put the tray down and leisurely filled the cups. After taking a whiff of the savory aroma, he said, "Mick, listen to me. You are not the only one suffering through this loss, so would you please stop the woe-is-me routine. You can only feel sorry for yourself for so long. We are all hurting deeply."

I looked away.

"Marci is putting on a strong front," Gerard continued, "but she is in the abyss of despair. Beau's grief is manifesting in its usual way - anger. As for me, I'm doing what I can to" - eyes closed, he bit his lower lip - "I'm trying to hold what's left of this family together. Marci and I have now lost two sons and a daughter in less than a year. Until you become a parent, you cannot know what that is like." Gerard sat down next to me holding a full cup of tea that he carefully set on the armrest. "There are no magic words that can ease your grief. In the end you're going to have to deal with the loss on your own - for the rest of your life. I will, too. So will Marci, Beau, and Gabby. To tell you the truth, and in fairness to you, I couldn't contemplate losing my wife. Marci and I have been married for a long time, over thirty years."

"It wasn't even a day for me," I mumbled. "Only a few hours." Feeling choked up, I reached for the tea and took a delicate sip.

"How is it?"

"Good," I said, trying to steady the emotional tide.

"It's imported from Sri Lanka."

Some quiet moments passed.

"Is Gabby here?" I finally asked. Gabrielle was Michelle's older sister by nineteen years. She and her husband, Vincent, were always busy traveling the world.

"She and Vincent got here this morning. They were in Cairo again. We've had an outpouring of condolences from friends and acquaintances. Over the last two days the chateau has had many sympathetic visits. In fact, there are people here now comforting Marci. I needed to get away from that for a while."

My back was getting sore, so I twisted side to side and touched my toes. "I have been feeling sorry for myself, but I can't believe Michelle's gone. We talked about how long we'd be married, hopefully seventy years or more - not seventy minutes."

Gerard gave me a sad, subtle nod.

"This was supposed to be a bad dream," I went on. "Michelle should be here with me, sitting where you are. I loved her so much, Gerard. None of this makes sense. She was only sixteen for Pete's sake! Her whole life was ahead of her."

"Don't look for any sense as to why things happen. I learned that long ago. There's no justice in the natural world. There never has been and there never will be. You have to accept life's events - that's all you can do. How you react to them defines who you are."

"What I feel like *accepting* is my own death," I said bitterly.

Gerard shook his head. "Don't talk that way. What if it was you who were dead? Would you want Michelle to throw up her hands and quit on life? - Would you?"

I looked away, hiding tears.

"Of course you wouldn't. You'd want her to go on. You'd want her to find love again - to get married and raise a family. Am I right? - Answer me."

"Yeah . . . I'd want her to."

"Michelle would want the same for you. Mick, you must honor that."

"Yes, I know. But I'm going to need time. A lot of time."

"Of course."

"Right now I'm just . . . I'm so upset. It feels like there are bombs going off inside me. Everything is shaking. All I want to do is scream my head off and smash things." I motioned behind me. "There's a hole here in the headboard. Sorry about that."

"Feel free to make more holes if you need to. Try not to break your hand."

"This must be what it was like for Queen Victoria when Albert died. She never got over losing him. – I better put on a lot of black."

"Maurice was like that with Yvette," Gerard said. "He moved on with his life but never found anyone else. - I'm not saying that will happen with you."

"It will. I know it. There can't be anyone else."

"I wouldn't be so sure. You're only sixteen. Time may not heal completely, but it always heals."

"Maybe I'll talk with Maurice about it," I said nodding. "He's gotta be waylaid by this. He was like a second father to her."

"He was."

I gave Sinn Fein a few gentle pats and ear scratches. "It's so crazy. How am I going to keep my sanity, Gerard? Maybe I've already gone insane? How would I know? I'm so . . . Jaysus, I can't think straight."

"You're not insane, and no one expects you to think straight. I'm not thinking straight either. How could anyone?"

After a few under my breath curse words, I said, "Last month Michelle and I were in the Balearics, having the time of our lives. A few days ago we were in Ireland, happy as could be - and then . . ." I gulped down a swig of tea. "How could she die? How is it possible? Michelle was in perfect health."

"I've learned much in recent days. This strain of influenza is fast becoming one of the worst in recorded history. It's a pandemic, infecting millions of people in Europe and the United States. They're calling it the Spanish Flu."

"Why that name? Is it from Spain?"

"Not from what I hear. News of the epidemic's virulence was first reported from Spain, however. They think it began spreading among soldiers in the trenches. From them it's moved on to the civilian population. I've been thinking that you might have caught this flu from the British soldiers you scuffled with in Dublin."

"Geez - yes," I said. "That's gotta be it. But why didn't the virus kill me?"

Gerard shrugged. "It very nearly did. Your body hung on; Michelle's didn't. Her lungs couldn't hold off the pneumonia. Doctors are mystified as to why so many young people are dying from it. Ordinarily the older and weaker of the population are more prone to succumb."

I finished off the tea. "Death just keeps taking everybody away from me. There's nobody's left. My mother died before I was potty-trained. All of my grandparents are gone. The Brits murdered Aunt Patti. Before you came in I was thinking about my father. He would have adored Michelle. - Man, I wish he was here. He promised me that I'd see him again, but that didn't work out."

* * * * *

Two years earlier, on the 19th of April 1916, I boarded a ferry and left Dublin to go stay with my aunt Patti in France. The Easter Rising was about to blow and my father wanted to make sure I'd have someone to look after me in case something happened to him.

"As soon as things settle down here you'll be back," he told me for the fifth time in the last hour - this time at the loading dock. "It could be a month, three, maybe more. I don't know the exact details yet, but a major action will take place. I'm envisioning another rebellion like the one in 1798."

"Could the whole thing fizzle?"

"I don't think it will. Pearse and Connolly are pretty fired up. They aren't in the mood to play nice with the Crown. Blood is going to be spilled."

"Just stay safe - ok?"

Seamus pretended to punch my chin. "I will. They won't lay a finger on me. Here's your ferry ticket and some money. You earn your keep with Patti, all right? Help her out as much as you can."

"Yeah, of course."

"I'll write you soon - let you know what's going on, ok?"

"Yeah."

"Hey, don't look so glum," my dad said, flicking the brim of my hat. "You know me, I always prepare for the worst. I have to do that, especially now."

"I just don't see why I have to go."

"Son, we've been over this."

"But I'm old enough to battle the Brits with you. I'm not a child."

"True, but you're all I got. Nothing is more important to me than your safety." The ferry's steam whistle sounded. "There's your call."

"I *will* see you again?"

Father forced a laugh. "Of course you will. Don't be daft. Now get going."

* * * * *

I never saw my father again. He died in the GPO on the last day of the Rising, the 29th of April. If he had been taken prisoner, he might not have survived for very long anyway. He could have gone to Kilmainham Gaol and been executed along with the other leaders of the Rising.

In the first volume of these memoirs (*The Emerald Ace*) I included my father's last letter to me. It arrived on April 30th.

Here it is again:

Dear Michael,

I hope you are faring well. Events here in Dublin have kept me inordinately busy. Danger is everywhere, and that's why visiting Aunt Patti was the right thing to do. Before you departed, I mentioned that an uprising was coming. It will take place during Easter week, beginning Monday, the 24th. My station will be inside the General Post Office, our main base of operations. Patrick Pearse will read the provisional government's proclamation in front of the GPO and then our flag will be hoisted.

I don't think the flag will be flying for long. In my opinion, and I believe also in the minds of Pearse, James Connolly, Thomas Clarke, Joseph Plunkett, et al., this uprising is doomed to failure. We cannot defeat the British in a conventional style of war. This rising plays to the British strength. I pray that our sacrifice will not be in vain. By the time you read this letter the world will know the outcome.

My thoughts are constantly with you. From the day you were born, you have made me the proudest father in the world. Youth still prevents you from being a pilot, but be patient. Hold on to your dreams and they will come true. With some good luck I will see you again soon. Give my best to Patti.

Seamus

My father's death was confirmed on the third of May. Since the arrival of his letter I'd all but given up hope for him. The previous day I'd seen a newspaper photo of the bombed out GPO that further darkened my outlook. Unconfirmed reports of casualties were rampant, with even the most conservative figures showing high rebel and civilian losses.

The Easter Rising had been thoroughly crushed by the British.

* * * * *

"In a way your father's death happened in stages," Gerard said, following my brief retelling. "You had time to process events, and to contemplate the next round of potential bad news. You were coping before you had to cope."

"I haven't thought about it that way before, but you're right. By the time the news came that he'd died, it wasn't a surprise."

"And you didn't have that with Michelle. Even while she was sick you expected her to get better."

"I did. It wasn't till we were inside Notre Dame that I thought the worst. I never thought about people dying from the flu before. You're sick for a few days and then you're supposed to get better, yeah?" I shook my head. "Michelle must have known she wasn't going to make it. That's why she wanted to get married. I thought she was being a little silly, but I couldn't say no to her. - This is cruel. With both of us being sick, we couldn't say goodbye."

"We didn't either," Gerard said dolefully. "Michelle was too incapacitated. Dr. Brodeur gave her some medication to ease her suffering, and . . ." Gerard stared at his teacup. "She passed away - peacefully at the end."

"While I slept."

"Yes."

Gerard stood up. "Let's get out of here, shall we?"

"Ok. I'll need a shower first and get presentable. I smell like an animal."

"You look like one, too."

"I bet." Cringing from stiffness and general weakness, I rose from the chair and said, "This can't be my body. Look at me . . . I'm a toothpick. I feel a hundred years-old."

"You'll get your strength back. It won't take you long."

"And then I'll have to figure out the next stage of my life."

Gerard put his hand on my shoulder. "There's no need to rush that. Take everything slowly. Don't think for a second that you're alone. You are a permanent member of this family. This house is your house for as long as you want it to be. You will always be a son to me - even if you do remarry someday."

"Geez oh Pete," I said, turning to the side. "You'd better stop. Talking like that's gunna get me teary again."

"I just want you to know that you will always have a home here."

I let out a long appreciative sigh. "That's a grand offering. Man alive, it's nice knowing that I'll always have a place for my stuff."

Gerard grinned at my lighthearted remark. "Like your Dickens books?"

"Yeah, those, the car, and all the other gifts you've spoiled me with."

"They are here to stay if you wish. Sinn Fein can stay here too. Furthermore, it should go without saying that you won't have to worry about finances in whatever you choose to do."

"Is there a time limit on that?" I asked jokingly.

"No time limit. I am, after all, one of the richest men in France."

"In *Europe* you mean, Mr. Modest."

Gerard chuckled. "See you downstairs."

"Right. – And thanks for talking to me."

"Don't mention it. You might soon be counseling me. This is a most trying time for all of us."

As soon as Gerard shut the door, I collapsed back into the chair and sobbed uncontrollably.

* * * * *

Michelle never wanted a traditional funeral. "They are depressing and no fun for anyone," she'd stated on several occasions. "When I die I want to be cremated and have my ashes thrown into the chateau pond. Simple, with no fuss, no fanfare."

On the windy, overcast afternoon of July 20th we carried out her wishes. It was a family-only ceremony that lasted a grand total of ten minutes. Some heartfelt words were said and some heavy tears were shed. Marci graciously asked if I would spread Michelle's ashes. So I rowed a boat out to the middle of the pond and, following a moment of reflective pause, I turned over the urn and let them go.

I had to be almost cold about it.

Ten months together. Life chapter closed.

"Goodbye Michelle," I said. "I will always love you."

The others soon left but I stayed in the boat for another hour, replaying the memories.

10
Universal Change

For the past half-year, I'd envisioned my life with Michelle. Being married, we'd eventually have our own place (or places), raise a family, and do whatever we wanted to do for the rest of our days. Along the way Michelle would always be there to support me in my fight for an independent Ireland.

Now she was forever gone.

Taken from me.

How could I ever recover? It didn't seem possible. When you hear stories about people who lose their entire family - spouse, kids, everybody - in a fire or some other kind of accident and yet they somehow manage to pick up the shattered pieces of their life and get on with it, you shake your head in amazement. How did they do that?

My father told me that when Mom died the only thing that kept him going was me. Otherwise he would have killed himself - with a gun or the bottle. Well I didn't have any kids. So what was I to do? Surrender on life and say to hell with it? Or fight back to embrace life again?

Though there was no real hurry to figure out how to do that, I *wanted* to hurry. I was in an anxious panic about it. And it didn't matter that I was only sixteen. So what! It was my way of coping. As soon as possible, I had to get my life into some semblance of order. What I needed was a completely new environment, a new universe so to speak, one with new goals, new ideas, and new horizons.

I set an arbitrary timetable of three weeks for me to leave the chateau - no later than August 10th. Why three weeks? I don't really know. Three weeks just sounded right. Less than a month; more than a fortnight. There was no need to inform Gerard and Marci of my intended departure date, for they surely would beg me to reconsider.

* * * * *

The first step was to get physically healthy. Beginning July 21, from 7 to 9:30 in the morning, I worked out like an obsessed Olympic athlete for 15 straight days. It was non-stop running, jumping, tumbling, swimming, rowing, climbing, and a myriad of calisthenics. I overdid it actually. The therapeutic aspects of such extreme physical exertion started to backfire at the end of two weeks. I had to ease off or the various hurts would have turned into injuries. My rebuilt but overly worked body welcomed the break.

Afternoons were spent on the golf course - 18 to 36 holes a day. Usually I played alone, but there were a number of occasions when the starter partnered me with another player - always, it seemed, a short hitting older gentleman who could split the fairways and was a wizard around the greens. Overall my game was good but not spectacular. When I was feeling especially fatigued from a morning workout my play could be atrociously erratic. There were a few times when frustration turned to laughter at seeing a chip shot shank into the water or a drive hook out of bounds.

During the most of the time when I wasn't exercising, playing golf, fending off sudden bouts of crushing sadness, and doing my best to be a sociable human being with the family, I was camped out in the library exploring the limitless possibilities for the next chapter of my life.

What a daunting task! My immediate future was restricted only by my imagination. The whole world was out there for me. *Carpe diem!* Seize the Day! It was almost beyond belief that at the age of sixteen I was already a widower and an internationally famous fighter pilot. On top of that, I had lucked my way into a source of money that could allow me to do essentially anything I wanted for the rest of my life. I would never have to 'make a living' like the vast majority of human beings. There would be no work stress, no boss breathing down my neck, no anxiety about making ends meet. Only people with generational wealth can say that. Though I felt some guilt about not having earned the money, it was there for me to use. I'd be a fool not to take advantage of the financial freedom. Besides, Gerard would have it no other way. And it wasn't like I was going to blow the fortune in a year's time. The money would always be working for me, growing through Gerard's wise investments and, eventually, my own.

* * * * *

Ireland's struggle for independence from Britain was never far from my mind. I could either return to Dublin now, or I could wait until the Great War was over. Being a currently wanted man for committing treason against the Crown, I decided to wait. Once the war was over, hopefully some of the heat would be off me. My identity as the Emerald Ace might not pose such a handicap while mixing about with the British on Dublin's streets.

The conflict couldn't go on much longer; Germany was certainly going to lose. Their last offensive, which I had been a part of with the Flying Circus, had run out of steam. America's fresh influx of men and equipment was proving too much to overcome. The Kaiser's army was exhausted and demoralized. The only reason they continued to fight was in the hope that they would get a better deal in the eventual peace treaty.

What about going back to school? The idea made sense in many ways, but I decided against it. I wasn't in the proper mindset for school. If I went back now I'd last maybe two weeks before wanting to break free. I had the rest of my life to further my education and attain a collection of nicely framed university degrees. Archaeology, philosophy, and biology were of high interest, as was civil engineering, architecture, and astronomy. But the long time commitment involved, and having to adhere to rigid class schedules was about as appealing as a dentist's drill. My formal polymath studies could wait a while.

So what was I going to do? Sitting in the library, trying not to think about Michelle (which was impossible), I arrived at a decision within the first ten minutes.

The answer was obvious, really.

I would travel!

Traveling would force me out of my current dark hole (or at least distract me from it) and expose me to boatloads of new experiences. I would surely grow as a person and gain new perspectives on the world and its people. Above all, traveling would give me the necessary time to mentally heal.

* * * * *

So it was settled - I would travel. But where to first?

The lure of golf immediately steered me toward Scotland and the Old Course at St. Andrews. A must-see, must-do location for sure! Any serious golfer's dream. But did I want to go there first? No, the home of golf would be a stop or two down the road. My first destination had to be somewhere more adventurous, a scenic, fascinating, and prudently challenging place. It had to be remote, but not *too* remote. For example, a trip to the Antarctic would take months, maybe a year or more, and I didn't want to bite off something so logistically iffy right out of the gate. Maybe I'd head to that icy world with Ernest Shackleton after visiting some major sites in the United States and a few places in South America.

An elegant bronze globe, framed in dark cherry wood, stood near the door. I thought about giving it a spin and going with wherever my finger landed. Though not at all committed to the result, I tried anyway just for fun. My finger hit the middle of the Indian Ocean on the first spin. The next spin gave me another watery location, this time west of the Hawaiian Islands. Not surprising, I thought. Two-thirds of the world is covered in water. A third spin found water again in the South Atlantic.

One more try, I thought.

The fourth spin of the globe fell on land - in Europe, somewhere between Austria, Italy and Switzerland. I lifted my finger and studied the spot.

Switzerland!

Not too far away - maybe a ten-hour train ride. Beautiful country. It had the Alps.

The Matterhorn!

Arguably the most famous, but certainly the most iconic mountain in the world, the Matterhorn had long fascinated me.

Yes!

I was going to climb it!

* * * * *

On the night of August 5 the last German zeppelin raid of the Great War took place. Five massive airships (including the newest and biggest *L-70,* the zeppelin I'd gone aloft in with Anton Dunkel and Peter Strasser) attacked the Norwich coast of England. The raid was a total failure. Of the five zeppelins, only the *L-70* perished. All 23 crewmen, including both Dunkel and Strasser, plunged to fiery deaths from 7,000 feet. The *L-53, L-56, L-63*, and *L-65* all made it back to Germany.

I would have been deeply saddened by the event if Michelle were alive. Now it seemed like nothing in the world could sadden me.

Another day, another friend gone.

* * * * *

A week or so after Michelle died I wrote Paul Coburn a long letter telling him the details of her illness. I would have called him on the telephone but I didn't want to break down.

During the afternoon of August 8 Maurice requested my presence downstairs.

"What is it?" I asked.

"The telephone. Your friend Paul Coburn is on the line."

I heaved a sigh. *Come on now, hold it together.*

"Hey, Paul," I said. "You got my letter."

"I did. - Mick, I . . . I don't know what to say."

"There's nothing really to say, so forget about it. It was a bad deal. Life kills us all man. It's relentless. - It's nice to hear from ya."

"Your letter - it told me what happened."

"Yeah you wanker, that's why I wrote it. Look Paul, I really don't want to talk about Michelle over the phone."

"Ok, ok, I understand. Is there anything I can do for ya? Anything at all? Want me to come down there for a while? It is my turn you know."

"You can do that if you want, but I'm leaving here real soon."

"Oh . . . when?"

"In a few days. I wanted to be out of here by the 10th, but I guess I can hang around a bit longer."

"Where are you going to?"

"Nowhere in particular. I won't be settling down, that's for sure. I'm gunna venture out and explore the globe. The only way I can move on from losing Michelle is to start over. I need to create a new universe for myself, you know, one full of new challenges and experiences. It'll get my mind off Michelle, and I'll meet gobs of new people that way. And I don't just mean someone to replace Michelle. No one's gunna be able to do that."

"For sure."

"It's the only way I can function," I said. "I'll never forget Michelle, and I don't want to forget her, but I have to put her in the past. If I don't it'll literally kill me."

"Yeah, I get it. - So what are some of the challenges you have in mind?"

"Well, first on my list is . . . are you ready?"

"Yeah, tell me."

"I'm going to climb a mountain - the Matterhorn."

"Huh? You're joking. - Seriously?"

"You bet I'm serious. It's only a half-day train ride away. - Hey, you wanna come with me?"

"You don't know the first thing about mountain climbing."

"I can learn fast. People are reaching the Matterhorn's summit all the time now. It can't be that hard to do."

"Yeah . . . suppose not. If you think about it, going from being an ace fighter pilot to mountain climber has got to be a lot less dangerous."

"Sure it is. There's no comparison. So come on, you wanna go?"

"Man, I don't know. It's pretty risky."

"Of course it is! It's the perfect amount of risk."

Silence.

"You big coward," I grumbled. "Grow a spine why don't ya?"

"Sheesh, Mick . . . pressure. - Oh all right, might as well. I'll climb it with you. But don't you push me off the top."

"Huh, me? No way. I might cut your rope on the way down, though. - Let's get after it. Why don't you take the train to Versailles tonight and we can get the trip ready."

"Ok. My parents are in need of a break from me anyway. - So tell me, what are your plans after the Matterhorn? Or do you have any?"

"Nothing's definite yet other than golfing at St. Andrews. You can do that with me, too. Get down here and we can talk. Make sure to bring your passport."

"All right. I'll be there by ten. - Hey Mick . . . I'm so sorry about Michelle."

"Yeah, I know. She was . . ." I put down the telephone for a few moments, trying to keep it together. "Hey man, I'll see ya soon ok?"

* * * * *

Gerard accompanied me for the drive to pick up Paul at the *Gare du Nord* train station. I drove the new Charron, the fancy car he'd given me for my sixteenth birthday back in November. I hadn't driven the 30 h.p. car much outside the palace grounds, so it was fun putting the pedal to the metal on a main road. During the speedy ride I finally told Gerard about my future traveling plans.

"We figured you'd be leaving soon," Gerard said, his wispy hair flying about in the wind. "It's not good for you to stay here too long. You've got to move on with your life. But please promise me that you will stop in once in a while. Marci and I would like to see you more than once a year if possible."

"It'll be more often than that. Like you said, this is my home. You're my family. And besides, Beau will blow a gasket if I don't visit often - and we certainly don't want that!"

Gerard laughed. "After you conquer the Matterhorn, will you come back here first or head directly to Scotland?"

"Well I'd have to buy new golf clubs if I didn't come back here to get mine."

"Bah! You could buy a string of golf courses, or build new ones, so I don't think buying new golf clubs will be a problem."

"True. I'll let you know when we leave Zermatt."

We pulled into the station parking area spot on time. Once parked it only took ten minutes to collect Paul and be on our way again. Paul asked if he could drive so I turned over the wheel.

"Don't kill us," I said. "That would ruin our trip."

* * * * *

I was itching to go. The mighty Matterhorn awaited! So the next morning, after a very late night of chit-chat (when I got pretty teary for a time), Paul and I loaded up our bulky backpacks and readied to leave for the resort town of Zermatt, Switzerland - but not before Marci, on a wild whim of an idea, shaved my head practically bald to give me a shocking new look to throw off any potential recognition. Talk about scary looking!

"You look like an ax murderer," Paul commented.

"It's probably best that I stay away from mirrors for a while," I joked. "Don't want to scare myself to death."

Marci giggled. "You're a *handsome* scary, Mick."

I said goodbye to Beau via telephone, Maurice, and my dog Sinn Fein, then hopped into the glistening Rolls-Royce Silver Ghost with Paul. Gerard was at the wheel, Marci beside him.

"Well, I'm Michael Fitzpatrick again," I said with a chuckle. "That bogus passport you made me for the Balearic Islands trip is grand."

"Don't get a sunburn on that bald head," Gerard said as we pulled away.

"Right. - You know I kind of look bald in the passport photo because you can't really see my hair."

"Do you guys wish you were climbing the Matterhorn with us?" Paul asked.

"Not in the least," Marci growled.

Gerard gave her a sour glance. "Well I do, Paul. But my risk-averse wife won't allow me such recreation."

Marci shook her head annoyingly. "If you were thirty years younger, I might let you. The climb is too dangerous for someone your age." Turning around to face us, Marci asked, "Are you novice climbers aware of what happened during the first ascent of the Matterhorn?"

"You mean Edward Whymper's group?" I answered.

"Yes. I've never forgotten reading about the story as a child."

"What happened," Paul queried uneasily.

"It wasn't good," I said.

"I'll tell you what happened," Marci replied forcefully. "Edward Whymper and six other climbers made it to the summit safely, but on the way down one of the men fell. - I can't recall his name."

"Hadow," I said. "Douglas Hadow."

"That's it. Hadow slipped and fell into another man, and in the process two others were pulled down with them. Whymper and two Zermatt guides, a father and son, held on, but a rope broke from the force of the fall. This breakage created a lot of controversy. Whymper was accused of cutting the rope to save himself."

"He didn't do that," I bluntly interjected. "I read his book of the account, *Scrambles Amongst the Alps* - you have a fist edition of it in the library. He said the rope that broke was the weakest one they'd bought before the climb. The accident was just bad luck." I turned to

Paul. "Rest easy. That's not going to happen to us. We'll use the strongest rope on the planet."

"I'm not climbing if we don't."

* * * * *

The train journey of nine hours and fifteen minutes to Zermatt was a smooth affair with only one minor delay in Beaune. We traveled through Basel and Bern and arrived in Zermatt at 10:30 p.m.

Paul and I were quickly given directions to the famous *Monte Rosa Hotel*, the oldest hotel in Zermatt and where Edward Whymper stayed before setting off on his tragic conquest of the Matterhorn in 1865. Room-service was still available, so we ordered some fruit-filled muesli and settled down for the night.

"Did you bring a gun?" Paul asked me just as I was beginning to nod off.

"Dumb question. Of course, I did. Gerard gave me one of his Lebel revolvers. It's in my backpack."

11
Zermatt

Attempting to climb the Matterhorn without the assistance of an experienced guide would be suicidal. During a delicious late-morning eggs and bacon breakfast in the hotel's restaurant, our waitress, a leathery-faced woman in her late forties with sunburn scars along both sides of her nose, overheard Paul and I discussing the climb. She offered her recommendation of a guide.

"You should seek out Umberto Lannelli," she said in a heavy French accent. "No one knows the peaks around Zermatt better than him. The Matterhorn is his second home. He's taken my husband to the summit twice. However, he is not cheap."

"Where can we find him?" I asked.

"I believe he is still living on the top floor of the *Monte Cervin Palace*. It's close by, just down the street on your right. You can't miss it. If he is not there he's either leading a climb or gambling in the casino. He does love the dice. The casino is across the *Vispa*, perpendicular from here."

"Thank you kindly. If by chance Mr. Lannelli is not available, do you have another guide in mind?"

"None that I would trust one-hundred percent with my life. Unless you must leave town quickly, I think it best for you to wait for Umberto."

* * * * *

Edward Whymper's tragic adventure made Zermatt world famous. A heavenly paradise for alpine climbers, skiers and hikers, the enchanting resort town is located at the foot of the towering Matterhorn (*Monte Cervino* in Italian, *Mont Cervin* in French). But the Matterhorn doesn't stand alone: surrounding the area are no less than 38 mountain peaks over 13,000 feet. Nothing says "Switzerland" more than a panoramic gaze from the bell tower of a Zermatt church. Tourism of course dominates the economy, so there are dozens of hotels, restaurants, and gift shops lining the cobblestoned streets. Pedestrians do not have to watch out for cars since all motorized vehicles are banned (still true today). Further adding to the charming atmosphere is the bisecting *Vispa*. The narrow river gives the village a little taste of Amsterdam.

"This is a fabulous place," Paul said as we headed out of the *Monte Rosa*. "If I was a dedicated skier I wouldn't mind living here. How much have you skied?"

I wiggled my index finger. "One time - when I was eleven. My dad immediately took me to the top of the run - the steepest one, mind you! It was wild. I'd never been on skis before and he expected me to be able to follow him down. Without any practice, and without any delay, we started off - zoom, right down the mountain. For some reason turning left came easy for me. I thought I was a natural. But I couldn't turn right very well. It was so frustrating! My ski tips kept crossing. If I did manage a right turn, it was never quite all the way, so I kept picking up speed, which then made it harder to turn left. So you can guess what happened after that. I ended up bombing down the hill full speed, out of control! Oh man - the crash was epic. Lucky I didn't break my neck. I almost took out this bloke who was skiing down the mountain all nice and easy like. Jaysus sakes, I coulda killed the guy! Dad laughed his back side off."

"Did you go down the run again?"

"Yeah, a few times more. The results were more or less the same. It baffles me why I couldn't turn right."

"No better time to fix the problem than now," Paul said. "We should ski after our climb."

I nodded. "Maybe take a real lesson. - You ever skied?"

Paul raised his index finger. "Same as you - one time."

"Did you do better than me?"

Paul grinned. "Let's just say that I can turn left *and* right."

"You're a wanker."

* * * * *

The tuxedoed front desk clerk at the *Monte Cervin Palace* informed us that Umberto Lannelli was not in his room. "Mr. Lannelli keeps me up to date on his climbing schedule," the clerk said, looking through a palm-sized notebook. "He has a Matterhorn climb set for tomorrow morning leading four people. After that he is open until August 19."

"Might he be at the casino?" I asked.

"I was just about to suggest that. Yes, check there first. Give me your names, contact information, and I will notify him of your interest in his services."

"Grand. Thanks, man. - Oh, what does he look like?"

* * * * *

With my natural older appearance coupled with the near chrome dome atop my head, I looked plenty adult enough for the *Casino Zermatt*. I thought Paul might have some trouble gaining entrance, but surprisingly no one batted an eye.

The place was jam-packed. There wasn't an open gambling table to be found. The rows of "Bell Machines" (slot machines) were reeling and dinging in a lively swirl of celebratory hoops and hollers.

All we had to look for was a black fedora hat with a red band around it. The desk clerk told us that Umberto always wore it in public. Otherwise the early thirties man had no distinguishable physical features: clean-shaven with black hair, medium build, medium height of 5-foot eight inches, and medium skin color.

"There he is," Paul said, pointing to a tight circle of people surrounding a craps table.

"He's rolling the dice. Come on, let's go watch."

We found a gap at the end of the table and squeezed our way in, just in time to see Umberto blow into the red dice and toss them with a skilled two fingered flick of the wrist toward us. "Give me an eight!" he commanded. The dice bounced off the padded green felt and knocked over a stack of orange chips that was sitting on the number ten. A dreadful moan arose from circle as the stickman uttered a depressed "Seven out."

"What happened?" Paul asked.

"He rolled seven. That clears the table when a point has been established. The point was eight."

"Huh?"

"Never mind. It's kinda complicated."

Umberto grabbed his drink in disgust and walked away, making a b-line for the exit. Nearing the door a man in a navy blue suit blocked his path. The two men exchanged some angry indecipherable words before Umberto shoved the larger man out of the way and burst out to the street.

"What was that all about?" Paul asked.

"You got me. That other guy was pretty cheesed-off."

* * * * *

"Pardon me," I said, catching up to him across the street. "I hear you're the best climbing guide in Zermatt."

Umberto turned around and glared his bright blue eyes at me. "You heard the truth."

"Mr. Lannelli, my friend and I would like to hire you to lead us to the top of the Matterhorn."

The annoyance on Umberto's face eased slightly. "Hmmm. Have you climbed before?"

"No we haven't, but I know we can do it. We're tough as iron."

"Tough's good, but are you in shape?"

"Tip-top."

"We could run a marathon," Paul added proudly.

Umberto nodded. "Do you take orders well?"

I playfully saluted him. "We'll follow your every command."

"Good. I won't tolerate disputers.   - When do you want to go?"

"The desk clerk at the *Monte Cervin* told us that you are leading a foursome up the Matterhorn tomorrow," I said. "So we can either add on with that group - if that's all right with them - or wait until you get back."

The guide's Italian accent was quirky. It sounded like he was trying to imitate an upper class Brit. "We can go the day after tomorrow. The foursome canceled yesterday. I'll need tomorrow to sleep off the hangover. I'm going to drink myself silly starting now until I pass out. The craps table slaughtered me. - Do you have enough money for the outing? The clerk probably also told you I charge an arm and a leg."

"He did tell us that. What's your price?"

"45 pounds each. In American dollars it's $265. I prefer those currencies, but if you have lira or francs that would be" -

"No bother," I said. "45 pounds each is fine." *(£190 in 1970 currency)*

"Good, because you'll pay me upfront. Meet me in the *Palace* lobby at 9 a.m. Monday morning."

"Right. What do we need to bring?"

"Just yourselves and whatever gear you've brought along. I supply most everything - even food."

I shook his hand, followed by Paul. "Grand, this is perfect. Thanks a ton, Mr. Lannelli."

"Call me Umberto. Your names?"

"This is my friend, Paul Coburn. And I'm Michael Fitzpatrick."

"Ok then - see you Monday morning at nine."

* * * * *

"Not the most personable of chaps is he?" Paul said when Umberto was out of earshot. Are you sure we want to go with him?"

"Yeah, I'm sure. He's the one we want."

"But getting drunk before a big climb . . . I don't know. That spooks me."

"Ah, he'll be sobered up. He's bummed about his losses, that's all." I motioned back toward the casino. "Since we've got nothing but time, how about we give the tables a try? Neither one of has ever gambled. Maybe we'll get some beginner's luck?"

Paul's face lit up like a neon sign. "Oh yeah! Why not? I know how to play blackjack - in fact I'm pretty good at it."

"Me, too. I want to give that craps a try, though. And some roulette."

"They give free drinks, ya know."

"Be my guest to that. I want a clear head."

* * * * *

We set a loss limit of £5 each (£21 in 1970 currency). Paul blew through his money in twenty minutes at the blackjack table. He made some dolt plays, like splitting eights and doubling down when the dealer was showing a nine. I played along with him, holding my own throughout and walked away about even. The craps table was still the center of the action, so I flipped Paul another pound and veered over to it. I knew the basics of the game, but had never played at a real table for money. My strategy going in was simple: play the pass line with full double odds. No sucker bets.

Talk about fun! No game in the casino can match craps when it comes to bringing out the emotions in people. Because the dice were kind to us for the next couple of hours, there were a few occasions when Paul and I found ourselves jigging about in triumph and hugging complete strangers. In the end my original £2 supply of chips turned into almost £10 (£8.5 to £42 in 1970 currency). Modest success!

It was a challenge to abandon our spots. But the longer you play a game where the odds *always* favor the House, the more certain it is that you will lose. It took me a while to convince Paul to walk away. He would have stayed there until his last chip was gone.

"Tomorrow let's hit the slopes," I said heading back to the *Monte Rosa*. "I'm going to master that right turn."

* * * * *

We ate a delicious fondue dinner at the *Dupont-Zermatt* (which we found out was the oldest restaurant in Zermatt) and then checked out a small theater show involving lots of elaborate puppets to carry us through the evening. The next morning we got up early, wolfed down an oatmeal and toast breakfast, and headed to the *Kliene Matterhorn* ski lifts. Zermatt has many choices for skiers. Most every run has a full view of the Matterhorn directly in front.

How did we do? Suffice it to say, Paul kicked my rear end. Practice is supposed to make perfect, as the saying goes, but *not* for me with skiing! Within an hour I was cursing like a madman. So frustrating! No matter how much I tried to copy what Paul was doing, and listening to a dozen or more different suggestions from Paul and other skiers, a smoothly executed right turn still eluded me. If my ski tips didn't cross to send me head over heels, then I more often than not ended up bombing down the run at break-neck speed. The result was always the same: a spectacular, body-busting, cart-wheeling crash that caused every skier on the slope to stop and see if I survived.

I threw in the towel by mid-afternoon. The mental torment and physical punishment was getting out of hand. For the next two hours I stayed in the lodge sulking, sipping down one whip cream-topped mug of hot chocolate after the other, all the while gazing out the big front window at skiers of all ages coming down the runs with ease. The ultimate humiliation came when I spotted a little girl no more than four years-old, all decked out in cute pink snow gear, skiing down the hill like a world champion.

Buggers! How was she doing that? How could an athletic person like me fail to master such a seemingly simple skiing maneuver?

Michelle and I had never gone skiing. I could only imagine how she would have skied circles around me.

"You can't be good at everything, Mick. Don't be so hard on yourself."

I could hear her sweet voice trying to uplift my pathetically sour mood. Michelle took over my thoughts until Paul stomped into the lodge all heelball cocky.

God how I missed her.

* * * * *

We got a good night's sleep and were up at the crack of dawn. I was stiff and sore from all the crashes (I had a nasty bruise on my thigh), but otherwise raring to go. Paul was nervous and excited about the climb. I was much calmer. All those near-death adventures with Richthofen's Flying Circus had inoculated me against such daring-do nervousness.

After a long buffet style breakfast, we packed what mountain climbing gear we'd brought with us into our rucksacks: six pairs of thick trekking socks, some warm underclothes, fur-lined hats, sunglasses, and gloves. I'd decided not to take the Lebel revolver; it was fairly heavy and I didn't think it'd be necessary.

We arrived ten minutes early at the *Monte Cervin Palace*, but Umberto Lannelli was already in the lobby going over his notes. "It's good that he's here already," I said under my breath. "This guy's a pro."

* * * * *

"Hi ya Mr. Lannelli," I greeted. "We're all ready to go."

"*Buongiorno* Michael," the guide replied, rising from a red leather lounge chair. "I like your rucksacks. Those will do perfectly. Let's have a seat by the fire. There is a lot for us to go over."

"How was your recovery day?" I kidded.

Umberto laughed with a hand on his forehead. "It was much needed. I have a love for your Irish whiskey . . . but oh what it does to me."

"*Jameson*, yeah?"

Umberto nodded. "The best there is."

We sat down at a table nearest the gas fireplace and got down to business. Umberto flattened out a map of the region. "The climb itself will take us two or three days, depending on how you're doing. What I mean by that is normally most beginning climbers spend anywhere from three to six days doing a series of progressive climbs to acclimatize to the altitude. Altitude headaches affect people differently. Some people can work through them while others are terribly debilitated by the pain and dizziness. - What do you have in the rucksacks?"

I told him, but he wanted to inspect.

"Some of this will work," Umberto said, rummaging through our stuff. "There is much more we'll be packing. I have it stored in another room. The Matterhorn is a tough climb, even though more and more tourists are ascending its summit. Deaths occur every year. The Zermatt Churchyard is full of Matterhorn fatalities."

"Yeah, we've heard about it," I said. "Haven't seen it yet, though."

"Many of the deaths happen on the way down - like what happened on the first successful climb of the mountain."

"Edward Whymper," Paul interjected.

"You've heard. One slip was all it took. Climbing up and down, you have to be aware at all times of the danger of loose rock. We don't want to hurry up the mountain, but we also don't want to lollygag. A steady pace is key. The weather forecast is good for us, so we shouldn't have any trouble with conditions. It's August, but temperatures up there can still get down to -10 Celsius (14 Fahrenheit). Here shortly we will load our gear and set out for Schwarzsee Lake, which is six miles away. It shouldn't take much more than two hours. From there we will hike to the Hörnli Hut to rest and spend the night. This will also take about two hours. The Hörnli Hut was built in 1880 by the Swiss Alpine Club to accommodate climbers for the next day's climb to the summit. The Hut sits at 3,260 meters (10,700 feet). The Matterhorn's summit is 4,478 meters - 14,691 feet. So, after spending the night in the Hut we'll be up at 0530 and setting off in the dark at

0600 for the hard part of the climb. It's a challenging 1,218 meters (3996 feet) which will take approximately five hours - assuming all goes well. The route we'll be taking is called the Hörnligrate, the easiest route and the most popular. There are other routes, but I'm not going to take beginners up any of those. The Hörnligrate is a ridge climb, with the first two-thirds of it basically what we call a rock scramble. Near the summit is the Solvay Hut, which was built three years ago for emergencies and short rests only. The Solvay Hut is 475 meters from the summit. It's a welcome rest stop, because the final 200 meters is *very* steep, with lots of ice and snow. We can linger at the summit for photos, but there is not much room there." Umberto folded the map. "Questions?"

"Not right now," I said. "I've read a ton about the Matterhorn, and some basic mountaineering stuff. We're going to need crampons, ice-axes, rope, helmets, and I'm sure other things, too."

"Correct. You'll need proper climbing boots, outer jackets, more underclothing, and some better mountain gloves. During the morning part of the climb we'll be using headlamps. I can assure you this equipment is the best money can buy."

"Food?" I asked.

"You'll have plenty - and it's *good* climbing food. At the Hörnli Hut you'll get hot meals."

Paul spoke up. "Are there fixed ropes on the Matterhorn?"

"There are in several of the steeper sections as we near the summit." Umberto smiled. "These ropes come in handy. We'll take a 50-foot rope and several shorter ones with us. They *won't* break. My ropes could pull the *Titanic* to the surface. Also, I'll be packing a Kodak camera to take some photographs of the climb. On day two, when we should reach the summit, we can either spend another night in the Hörnli Hut or, if you feel all right, we can push on to get back here. There is no time crunch once we get back to the Hörnli Hut."

"We'll just play it by ear," I said. "You ready for this, Paul?"

"I'm so excited my legs are shaking."

"It will be a great accomplishment for you," Umberto said. "I never tire of seeing the reactions of people when they get to the summit. - If you have no more questions for me, we can go load our gear."

* * * * *

Thirty minutes later we were fully loaded and equipped for the trek. Every cubic millimeter of our rucksacks was filled to the hilt. We tried on every piece of gear.

"This will keep us nice and toasty," I said to Paul, modeling my spiffy alpine attire. "Japers, we'll look like master mountaineers up there."

"The boots feel fantastic," Paul replied, tapping his heels. "I've got really high arches, too. Wouldn't mind keeping these."

"I'll give you a nice price for them," Umberto said with a grin. He checked his gold *Omega* wristwatch. "It's half past ten now. Do you want to have an early lunch before we go?"

"I'm still full from breakfast," Paul answered.

"Me, too," I said. "But I'll take some hot chocolate."

Umberto nodded. "I'll join you with that. Then we'll be off."

* * * * *

The easy hike through the quiet, sun drenched Zmutt Valley was picture book gorgeous. The lush green forest meadows were decorated with gently flowing idyllic streams and small wooden huts. Most of the huts were built on stilts due to the area being a floodplain.

Paul and I had never seen marmots before. These large squirrels kept darting across our path, stopping ahead for a curious look at us before scampering away again. We passed through the tiny villages of Furi and Hermettji, saying hello to several of the friendly residents, one of whom insisted that we try a cup of her locally renowned 'Summit Cider.'

"My apple cider will give you the stamina to make it to the top," the old woman informed us. "I can't tell you the secret ingredient. It's *magical*."

"She's not lying," Umberto said. "I've had it many times. Try it."

Man it was tasty! The perfect blend of sweet tartness. It was so good that I couldn't help but ask for a refill. Paul did too. For her hospitality I slipped her a wad of Swiss francs. I've never been able to figure out what she put in it. The woman could have made a pretty penny selling the cider in a big city like Zurich.

We stopped briefly in the little hamlet of Zmutt to eat a salami sandwich lunch and then continued on, now using trekking poles. During this part of the hike we got the most scenic views of the enormous Zmutt Glacier as the terrain steepened toward the ridge where Schwarzsee Lake was located. Our pace kept steady and quick, fueled by a pouch of trail mix. We passed several small groups of hikers. Heading straight into the sun, we were now into the clouds. As we trekked ever higher along the rocky trail the sky scraping Matterhorn grew ever larger, daring us to approach its snow-encrusted slopes.

12
The Hörnligrate

We got to the empty Hörnli Hut at 3:30. I felt great, the skiing soreness all but gone. Paul was still full of energy as well. So I asked Umberto: "What's to stop us from continuing on? There's still plenty of the day left to make it to the summit."

"It certainly can be done, but I strongly advise against it. The climb to the summit and back would take a minimum of nine hours. We would be climbing down in the dark, utterly exhausted - and that's the biggest danger. Most likely both of you would be dealing with altitude headaches. - No, not a smart idea. Are you in a hurry?"

"Oh, I'm not in a hurry. I do enjoy pushing myself physically. Just knowing we *could* do it is all right."

"He's nuts that way," Paul blurted. "We need to stick to the plan. I want to relax here. We've paid to stay anyway."

"You might as well take advantage of it," Umberto said. "Space is limited inside. Most climbers sleep outside in a tent."

The Hörnli Hut (*Hörnlihütte* in German) was a simple two-story building. The first floor was made of stone and the second with wood. There was no running water supply, so climbers had to gather snow and melt it. An old wood stove and a sooty fireplace provided a surprising amount of heat. Outside, the view of the Matterhorn and the surrounding area was a feast for the eyes. For many less ambitious tourists, a hike to the Hörnli Hut is plenty enough to satisfy their alpine experience.

* * * * *

An hour later we had company: a quintet comprised of two forty-something Norwegian brothers, a middle-aged, upper-class British man who reminded me of Phileas Fogg from Jules Verne's *Around the World in Eighty Days*, and a Portuguese guy whose age I couldn't quite peg. He could have been thirty; he could have been forty. They were led by an experienced guide Umberto knew well, a lanky-built Frenchman named Mathéo (pronounced MAH-tay-o). In his late-twenties, he was one of those people who tried to turn everything he said - and I mean *everything* - into a joke. He was a friendly guy for sure, but try as he might he wasn't that funny. I didn't want to be rude (in fact I felt a bit sorry for him), so I gave Mathéo varying degrees of obligatory laughter throughout the evening. Paul was less tolerant, and Umberto even more so. He'd suffered through the act too many times.

The two Norwegian brothers, Jørgen and Lars, were a quiet lot; same with the British gent, Gregory R. Thurman IV. The Portuguese man, Arnaldo, was more talkative. Paul and I took to him right away. The guy was smart, and his self-deprecating wit was hilarious. Everyone in the group could speak English well, and none of them seemed to mind Mathéo's trying verbal antics.

With our gear ready for the morning, we doused the lanterns at 10:00 p.m. The night was short, but not for Umberto. For some reason he couldn't sleep, and it wasn't due to the smelly, paper-thin mattresses. I heard him get up a couple of times before midnight, and after that he stayed on the first level for the rest of the night reading Gabriele D'Annunzio's *Triumph of Death* by lantern light - or so he told us. I had no reason to doubt him.

* * * * *

All eight of us were up by 4:30, eager to get going. Nervous tension filled the Hut; there wasn't much idle talking. Game faces were on. Even Mathéo had ceased his blather. *It's a dawn patrol on the ground*, I thought. We filled our hungry stomachs with eggs and bacon, lots of buttered toast, and hot tea.

Fully dressed, we'd officially become one large group with Umberto, the most experienced Matterhorn guide in Zermatt, assuming the role of leader. There wasn't a hint of protest from Mathéo. We paired off to utilize a popular method called short roping, where a stronger climber is placed in front of a weaker climber linked together by a rope. The pair tries to maintain a 20-foot separation as they make their way up the mountain. The stronger climber does his best to use both fixed and natural anchors to help his weaker partner (called *belaying*) up the steeper and more challenging sections.

"I know every millimeter of this ridge," Umberto told us. "Mathéo does, too. I'll take the lead with Lars. Behind us will be Michael and Jørgen. Mathéo and Gregory will follow. At the back will be Paul and Arnaldo, but I don't care who's in front. You both look to be about the same strength."

Paul slapped Arnaldo on his shoulder. "I know I'm stronger, but you want to flip a coin?"

"You stronger? I don't think so. How about we arm wrestle."

"Sure mate - you're on."

The contest wasn't close. It was over in five seconds. Paul lost.

* * * * *

As we began to climb with headlamps aglow, it occurred to me that we must have looked like a bizarre line of florescent sky insects to those far below. *Aliens from outer space*, I thought. This part of the Hörnligrate ascent wasn't difficult. It was profoundly easier than my rescue climb up the slick, vertical stonewalls of Seve Manon's residential hideout (described in volume 3, *Dangerous Duty*). I quickly came to the opinion that, in this early going, short roping wasn't necessary for competent climbers.

It wasn't long before I had to slow down. Jørgen Gulbrandsen was working hard, but he couldn't keep up with me. It was the same for his bother Lars trailing behind Umberto Lannelli. However, Gregory R. Thurman IV, the oldest and outwardly the most ill-conditioned member of the group (he had quite a paunch), seemed to easily match pace with Mathéo Sarchet; and of course Paul and Arnaldo made child's play of this first section. Lest Jørgen and Lars feel like hindrances, Umberto reassured them that they were doing fine. "Take as much rest as you need," Umberto said. "No one is pushing us, and we are making excellent time." I chipped in too with a few lines of encouragement.

After an hour of steady climbing, the sky began to lighten. We could finally see the mountain without the headlamps. During another timeout waiting for Jørgen, I took a scrutinizing gaze around the wondrous Zermatt valley. Amazing view! The surrounding *Monte Rosa* peaks (too many to count) floated above a blanket of soft clouds in a magenta-tinged backdrop of pre-dawn sun.

* * * * *

Higher and higher we climbed, making steady progress. No one was running low on energy or confidence, but except for Umberto and Mathéo, we were all feeling the effects of the thinner air. Jørgen, Lars, and Gregory felt it in the lungs and head; the rest of us only in the head. The altitude headaches had to be ignored.

As we neared the 13,000 foot mark with the Solvay Hut just coming into sight, the mountain began to bare its teeth. It got steep. Very steep. Our ascent slowed drastically despite the use of several handy fixed ropes. Guarding the Solvay Hut, both above and below, were the infamous 'Mosely Slabs.' Named after William Moseley, a 29 year-old American doctor from Boston, these steep sections of rock required concentrated patience. There wasn't a Matterhorn guide worth his salt who would allow a member of his group to negotiate the slabs un-roped. Unfortunately, this is what Moseley tried to do.

The journey to the summit had gone well, and Mosely had climbed strongly throughout. During the first encounter with the slabs Moseley, feeling full of vain confidence, was sure he could scale the slabs without being roped. His three companions persuaded him against it. After twenty minutes at the summit, the group began their descent. Moseley ignored the protests of the others and unhooked his rope. Near where the Solvay Hut is today, the good doctor slipped and fell to his death.

Interestingly enough, it *is* possible to climb the slabs un-roped. I came to this conclusion half way up the lower Moseley Slab. But there was no way in hades that I'd have unhooked the rope!

* * * * *

The dinky Solvay Hut sits precariously at 13,133 feet, roughly 1,500 feet from the summit. Though the 225 square foot shelter can sleep 10, its intended use is for emergencies and brief respites to and from the summit. Umberto and Lars reached the Solvay at 8:40. The rest of us were all there by 9:00.

While gazing out at the pointed snowcapped world around me, I had another sad reverie moment about Michelle. It had been brewing for a while. The flood of emotion almost broke me down. For a second or two I felt a wave of dizziness that caused me to fall back against the side of the hut.

Janey mack, get ahold of yourself! Michelle is gone. Don't dwell on it.

"Hey, you all right?"

I stood straight, grabbing hold of my sunglasses. "Yeah, Paul. I'm grand. Just thinking about things, ya know?"

Paul smiled, nodding.

He knew.

* * * * *

Inside at a small table we chowed down like a pack of ravenous wolves. Once refreshed, Umberto took out his heavily scratched Kodak "Brownie" camera. He snapped various photos of the group posing on the narrow sidewalk beside the hut. "Believe it or not," he said after the last photo was taken, "we still have more than two hours of hard climbing left before we reach the summit."

"You're joking," Jørgen blurted, shocked at what he'd heard.

"I wish I was joking. This is the steepest and most difficult section of the Hörnli route. The last 470 meters will require us to use crampons and ice axes. The fixed ropes do not go up all the way. Past the upper slab we'll have snow to the summit. Tread carefully and do not take a single step for granted."

"Onward and upward then," Gregory said. "The summit awaits." The stoically reserved Englishman had been a pillar of quiet determination throughout the climb. I liked and admired him. In fact, I'd grown to like everyone in the group. Jørgen and Lars had opened up and had turned downright chatty. Mathéo could actually be funny when he wasn't trying to be. He was a great guide, almost the equal of Umberto. Their overall knowledge of the mountain and skill levels were equivalent, but I gave a slight edge to the Italian in the leadership department.

"We should get to the summit around noon," Umberto said before we set out. "Look out for each other, and don't get summit fever. It can make you careless. The urge to rush to the very top of the mountain can be strong. - Let's go."

* * * * *

It was a tedious process from here on out. Once past the upper Moseley slab I could have easily un-roped to climb past Lars and made speedy headway to the summit. Jörgen even told me to go ahead and do so. "I can make it without any assistance," he assured. "You do not need to babysit me." But I knew Umberto wouldn't have gone for it. He was a team player all the way, and no one was going to break the team chain. I had no problem with that.

The crampons made easy work of the icy snow. It was almost impossible to slip. I got a steady rhythm going in several sections combining the use of fixed ropes and my ice ax - pull, hack, pull, hack, pull, hack . . .

So far, our climbing group had suffered no setbacks. *We've cruised right up this puppy,* I thought with the summit in sight. *The Matterhorn is a tough haul, but not overly so.*

Of course we couldn't have asked for better climbing conditions: warm temperature, not much wind, and no congestion on the mountain. And we couldn't have asked for a better pair of guides. The mighty Matterhorn on this day was pretty much defenseless.

* * * * *

The icy ridge narrowed near the summit. Even so, team speed was picking up as everyone could taste the thrill of conquest. Ten yards from the finish line, Lars was shuffling along in a peculiar crampon trot, his rope unhooked. Umberto let him pass, and I did the same with Jørgen, who was imitating his brother to a tee.

"We did it!" Paul shouted in triumph behind me. "*Sacré Bleu,* we climbed the Matterhorn!"

Gregory Thurman IV, his countenance restrained as usual, soon caught up with me. I'd slowed way down, basking in the moment, soaking in the grand perspective. "Hi ya Greg," I said. "Congratulations."

"To you also. - A walk in the park, really, don't you think?"

I shrugged. "Yeah, maybe. It wasn't as tough as I thought it'd be."

"I concur. We'll have to give Everest a go next, eh?"

"Good luck with that. I'm gunna try something different - maybe swim the English Channel."

Mathéo, Paul, and Arnaldo joined us. We shook hands all around.

"I don't want anyone looking taller than me in the photograph," Mathéo joked.

"We'll kneel before you," Paul fired back with mock reverence.

13
It's a Long Way Down

The Kodak Brownie had a timer on it so we could all get in the picture. We took three shots, each one with a slightly different background. For each photo Mathéo built himself six-inch snow platforms to boost his height. Afterward, Umberto snapped a couple of pictures of Paul and me: one serious, and one with Paul pretending to stick his ice ax in my nostril.

Taking a load off my feet, I sat down and unpacked a crushed turkey sandwich. Instead of inhaling it, I tried to go slow and savor each bite. It worked for the first half, but the other half went down my gullet almost whole. My extra large canteen still had lots of water in it. I was in mid-gulp when a blood-shrieking cry of terror shattered the crisp alpine air.

Twelve yards behind me, Arnaldo was on his hands and knees with an arm dangling over the steeply sloped edge.

I shot to my feet as everyone bolted toward the scene.

"He fell!" Arnaldo cried. "Oh my god, he fell!"

Lars got there first. I was second. The rest gathered seconds later.

"What happened?" Mathéo shouted, falling on all fours to look over the edge.

Arnaldo could hardly talk. "I . . . I don't know! One moment he was there, and the next he was gone."

"Did anyone else see anything?" I asked of the group, scanning down in vain hope of seeing a glimpse of Umberto's yellow-hooded coat.

"I didn't see anything," Lars said.

"I didn't either," echoed Jørgen. "We were on the other side."

Paul shook his head. "He was checking his backpack the last time I noticed him."

"I can't believe what just happened," Lars mumbled in disbelief.

"This is most unusual," Gregory postulated, his voice dispassionately calm. "A man of his experience doesn't suddenly fall off a highly familiar summit in broad daylight."

"It's a long way down," Jørgen said gloomily. "Is there any chance he could still be alive?"

"Impossible," the Englishman replied. "It's a sheer drop. He fell thousands of feet down to the glacier."

Mathéo, now standing again, continued to stare at Arnaldo. The Spaniard, still on his knees, felt the guide's searing eyes upon him. He finally looked up at Mathéo.

"What are you doing? Why are you staring at me?"

"How close were you to him when he fell?"

Arnaldo stood up, brushing the snow off his pants. "I don't know for sure - perhaps eight feet." He pointed to an indecipherable mess of crampon footprints. "I was standing there. You can see where I was."

Mathéo gave the area in question a cursory inspection. "I don't see any proof."

Arnaldo threw his hands out in frustration. "Would you stop! I mean it! You're interrogating me. Stop! This is unfair. He *fell*! It was an *accident*! He must have been preoccupied with something on his mind and not realized how close he was to the edge."

"No, no. Not Umberto."

"Tell the truth Arnaldo," I barked. "Come clean, mate. This isn't looking good for you."

Mathéo took a step closer. "Mick's right, because I don't believe a word you've said."

"What? I'm not lying! Believe me, I'm not!"

"You are."

"So what are you saying? Huh? Go on, tell me! You accusing me of murder?"

Cold silence.

Mathéo took another step, putting him at arm's length distance from Arnaldo.

In a frantic search for sympathy, Arnaldo bounced desperate glances off everyone in the group. "Ok, ok. - Let's be reasonable here. All of us are un-roped. A misstep can happen. Umberto might have slipped and lost his balance. It doesn't take much. It all happened so fast."

Mathéo inched closer. Arnaldo nudged back.

"You're lying. You pushed him. I know you did."

"I did not! For god's sake, I'm telling the truth. - You better back off."

"No."

"I'm warning you!"

"You killed Umberto."

In the next instant Mathéo charged.

Arnaldo wasn't caught off guard. He twisted his body like a flamenco dancer and grabbed Mathéo around his waist in an attempt to throw him over the precipice. It didn't work.

Mathéo collapsed to his knee and stopped the momentum.

I bounded forward (as did everyone) and prepared to dive for Mathéo's outstretched right leg.

No one was quick enough to prevent what happened next.

Arnaldo countered Mathéo's move by widening his stance. He bent down to gather leverage, and while doing so his left foot slipped. The two men fell sideways toward the edge, neither one letting go of the other.

Then gravity latched onto them with an unbreakable hold.

My leap for Mathéo's leg missed.

The last image I saw of them was the spikes of their crampons plummeting over the abyss. Arnaldo's guttural scream faded quickly.

* * * * *

Tell me that didn't happen, I thought. *You've got to be kidding me. Three men dead, including our guides?*

I lay there face down in the snow for half a minute, surrounded by Paul, Lars, Jørgen, and Gregory. No one said a word. The only sound was that of a brisk, howling wind flapping our clothing.

"We're staring as if they might come back," Lars finally said. "They're dead. We can't stay up here all day."

I lazily rolled over and squinted into the cold sun for a few seconds. Nodding, I said, "We best get back. In Zermatt we'll report this to the authorities. I don't know about you guys, but I'm convinced Arnaldo was a murderer. Umberto didn't misstep. That's a crock." Gregory held out his hand and helped me to my feet.

"No question," Paul agreed. "But why would he want to kill Umberto?"

"He had enemies. Remember that altercation when he was leaving the casino?"

"Yeah, the guy at the door was fuming. Do you think Umberto owed him money?"

"That'd be my guess. Maybe he hired Arnaldo to stage an . . . *accident.*"

"An unholy shame," Jørgen said. "I'd gotten to like Mathéo. But last night his ceaseless jabber made me wish I was deaf."

"I wanted to gag him," Paul quipped.

"Mathéo was a good guy," I said. "He would have given his life for any of us."

"We can chat and speculate more when we reach the Hut," Gregory said, hooking his rope back on. "Should we link ourselves all together?"

Uncertainty sped around the group.

"I think we should, at least to the Solvay Hut," Lars said.

"I agree," his brother concurred.

Paul nodded.

"All right then," I said. "We're a chain. Let's head down."

* * * * *

I led the way, followed by Jørgen, Lars, Gregory, and Paul. The tragic events atop the summit had taken all the beauty out of the alpine scenery. The descent was nothing more than a dangerous, calculatingly tedious chore. There was hardly any talking amongst the group, and what little there was dealt only with the mountain. For the first eighty minutes of the journey we progressed down in quick time without a whit of trouble. Nearing the Solvay Hut, I was all set to jump down the last half-meter to the narrow sidewalk when a heart-stopping shriek echoed from above. Gregory's cry so startled me that both my feet slipped off the sheet of ice. I held onto the rope as my body twirled around and bounced off a jutting section of rock. Being so close to the sidewalk, I let the rope slide through my hands and safely touched ground. By the time I looked up, the crisis was over. Gregory had slipped twenty feet down the slab face and was now at arm's length from Jørgen. Failing to hold tight to the rope, he'd used his ice ax to slow down his rapid slide - just like Umberto had taught us to do in such a situation. He was never in any mortal danger because of the combined strength of the rope chain.

"Are you all right?" Lars hollered above him.

"Oh yes, ship shape. Had a bit of a slip, that's all."

"Jaysus Greg, what were you trying to do, beat me to the hut?" I jested.

The coolly low-key Englishman laughed. "The thought crossed my mind. But no, I was just giving this ax a thorough tryout. Gentlemen, it is quite satisfactory."

* * * * *

While sitting around the cramped table inside the Solvay Hut, I informed the group that upon reaching Zermatt I would seek out the man who'd confronted Umberto in the casino.

"I'll try and coax incriminating comments out of him."

"With the police overhearing your conversation, of course," Gregory said.

"Yeah, sure. They could arrest him on the spot if he gives away anything."

"Be careful with what you say. You don't want to incriminate yourself."

* * * * *

Once we cleared the lower Moseley Slab, our crampons came off and we had an easy, uneventful scramble down the ridge to the Hörnli Hut. A nine-member group of Japanese climbers was at the Hut to greet us. Their guide, a short blond English speaking German named Stefan, immediately asked about Umberto and Mathéo. Gregory took Stefan aside and told him what had happened. The rest of us soon joined the discussion.

"Umberto and I were good friends," Stefan said, his head hung low. "I knew he was having money troubles, and stupidly he was involved with a married woman. The husband had found out about their relationship."

I then described the angry man in the casino.

"That's the husband. His name is Tolson Jerns. - This is so sad. Inevitable, really." Stefan took a heavy breath. "What's more is that Umberto owed Tolson a great deal of money. He was in debt to him even before he began seeing his wife. Tolson has many friends, many connections."

"We're going straight to the police when we get to Zermatt," Jørgen said.

"You must do that, but I do not trust the police. They look the other way on many things. It wouldn't surprise me if Tolson has bought them off."

Upon hearing this I dismissed my plan of confronting the man. Taking the law into my own hands wasn't a good idea - not this time.

I don't need more people after me, I thought.

"Then what do you suggest we do?" asked Gregory.

The guide shook his head. "I'm afraid there isn't much you can do. Tolson will not be in Zermatt. He is too smart to remain there. He's already gone."

* * * * *

Once back in Zermatt, I treated our group to a well-earned fish dinner, and then we headed for the casino. There was no sign of Tolsen. The guy most likely had gotten away with murder.

None of us did well at the tables. Blackjack was especially cruel to me. It's amazing how often the dealer will be showing a bad hand like twelve or thirteen and then draw two or three cards to hit twenty-one. And then, when you do have a run of good luck with one dealer, they'll change him out for another who will then proceed to bleed your money dry. I don't get it.

* * * * *

"So what's next, back to the chateau and on to St. Andrews?" Paul asked in our room that night.

"Yeah, might as well. I was kicking around the idea of heading to Genoa and going by ship. Sounds grand, yeah? But it would take forever and a day to get there because we'd have to make a bunch of transfers. And then there's the risk of submarines. Believe me, you don't want to go through a torpedo attack."

* * * * *

I didn't sleep a wink that night. I lay there trembling, eyes wet, feeling sick, thinking about Michelle. This hadn't happened to me for a week - the longest span since her death. No matter how much I tried to keep busy, I could only go so long before the emotional bubble burst. Handling downtime was the hardest part of coping. If only there was a way to bring on instant sleep. Sleeping tablets? They only made me feel drugged.

In the morning I sent Gerard a telegram informing him of our return. We were back at the chateau by dinnertime.

14
The Auld Grey Toon

At 1:00 in the afternoon the next day, Paul and I boarded an escorted ferry from Calais to London. I hadn't been to London since a 1912 trip with my father. Paul had been to the metropolis once, a short stay when he was eight, so he wanted to spend some time seeing the major sights. I put aside my hatred of the British Empire and reluctantly agreed. We checked into a convenient hotel in the West End, unloaded our luggage (instead of the Lebel revolver, I'd brought a British Webley Mk VI with a shoulder holster), and spent the rest of the day zipping around town on the Tube. Paul, being an art lover, couldn't get enough of the National Gallery in Trafalgar Square. It was the same with me in the Natural History Museum. We did some window shopping on Oxford Street, ate dinner at a fish and chips pub in Piccadilly, and finished the day with an hour long Jack the Ripper tour and the musical comedy *Going Up* at the Gaiety Theater.

Early the next morning we caught a train at Waterloo Station and headed for Edinburgh. Paul new the city well, but I'd never been there before. Scotland had always fascinated me, and the thought of the country made me think about Edgar Burke, the fiercely proud Scotsman who'd hidden me, Anton Dunkel, Lee "Leaky" Jensen, and Jason Dwyer after our escape from a prisoner or war camp in Amiens (detailed in *Richthofen's Knight*).

I had to thoroughly explore the town, so we used the rest of the day wandering up and down the Royal Mile, visiting Edinburgh Castle and Holyrood Palace, and hiking to the top of Arthur's Seat, an 823-foot extinct volcano. We stayed the night in a five star hotel on Princes Street next to Usher Hall. In the morning Paul went with me on a long run, and after breakfast we took a train to Leuchars. From there we hopped on a bus for the short journey to St. Andrews.

* * * * *

The undisputed most famous golf course in the world is the Old Course in St. Andrews. It's holy ground, with over five-hundred years of glorious history. Every serious golfer aspires to play the Old Course at least once in their life.

The first mention of golf in St. Andrews (the 'Auld Grey Toon) dates back to 1457 when King James II banned the sport because it was interfering with his soldiers' archery practice. Golf was a serious threat to national defense! King James IV removed the ban in 1502 when he bought a set of golf clubs in the town.

The Royal and Ancient Golf Club of St. Andrews (the R&A) has played a vital role in the evolution of the modern game throughout the world. Stroke play was introduced for the first time in 1759 on the original 22-hole course. By 1764 some of the holes were considered too short, so they were altered to make the course 18 holes - the standard round of golf today. The first Rules of Golf committee was appointed by the R&A in 1897, giving it world authority in the game - apart from the USA, Canada and Mexico, which are governed by the United States Golf Association (the USGA).

* * * * *

Paul and I checked into the *MacDonald Rusacks Hotel*, located only a chip shot away from the historic R&A clubhouse and the 18th hole.

Perfect!

"The first thing we need to do is buy some clubs," I said as we unpacked. "We can go the *Tom Morris Golf Shop*. It's right next door."

"Is there a price limit?"

I laughed. "Only for you."

Then I tackled him.

* * * * *

Paul hadn't played a lot of golf recently, so he didn't have any trouble picking out a set of clubs and a putter. All the sticks felt grand to him. It wasn't so easy for me, however. When the dust settled, there were three sets that I really liked. The clubs felt fantastic from long to short. "Why don't you buy all three sets?" Paul asked impatiently. "Then you won't have to choose." With a big grin he added, "Or better yet, you could buy the entire store."

"That's a golden thought," I replied while standing in front of a mirror addressing an imaginary ball with one of the drivers. "Maybe I'll do that someday when I'm old and crinkly."

Paul tapped his watch behind me. "We've been in here over an hour. Make a decision. We're wasting the day."

"Yeah, I know." I took one more full swing. "Ok, I'll go with these clubs. They seem like the offspring of the other sets in looks and feel."

"Great. I'll meet you outside."

"You might have a long wait."

"Huh? Why?"

"I haven't picked out a putter yet."

* * * * *

We couldn't get on the Old Course until later in the afternoon. A local tournament had to finish that had been delayed from the previous day. With a minimum six hours to kill, we divided the time between getting our photograph taken standing on the Swilcan Bridge, hitting on the practice range, and touring the remains of St. Andrews Castle, St. Andrews University (the oldest university in Scotland), and the ruins of St. Andrews Cathedral where both Old and Young Tom Morris are buried.

On the range Paul's rusty swing took a while to loosen up, but when it did my friend was hitting the ball long and straight. "Your ball flight is low and punchy," I commented. "That's good with the wind blowing today."

I couldn't have been more pleased with my new sticks. They performed magnificently. Japers I was hitting it far! The perfectly balanced drop-toed putter I selected (in only *five* minutes!), with its shiny gold face and fancily embellished top-line, was also money on the practice green. It rolled them true every time.

It was while chatting with the Old Course official starter about what time we'd be teeing off when, out of the corner of my eye, I spotted something that spun me right out of my shoes.

Janey mack! It's him! It has to be!

Just off the 18th green, standing over his ball in the notorious swale known as the 'Valley of Sin', was none other than Edgar Burke. He chipped his shot onto the green and the ball rolled to a stop six feet from the hole. Burke seemed disappointed with the results. "Confound it, I looked up!" he complained to his playing partners. "I've done that all day!"

I tugged on Paul's arm. "Come on. I got to introduce you to someone."

"Who is it?"

"An old friend."

We sat on the R&A Clubhouse steps and waited for Burke to finish his round. He drained the six-footer to save par, removed his red *tam o' shanter* cap and then shook his two playing partners' hands. "Thank ye kindly lads," the Scotsman said in his thick, deep toned brogue, an unmistakable voice as familiar as my own. "You almost came back and beat me! Fine round it was! If you have the time I'll treat ye lads to the best scotch in town at the 19th hole." The men, both middle-aged Orientals, politely declined his offer and went happily about their way. Paul and I were standing at the edge of the green as Burke walked off. He gave me a slight double-take glance when I removed my hat, and strolled past with his clubs strapped over his shoulder in a tattered, white canvas bag.

"Jaysus Edgar, you got something against bald guys?" I called out.

Burke abruptly stopped and turned around wearing a befuddled expression behind his Santa Claus white beard. "What was that laddie?"

I stepped closer. "How's Mayling?"

Squinting into the sun, the Scotsman continued to study me.

"That was quite the hole in the ground at your place," I said. "Maybe next time I can sleep *inside* your house."

Burke's face lit up. He grabbed his *tam o' shanter* with both hands and let out a battle cry holler of joy. "Mick! You Irish rogue! Come here ye my boy!"

Edgar Burke bear hugged me half to death before I could say another word. "It's great to see you!" I finally said. "Wasn't sure you were still above ground."

Burke let me out of the python squeeze and extended his hand to Paul. "You worried about me for nothing. Mayling and I have never been better. We love livin' in St. Andrews. - Who's your friend here?"

Paul shook his hand. "I'm Paul Coburn, Mick's best friend . . . I think."

Burked laughed. "You think, eh? Well he's a good friend to have."

I pushed Paul away. "No I'm not. Say listen Edgar, I'm still lying low. Gotta keep the Brits off my tail."

"Oh, of course. That bald head'll hide ya good."

"Yeah, the shine is blinding. I've been using the name Michael Fitzpatrick, so Mick's ok, but Mike or Michael is better."

Burke patted my head. "Ah, how 'bout I call just call ya Killer? That's fittin', eh?"

"Killer's grand. I like it." I pretended to slug him in the stomach. "What a treat to see you! Janey mack! We didn't know what to think when we found your house ransacked. What did the Brits do to you and Mayling?"

My inquiry stoked Burke's ire. He set his clubs down with a thump and let them drop to the ground. "Ooooh - curse 'em! They barged in about two in the morning. The brutes threw us out of bed and had a happy time roughing us up. We were hauled to a smelly shoebox holding cell and they interrogated us for about three hours. They finally let us go the next day. Didn't even give us a ride back to our place. No help cleaning up either. As you probably noticed, a lot of our belongings were pilfered. The rat-chufters played dumb about it and said there was nothing they could do. Can you believe that? I'm still steamed. Without Mayling to control my temper, I'd have gotten myself killed over it."

"But here you are, living in St. Andrews. Can't beat it man!"

"Aye to that!"

I motioned to the official starter's box. "We were getting ready to have a first go of the Old Course."

"Ooh, she's playing beastie today. You can't feel the wind too much right here and now, but out near the turn she's a blowin' a gale force." Burke pointed out to sea. "There's a front comin' in, see? You'll be wishin' you were in a pub drinkin' *Guinness* within the hour."

"Buggers." I turned to Paul. "What do you think?"

With a dejected heavy sigh, he replied, "We probably ought to heed his advice and play another time."

"I think so too."

"Come on with me lads," said Burke. "I'll take you inside the R&A clubhouse. Give ya a tour of the place. I'm a member ya know. And later maybe we can track down Vardon."

"What?" I exclaimed. "Harry Vardon is around?"

"He's in town, and John Taylor as well. They'll be here for a couple days. I'm good friends with them - and James Braid too, but this time he's not here. - Ah, if only! 'Member me telling ya back at the house about these lads?"

"Yeah, of course. You gave me that set of clubs. You said Vardon didn't like the balance on them."

Burke's face soured. "Those sticks are gone. But I see you got a grand set there. You got 'em at the Morris shop. I've had my eye on that set for a while now, and was thinking about buyin' 'em. Ya beat me to 'em, ya scoundrel! - Looks like Paul got himself a nice set, too."

Paul smiled. "I don't think I'm worthy to play these clubs. They're too good for me."

"Nah, you'll hit 'em fine! Come on lads, let's go in the R&A."

* * * * *

The Swilcan Bridge and the R&A Clubhouse are the two most iconic structures in the world of golf. Even many non-golfers can recognize them and know that they are in St. Andrews, Scotland.

Once inside the clubhouse I was immediately surprised by the fact that the main windowed area in the front of the building wasn't a lounge per se. It sure looked like it would be from the outside.

"Though there are tables and chairs, it's really a locker room," Edgar informed us, standing in front of a line of portraits and photographs of famous R&A figures. "The dining-lounge area is upstairs. See those stairs over there?" Burke frowned with a subtle headshake. "Ten years ago Old Tom Morris fell down them and fractured his skull. He died a couple months later from his injuries. He was 86."

"We visited his grave, and Young Tom's too," Paul said.

Burke turned and gazed out the main window. "This view never gets old. Take it in lads. You gotta love it. The Swilcan Bridge is right there, the 17th green - the road hole. Lovely! This is the best view in the world if you ask me."

"Not gunna argue with that," I said. "But it's frustrating we can't get out there and tee off."

"Patience laddie, patience. You'll be out there tomorrow. - Come on. Be careful on the stairs. Let's go get something to eat."

* * * * *

The dining area was sparsely filled of people but not of cigar smoke. Burke picked out his favorite corner table next to an exact replica of the *Claret Jug* - the trophy given to the British Open champion. Behind the display were various photographs of past winners, including Willie Park, Old Tom Morris, Young Tom Morris, and the 'Great Triumvirate' - Vardon, Braid, and Taylor. Soup and ham sandwiches were ordered, and then Burke and I bounced our past months' stories off each other for the next hour. I avoided the topic of Michelle until Burke brought it up.

"Are you still romancing that beautiful French girl?"

"Oh . . . well, things didn't work out between us," I replied bluntly. "It was for the better." When Paul gave me the strangest of glances I kicked him in the shin. There was no way I could tell the truth about Michelle without spilling tears.

* * * * *

Long after our plentiful supply of food was consumed, a commotion of voices suddenly echoed into the dining room from downstairs. Burke smiled and checked his watch. "This is about the right time."

"For what?" asked Paul.

"You'll see. The answer should be coming into the room momentarily."

We all focused on the red-felted stairway as the banter grew louder.

"And there they are," Burke announced as he rose from his chair. "Eleven Open championships between them!"

Jaysus sakes . . . Harry Vardon and J.H. Taylor!

I couldn't believe it!

The living legends of golf saw Edgar immediately.

"Burke, you old highlander!" the stocky, 47 year-old Taylor greeted from the top stair, Vardon beside him.

"The rumors are true," Vardon said placidly with a tip of his flat cap. "You are alive. And living in St. Andrews to boot."

Burke laughed. "I told ye years ago this town would be my last home. What'd ya do, leave Braid out of the party?"

"He couldn't make it," Taylor said. "He's up in Yorkshire designing a new course."

"Too bad. - Please come join us. Big table here."

* * * * *

The Great Triumvirate.

It's amazing when you look at the run of Open championships that Harry Vardon, J.H.Taylor, and James Braid strung together between 1894 and 1914:

Taylor: 1894, 1895, 1900, 1909, 1913
Vardon: 1896, 1898, 1899, 1903, 1911, 1914
Braid: 1901, 1905, 1906, 1908, 1910

Sixteen wins!

Their win totals would most likely be higher if the war hadn't cancelled the Open from 1915-1918. As it turned out, Vardon, Taylor and Braid remained highly competitive until the late 1920's when age (and the effects of tuberculosis on Vardon) finally caught up with them. Taylor tied for 5th and 6th place in the 1924 and 1925 Opens. Braid was in the money through most of the decade, and even played in the 1938 Open at age 68! Vardon always played well in the Open and came close to winning his second United States Open in 1920 when he tied for second place.

* * * * *

The mustached Harry Vardon, 48 years-old, dressed in his patented olive tweed coat and 'plus four' knickers, casually strode over to the rounded table. Taylor spotted another close friend and made brief conversation with him before following suit.

Burke introduced us, remembering to call me Michael Fitzpatrick. He also used the new nickname 'Killer'. Vardon sat down to my left, and while scooting in his chair he said to me, "So Killer Michael, how many years before your name is on the Claret Jug?"

Still a bit star struck, I was surprised by his friendly question. "Oh man - I'll be lucky if I *ever* qualify for the Open, Mr. Vardon."

"I wouldn't say that young man. You're only in your teens. Imagine how good you can be by the time you're thirty. Earlier today I was watching you hit on the practice range. Your swing caught my attention, and that usually only happens when I'm watching fellow competitors in a big tournament."

"Aye, Killer, are ye *that* good?" Burke asked me.

"Oh . . . I'm all right - at least I was on the range today. The new clubs were feeling pretty good."

"But the question is, can you *play*?" Taylor piped in rather challengingly. His glare matched his tone.

I didn't know quite how to take his comment. Vardon didn't seem to care for it. "Maybe he can play better than you, John? Francis Ouimet sure could play when he beat me in the U.S. Open five years ago."

"Bah - I still think that was a fluke."

Vardon shook his head. "No, it wasn't a fluke. The kid was good."

"All right then," Taylor said, "Let's have a contest - yes? Old Course tomorrow morning? We could -"

"Wait - wait a moment John," Burke cut in. "How would that be fair?"

"Easy - you get strokes. How about five for you, and maybe twelve for the Killer here?"

"Hmm . . ." uttered Burke inquisitively.

"Or here's another idea," Vardon proposed. "How about we team up for match play? 18 holes with extras in case of a tie. For teams, I'll take Killer. John, you can have Edgar."

"Yes, I'm all for it!" Burke declared, raising his mug of beer. "It'll be fun!"

"Suits me," Taylor replied with a confident smirk.

"We'll get a 9:30 tee time or thereabouts," Burke said, turning to me. "You got a dream match coming your way, Killer. You ready for this?"

Holy schmykees! This could be ugly. What if I stink it up?

I gave a pensive nod and looked at Paul nervously. "You want to be my caddie?"

15
The Ultimate Round

"What time will you get to the course?" I asked Vardon before he left the table.

"I would prefer to get there early to practice some shots, but Taylor and I have an R&A breakfast engagement to attend. It'll be held in this room. If necessary, we'll leave early in order to make our tee time." He shook my hand, and with a chuckle added, "You may have to carry me for the first few holes until this old body warms up. See you in the morning partner." Vardon motioned at Edgar. "The tab for the food and drink is on me."

The bad weather didn't let up, which nixed any possible evening practice. There wasn't much to do except head back to the hotel and relax. *Try* and relax. I was pretty keyed-up. Never having played the Old Course (with all its quirky blind tee shots, hidden pot bunkers, knee-high fescue rough, fairway slopes and mounds, huge double-greens, and the infamous #17 'Road Hole') was my biggest concern. Vardon would help me out all he could with course management, but I sure would have liked some actual playing experience on it.

Trust your swing and alignment, I kept thinking. *Your nerves will settle down.*

"Do you think you might lose the first hole?" Paul asked during a late evening dinner on Market Street. "Vardon will be cold and you'll be nervous as all get out."

"Thanks a lot for the boost of confidence, ya biffo. It's match play. You gotta win ten holes."

* * * * *

Paul and I got to the course at the first hint of daylight. The weather was glorious with only a trace of wind. I hit range shots for an hour and putted and chipped for another. Everything was clicking, and my ball striking was pure cream. Putts were rolling true, with excellent lag on the long ones. *Very* long putts, even for the world's best golfers, were a guarantee on the Old Course. Putts of 70 plus feet were commonplace on gigantic greens measuring up to 100 yards long!

"If my practice session carries over to the round I should be all right," I said to Paul while making our way to the first tee.

We got there at 9:15. Edgar Burke was milling about chatting with friends on the front steps. "Vardon and Taylor will be out momentarily," he announced. "We couldn't have asked for a better day, eh lads? The course is ripe for the taking!"

Nodding, I looked out at the first hole, a 370-yard par 4 nicknamed the *Burn* due to the narrow channel of water that snakes across the entire 18th and 1st fairways. "It'll be the three of you taking it, not me," I replied modestly. "Our playing partners still inside?"

"They'll be out any minute now. We're cleared to go from the Starter."

At that moment Taylor and Vardon came trotting out of the R&A. "As promised, right on time," announced Taylor, buttoning the sleeve of his white silk shirt. Vardon stayed true to form with his olive-tweed jacket and knickers.

"No respect for the god of summer, I see," joked Burke.

"What can I say, it's my uniform," Vardon replied. "You two ready to play?"

Burke motioned to his caddie, a bubbly middle-aged fellow who could have passed as Burke's brother. "We're more warmed up than you for sure."

"The honors are yours," Taylor said, waving over his much younger caddie.

I turned to Paul. "Your most important job is to help keep my emotions in check, yeah? Slap me upside the head if I get all mopey. Got it?"

"Check. I love peltin' ya."

* * * * *

Seen from above, the Old Course looks like a giant seahorse. A golfer plays straight out, curves around the 'head,' and comes straight back. Every hole except the 1st, 9th, 17th, and 18th has a double-green.

What follows is a synopsis of the match on that hot August day - not shot by shot, but hole by hole. You'll notice that each hole has an interesting nickname.

Japers, it was a contest for the ages!

(For those readers who aren't particularly interested in the sport of golf, you may want to skip to hole #18 for the climax.)

* * * * *

\-   #1 - 470 yards/par 4 (The Burn): A throng of 20-plus people lined up to watch us tee off at 9:30 sharp. Man was I nervous! Here I was, a 23 victory ace fighter pilot getting nervous about a leisurely recreational game! And buggers if the jitters didn't get the best of me! On a hole with one of the biggest fairways in the world, I *missed* the fairway! My drive banana-sliced right. A balloon ball. Vardon's shot also went right, but it was more of a fade and still found the fairway. Neither of us had good approach shots to the relatively flat green. Vardon had a tough chip and two-putted from 12 feet. I three-putted from the back fringe. J.H. Taylor took a routine 4 while Edgar Burke sank an 8-footer for bogey.   We'd lost the first hole.   Score: Taylor/Burke (TB) 1up

\-   #2 - 406 yards/par 4 (The Dyke): The four of us all made par. Vardon's wildly breaking birdie putt lipped out from 20 feet. Even though I parred the hole, none of my four strokes felt good: no rhythm, all-tight, out of sync. It's a wonder the ball went where I wanted it to. Score: TB 1 up

\-   #3 - 398 yards/par 4 (Cartgate Out): Harry Vardon had a tap-in birdie 3 to square the match. I hit a nice drive, but my approach shot landed six-inches outside Cartgate Bunker on the left side of the green. With one foot in the sand, my extremely awkward chip shot was stellar and left me with an easy up hill one-footer for par. Taylor and Burke made 4's. I felt better now. Score: All square

\-   #4 - 458 yards/par 4 (Ginger Beer): Before teeing off, Vardon told me: "This is the hardest hole on the outward nine. The drive is key. Try and go left of the grassy ridge." Well I tried, but again went right - right into some gnarly knee-high fescue. It took me 3 shots to get out of it and I ended up taking a bloody 7 on the hole! Vardon made 4 to keep the match even. Burke had a shot at birdie but choked his short putt. "It's early man," Paul reminded. "Keep your head about you. You're fine." I wasn't so sure. Score: All square

-       #5 - 550 yards/par 5 (O' Cross Out): J.H. Taylor really shined on this one. He made the hole look easy: great drive, perfect second shot, beautiful approach to 10 feet, nice birdie 4. Edgar Burke took a 6, Vardon a 5, and I two putted from 75 feet. Whew! The double green is almost 100 yards long! Besides the putting, I was relieved that my drive didn't go right again. If it had, one of the "Seven Sisters" would have snagged my ball. The Sisters are a group of bunkers that await drives veering even slightly to the right. Score: TB 1 up

-       #6 - 410 yards/par 4 (Heathery Out): On this relatively easy hole Taylor and Burke blew it. They both made bogey 5's. I also made a five *(I chunked my approach)* but Vardon took a 4. Score: All square

-       #7 - 370 yards/par 4 (High Out): Vardon hooked his drive left into some prickly whins. My blind tee shot was short but straight. Once again I blew the approach shot with a mid-iron and took a 5 on the hole. Vardon's adventure in the whins resulted in double-bogey 6. Taylor scrambled for a 4 and Burke three putted for a 5. Score: TB 1 up

-       #8 - 178 yards/par 3 (Short): Vardon is such a surgeon with his irons! He made a 2 to win the hole. I made a stupid 4, all caused by an errant tee shot that came up a mile short. My approach was all right, but I missed the 15-footer. Taylor took a 3 and so did Burke. Score: All square

-       #9 - 355 yards/par 4 (End): This hole offered another prime scoring chance, being one of the easiest in the 'loop'. We all had birdie putts, but only Burke's went in for a 3. The rest of us had 4's. Opportunity blown. Score: TB 1 up

-       #10 - 380 yards/par 4 (today called *Bobby Jones*): Ahh, buggers! Not good for us! My ghastly shank resulted in a lost ball. I took a double-bogey 6, and Vardon made bogey from being caught in bunker. Taylor got the par 4 to win the hole. Burke made 5. Score: TB 2 up

-       #11 - 171 yards/par 3 (High In): Vardon saved the day again with a birdie 2. I made another double-bogey 5. I landed in the same bunker that Bobby Jones did a few years later in 1921. Nicknamed the Hill, this bunker so frustrated Jones that he picked up his ball, tore up his scorecard, and walked off the course. I got out of the sand all right, but was left with a tricky downhill 30-foot putt. A lousy first putt set up a double-bogey 5. Taylor and Burke made par. Score: TB 1 up

-       #12 - 315 yards/par 4 (Heathery In): With the advent of more modern equipment, many of today's top professionals can drive this hole. The first to do so was Craig Wood *(using a steel shaft)* in the 1933 Open. Sam Snead also did it when he won in 1946. Obviously none of us drove the green, but all of us hit spot-on drives. My approach, however, didn't quite conquer the steep slope that protected the flag. The ball rolled back into the fringe. Luckily I two-putted for par, just like everyone else. Score: TB 1 up

-       #13 - 427 yards/par 4 (Hole 'O Cross In): Vardon, Taylor, and me all found one of the "Coffin" bunkers in the center of the fairway resulting in bogey 5's. Burke made nice work of this hole and took an easy par. Score: TB 2 up

-       #14 - 553 yards/par 5 (Long): I made par on this hole, managing to keep away from the dreaded "Hell" bunker. One of the biggest bunkers in the world, this monster of a hazard is almost 7 feet deep and covers 300 square yards! You can get lost in the thing! However, Taylor won the hole with a long birdie putt. Vardon made 5 and Burke took a 6. Score: TB 3 up

(At this point I was thinking the match was as good as over. Paul did his duty by not letting me throw my clubs over the fence. "You wouldn't give up in a dogfight," he said. "So you're not going to give up now. You still have four holes left.")

-       #15 - 457 yards/par 4 (Cartgate In): I aimed my drive where Vardon told me to - the right hand steeple of the city skyline - but the shot didn't quite keep the line. It found one of those nasty hidden bunkers that can't be seen from the tee. My sand shot was nothing brilliant and I made another bogey. Thank heavens Vardon chipped in for birdie to best Taylor's par. Burke made bogey 5. Score: TB 2 up

- #16 - 425 yards/par 4 (Corner of the Dyke): My first birdie of the day! Japers, it was about time because I'd been pretty much a burden to Vardon the entire round. I was 13 over par coming into the hole. My drive was grand! I aimed a little left to avoid the drivable bunkers known as the "Principal's Nose" positioned down the middle. Taylor and Burke both found trouble on the right - Taylor landed in some rough and Burke's shot went out of bounds. My second shot was also a doozie and stopped a mere 8 feet from the hole. And, to top it off, I sunk the putt for a 3. Vardon made an easy par. Score: TB 1 up

- #17 - 460 yards/par 5 (Road Hole): This hole is one of the most difficult par 4's in the world. But it only became a par 4 after the 1964 Open. The tee shot is quite demanding because you have to hit the ball over the "Black Sheds" *(used for storing hickory)*. Today the *Old Course Hotel* sign is there, and the ideal tee shot should be aimed to go over the 'o' in *Course*. A low stonewall off the back of the green punishes approach shots that come in too hot - which happens all the time. To come away with a par 4 feels like hard-earned birdie.
    Man did I smack the drive! It was the longest of the day. And perfectly placed, too. My mid-iron shot came in nice and high, dead on for the flag. Unlucky for me, the ball landed on a dry hard spot and barely held the green. The 33-foot putt I was left with was a wicked double-breaker left and right - practically impossible to make. But after a million readings of the line, and some sage advice from Vardon about speed, I finally struck the putt. Holy schmykees! I made it! An Eagle 3! To this day it's the best - *and most memorable* - putt I've ever made. Taylor made a birdie 4 while Vardon and Burke took par 5's. Burke survived his adventure by the stonewall by hitting his ball into the wall and bouncing it onto the green. Fantastic shot! Score: All square.

- #18 - 354 yards/par 4 (Tom Morris): Just like that, the match had turned around. We'd won three holes in a row! Talk about new life! And now we were at the most famous finishing hole in golf. The hole isn't that difficult unless you make it so. I aimed directly at the R&A Clubhouse's clock and mashed it straight. In fact, we all mashed great drives. Right after Burke hit, Paul took a speedy detour back to our hotel to grab my camera. Once back he snapped some photos of me posing with Vardon, Taylor, and Burke on Swilcan Bridge. One of the spectators then offered to take over the camera so Paul could get into the picture.

Though Harry Vardon and J.H. Taylor had been fierce competitors for over 20 years, the two men were good friends. It certainly showed on the golf course. They were just having another day of fun doing what they love to do. Edgar Burke, too. Seemingly immune to pressure and frustration, he'd cracked jokes all day, laughing at everything, even his own mistakes, all the while dishing out optimistic praise and unique observations. Up until #16, I'd treated the match as a matter of life and death while trying my best not to show it. All that tension certainly affected my golf game. That birdie on 16 helped a lot. If we had played another 18 that day I'm sure my score would have been far better.

Anyway, back to how the 18th hole played out. Using a mashie *(loft of a modern day 6 iron)*, my second shot rolled off the green into the "Valley of Sin" - a large swell in front. Burke and Taylor's shots landed pin-high to the left and right around 9 feet away. Vardon's approach was something else! The ball nearly slam-dunked into the hole! It hit the flagstick and careened left, settling two-feet off the green. My chip wasn't the best, but it gave me a fair shot to save par. Vardon needed a long time to study his chip, so he told Taylor and Burke to go ahead and putt. With a two-deep circle of onlookers now surrounding the hole *(almost like what you see in photos of the Open Championship!)*, Burke went first. His attempt veered off-line from the start leaving him a testy three-footer that he went ahead and smoothly sank for a 4. Taylor's putt was dead-on for the cup. It looked good but stopped a half-inch short. "Blow wind blow!" he hollered to his ball. The crowd groaned, and then enthusiastically applauded the attempt. Now it was my turn. I had a gentle right to left putt, slightly downhill. The stroke knocked it on line but a tad too firmly. The ball hit the back of the cup and bounced left. The five-foot comebacker was a tester, but I kept my nerves in check and made it to save par. I received rousing applause despite the crowd not knowing who I was. "All right now, knock it in the hole," I said to Vardon with a pump of my fist. The living legend then stepped up to his ball with a putter in hand. He could have used a Benny *(modern day 7-iron)* to chip, which is what I would have used and what his caddie had suggested. Trusting his gut, Harry Vardon stared down the hole for the longest time. At last he smoothly stroked the 20-foot putt. You could have heard a pin drop as the ball silently rolled on a crescent-shaped line toward the caddie-tended flagstick. There could only be one outcome.

Of course it went in. A birdie 3 to win the hole and the match! I must have jumped 50 feet high. It wasn't a world championship we'd won or anything, but japers it felt like it!

My score was 10 over 83 - not bad considering it was my first go on the Old Course. The first 9 holes had stung me. On the inward 9 holes I was only 4 over, and had played the last four holes at 3 *under par*. Edgar Burke fired an 8 over par 81, while J.H. Taylor shot plus 1 for a 74. Harry Vardon won the individual score with an even par 73.

* * * * *

On the steps of the R&A Clubhouse, only a few minutes after the match had concluded, Vardon said to me with his pipe in hand: "You have the game to be a successful professional golfer, Michael. You can easily qualify to play in next year's Open - assuming there is one. Bloody war."

"Thanks for the kind words," I humbly replied. "The Open will definitely be on my mind. I got to find the time to put in some serious practice if I want to compete in the tournament and not just play in it."

Vardon shook my hand and Paul's. "How long will you two be in town?"

"For as long as we want, really," I said. "No time restrictions at present."

"Then take advantage of it. Play as much as you can. It certainly was a pleasure today. Unfortunately, Taylor and I have to leave this afternoon, so there won't be time for another round today. But let's do try and play again *before* next year's Open, yes?"

"For sure."

16
The Invitation

After a turkey sandwich and tomato soup lunch on Market Street, Paul and I ventured back into the *Tom Morris Golf Shop* for no other purpose than to spend some more money. While comparing some stylish V-neck sweater vests, I received a light tap on my shoulder.

"Pardon me so," said a voice in a German-tinged British accent. A fleshy-faced man with rimless glasses and a neatly trimmed red-beard stepped to my side.

"Yes, hi ya," I said.

"Hello. I want to tell you that I watched the beginning and end of your round today. You are a talented golfer."

"Thanks mate. Do you play?"

"No, never."

"Oh, that's too bad. - What can I do for ya?"

The stranger lowered his voice. "Is there a place where we can sit down and talk?"

"I don't know. It depends on what kind of talk."

The man grinned, adjusting his bifocals. "Yes, certainly. What I can promise you is that your time will not be wasted."

I pondered the enticement as Paul came over. "What's going on?"

"This fella here - sorry, I didn't catch your name?"

"Rölf, Rölf Schreiber."

"Rölf says he has something interesting to tell me. All right, Mr. Schreiber, I'm game. We can leave here. Where do you want to go?"

"I am quite hungry; didn't get any breakfast. Have you eaten lunch?"

"Yeah, but we could squeeze in some extra tidbits."

Schreiber looked at Paul uneasily. "My intention was to speak with you alone."

"Well that's not gunna happen. Whatever you have to say to me, Paul can hear it too."

Adjusting his glasses again, the man mulled my demand. "Very well, as you wish. We can go to an eatery a short walk from here."

"Lead the way, Rölf. We'll keep some distance behind you."

When Rölf was out of earshot, Paul asked, "Have your gun?"

"No. I'll run back and get it and catch up with you. If he asks, feed him an excuse."

* * * * *

Who was this German? A spy? A British agent? My guard was up.

The three of us sat down in a lively old pub called *The Duffer* located on the corner of Golf Place and North Street. The dark timbered interior was festooned with all sorts of golf paraphernalia. Schreiber ordered steak and ale pie with extra mashed potatoes. Paul wanted some more chips (french fries), which was fine with me. The order came quickly.

Sipping a mug of *Shepherd Neame* ale, Schreiber, his voice barely audible in the merry chatter around us, said, "Your appearance is remarkably different than the pictures I've seen in newspapers - pictures of the . . . *Emerald Ace*."

My right hand was hidden under the table. I gripped the Webley revolver tight, ready to draw. A butter knife occupied my visible left hand.

So you are a spy . . .

Giving him a cold stare, I tossed the knife into the breadbasket and leaned back a little. "Well, well. How long have you known?"

"For several days. Not to be boastful, but my talent for recognizing details, especially faces, is extraordinary."

"Like Sherlock Holmes. Comes in handy in the spy business."

Schreiber broke off a piece of his bread. "It does. I first noticed you in London, which is where I live. By chance we were standing by each other near Leicester Square waiting to cross a street. Do you remember seeing me?"

"I don't. - Did you see him, Paul?"

"Didn't notice him."

"I discretely trailed you for the next thirty minutes as you wandered through Chinatown heading toward Piccadilly Circus," Schreiber continued. "Though I couldn't be positive, I thought you were probably Mick Gallagher - with your head shaved."

"Saves me time in the morning."

"I needed to be sure, so I trailed you to Edinburgh and then to here. I shaved off a large portion of my beard to keep you from recognizing me on the train." Schreiber pointed six inches below his chin. "It was down to here."

"Uh- huh. - So Rölf, brass tacks here. Are you a good guy or a bad guy? If you're the latter, this won't end well for you."

"At ease, Mr. Gallagher," Schreiber replied, his palms raised defensively. "Do not reach for the gun I know you have. I assure you I am not your enemy. In fact, I am an avid admirer of yours and have read much about you. Your fighter pilot exploits with the Flying Circus are legendary. You were on the mission with Richthofen when he was killed in April."

I nodded. "A bad day."

"Germany is still weeping over his death." Schreiber took another sip from his mug. "After I positively identified you in Edinburgh, I sent a coded message to Berlin. They've been extremely curious as to your whereabouts these past months. Berlin sent word to *Jasta 11*, where Hermann Göring is now in command."

"Göring? - Jaysus. Didn't figure him to ever be the headman. But he has friends in high places. Do you know what happened to Wilhelm Reinhard? He was in command when I left."

Schreiber grimaced. "Reinhard is dead. He was killed in early July while test flying at Aldershof. I don't know any details."

I reflected on Reinhard for a few moments, thinking back to the last time I talked to him. "That's a bummer. He was a good man, a good pilot. - Test flying is so risky. I was nearly killed at Aldershof in January."

"A parachute saved you - yes, I heard the story," Schreiber said. "Göring and Ernst Udet were most happy to hear that you were well. And that's why I was ordered to follow you and give you a message from them."

"I see. - Well, you're right. I am intrigued."

"I told you it would be worth your time."

"So what's the message, Rölf? Best wishes?"

"They send that – and something else. You've also been sent an invitation to receive the *Pour le Merite*."

I chuckled. "The Blue Max."

"Why'd they wait so long?" Paul asked. "It's about time! Mick should have gotten it long ago."

"Yes, I agree with you," Schreiber replied.

"Why do they want me to accept it in person? I'm sure they could get it to you for a handoff to me, yeah?"

"Most likely, yes. - I don't know why they want you to be present to accept it. I am just the messenger."

"Maybe they hope you can be talked into staying and fighting for the Circus again," Paul speculated.

"Yeah - that could be," I said. "They certainly need pilots, and planes. But the war's hopeless now. You agree Rölf?"

Schreiber dipped his chin. "Germany's situation is dire."

"They've *lost*, you mean."

"Why Germany keeps on fighting is insane," Paul said.

I poured myself another glass of water. "The heads must think that fighting on will give you guys a better position in the final peace treaty. In my opinion you'll get a better deal from President Wilson than the French and Brits."

"I again concur," replied Schreiber.

"Let's say I agree to go to Germany for the Blue Max. Exactly how would I get there from here?"

Schreiber quickly scanned around before answering. "By boat from London. I have a fishing boat that I use for work and leisure. It's 58 feet long and can handle rough water with ease. We would sail across the Channel to Amsterdam. From there my contacts would get you to Berlin."

I nodded. "All right, sounds like a pretty good plan."

"It's as close as you can get to a sure thing. You can get out of Germany through Denmark."

"Tell me Rölf, how long have you lived in London?"

"Since July of 13. "I came here looking for something new in my life."

Glancing at Paul, I said, "I can relate with that."

My marriage had failed, which I admit was my fault. I'd lost custody of our two children, and I was drinking heavily." Schreiber raised his mug and took a big gulp. "My drinking is under control now, I can assure you."

"Whatever you say, Rölf."

"It's understandable if you don't believe me. I'm used to it. - So, I came to London and lived with some relatives. I found a well-paying fishing job and have been doing it ever since. I do miss Germany, however. Badly."

"How long have you been -"

"Since June of 16," he cut in, guessing the spy question. "Another agent befriended me on the docks, and before I knew it I was in the game."

"And how do I know - *for sure* - that you're not a double-agent trying to lure me into a trap?"

Schreiber smiled with a slight shrug. "You will have to trust me. - I'm *not* a double. If I was working for the British or French, you would have already been captured. You wouldn't have gotten out of London." Schreiber pretended to shoot me with his hand. "You probably would have been shot by now."

He was right. And there was something about Rölf that made me trust him. The guy had to be legit. "When do you need a decision?"

"Within a few hours. I'm leaving for London on the six o'clock train from Waverley."

I pictured the Blue Max around my neck. It would be a grand medal to have. "All right, Rölf. I'll come with ya."

Schreiber smiled as he stood up and slipped on his black jacket. "Pleased to hear it. I will meet you at the bus station in one hour."

"Right. See you then."

* * * * *

Paul understood my decision, but he wasn't convinced that I could resist the urge to fly my green Fokker again with the Flying Circus. "Something will happen, and you'll feel obligated to help out the squadron," he said during the ten minute walk to the bus station. "Mark my words. You'll be flying combat before you know it."

"You're full of it," I retorted. "The Emerald Ace is retired."

"Yeah . . . yeah right."

* * * * *

Light traveling Rölf Schreiber arrived at the station five minutes after us, wearing a small blue backpack and holding a folded newspaper.

We boarded a sparsely filled bus to Leuchars and promptly caught the sparsely filled train to Edinburgh's Waverley Station. From there we boarded a packed night train to London. Paul and Rölf slept most of the way during the seven-hour journey. I tried to get some zzzzz's, but it wasn't happening.

Jaysus, I'm going back! I thought. *Back to Germany to get a medal! Back to some obscure farm field airstrip and the organized chaos of the Flying Circus!*

But not to fight!

Just to visit!

V-i-s-i-t

"Jaysus!" I said aloud - and too loudly at that! My voice disturbed an older gentleman from his slumber sitting across from me in the lounge car. I politely apologized and then occupied the time reading Rölf's newspaper in an effort to pull my mind off *Jasta 11*.

It sort of worked.

At a smidgen past 0600 we arrived at London's Paddington Station.

* * * * *

"My boat is docked near Greenwich north side," Rölf told us during the long taxi ride. "Barring any unforeseen delays, the voyage should take us about 12 hours averaging 10 to 12 knots. The weather forecast for tonight is ideal: clear with light winds and calm seas. I have made the journey several times over the years, so I have the route charted with precise coordinates."

"What about patrol boats?" I asked.

"That won't be a problem. I have all the necessary documents - for Allied or German. My boat has comfortable sleeping areas, a small but diverse library, and plenty of food, water, and petrol."

* * * * *

12 and a quarter hours later, in the middle of the afternoon on August 15th, the *Gormlaith* sailed into the ever-busy port of Amsterdam. Other than Paul's stomach turning a bit queasy, the journey had been smooth and without incident. We'd encountered one

British patrol boat that gave us a cursory inspection, document check, and let us be on our way.

The three of us took a boat ride through several narrow canals to the Amstel River and continued all the way to the gloriously red-bricked *De L'Europe Hotel* in the center of town. Paul checked out my fifth floor deluxe suite before flagging down a taxi to take him to the train station. "I might as well get back home," he said. "Unless you want to recruit me to join the Flying Circus."

"You'd be a star fighter pilot in no time."

"Maybe. But you couldn't get me up there without a parachute." Paul hopped into the taxi and closed the door. "How long will you be there?"

"Not sure," I said. "A week at most? Shouldn't be more than that."

Paul laughed. "Uh-huh, sure. See you a year from now."

I popped him in the chin. "I mean it ya gobshite. In a few days we can be off on our next adventure. Maybe Brazil. Rio. A boat trip on the Amazon. Yeah?"

"Only if you hurry back. School's gunna be starting soon."

* * * * *

After Paul left I grabbed a bite to eat at a close-by sandwich shop. I got to yapping with a couple of the locals and the time slipped away. Rölf had told me that the two contacts would meet us at 16:30 sharp in his room on the fourth floor. Racing back to the hotel, I took the stairs two at a time and got to Rölf's room with five minutes to spare - or so I thought. My watch must have been a little slow because as I knocked on the door a nearby elaborately crafted coo-coo clock announced the half-hour.

"Did you get lost?" Rölf asked, somewhat perturbed.

"Na, took the stairs. They're not here are they?"

"Any second now."

I checked the hallway once more before entering the room. "No worries then. They probably saw me enter the hotel. I came in fast." Once inside I joked, "Janey mack, this is a dinky room compared to mine."

Rölf ignored the comment, listening intently at the door with his Webley revolver drawn. "I think they're here. That was the elevator bell." Three seconds later he said, "Yes, footsteps. It has to be them."

Rölf lowered his gun waist high and moved to the left side. I took the right side with my hand on the Webley ready to draw.

Knock, knock . . . KNOCK.

Rölf nodded, relieved. I stepped farther to the side as Rölf slowly opened the creaky door. "*Guten tag,*" he greeted warmly, recognizing the visitors.

A tall man wearing glasses and a black leather jacket entered followed by a much shorter companion sporting a white Panama hat. "*Guten tag, Rölf,*" replied the first man. They were only a few steps inside when suddenly they both shot forward as if hit by a locomotive. The man with glasses plowed into Rölf, knocking him and his gun to the floor. I instinctively jumped back and crouched into firing position as the man in the Panama hat fell sideways into a nightstand.

The two intruders who'd barged into the room and shoved the other men now separated from the blur of movement, their Colt 1911 pistols waving rapidly 180 degrees from side to side. "Everyone freeze!" the man closest to me shouted in a Liverpool accent. It was the last thing he ever said. My bullet hit center mass, killing him instantly. The other intruder then pointed his gun at me and fired, but I was already into a diving roll toward the foot of the bed. The bullet splintered the wooden bed frame post, barely missing the back of my leg. Before he could get off another round I let loose a shot that hit him in the right shoulder. It caused enough of a delay to allow me a follow up shot. This one found the fatal mark, though it wasn't the mark I'd aimed at. Because the guy was twisting downward, center mass became center forehead.

By this time Rölf and the expected visitors were rising to their feet. "We're ok," Rölf said, picking up his pistol and adjusting his glasses. "These men are true."

Nodding, I then poked my head out the door in time to see a glimpse of someone in gray scampering around the hallway corner sixty feet away.

The lookout!

I took off full speed after him. Nearing the corner I didn't slow down. Instead I slid baseball style on the slick hardwood floor with the Webley in position to fire, just in case the guy was hiding in ambush (that's what I would have done).

Where are you . . .

He was there!

Waiting with his back flat against the wall!

But I'd appeared so fast, and in a position so unexpected, that the ambusher was caught off-guard. My Ty Cobb pop-up slide carried me into the base of the hallway wall with the perfect amount of force to allow me a smooth push-off into a reverse direction roll. Now positioned flat on my stomach, I quickly took aim at the stupefied man, who was in the process of trying to fix his pistol on me. Too late. My shot hit him square in the chest. He dropped his gun and fell mortally wounded, landing with a sickening thud on the very top of his head.

To my knowledge no one had seen me, but most of the hotel had to have heard the gunshots.

I sped back to the room.

"You get him?" asked Rölf.

"Yeah, he's toast. - We got to get out of here."

The tall man in glasses nodded. "Yes, immediately."

"I'll stay here," Rölf said. "I'll say these men tried to kill me. It was self-defense. I then pursued the lookout and got him, too."

"That works. We gotta switch pistols, then." I handed him my revolver and holstered his gun, a smaller Webley model called the Bulldog.

"We will play the part of shocked bystanders," said the tall man. "We can then make our way out of the building through one of the back doors. There could be more British agents in the lobby. We must go now."

"Good luck to you," Rölf said. "*Auf Wiedersehen.*"

Footsteps thundered down the hall. I stepped out of the room and, beginning the charade, hollered at the onrush of hotel staff, "In here! Call the police!"

* * * * *

Though we'd been first on the scene, we pretended not to know Rölf. The tall man with glasses (I didn't know his or the other guy's name until later - Stefan and Helmut) explained our situation by making up a convincing story about meeting me at the hotel for a job interview: We were in the stairway, heard shots, and when the shooting ceased we headed Rölf's call for help.

Following some basic questions from the hotel manager and an off-duty police officer, the two German agents and I blended seamlessly into the panicked throng of hotel guests. A few minutes later the three of us were exiting the *D L'Europe* through a second floor fire escape door along with an anxious mother and her young daughter.

* * * * *

Without delay we drove 28 rutted miles to Utrecht. After quickly switching from the rough riding cargo lorry to a speedier car, we drove another 40 much smoother miles to Arnhem. There, at a city park roundabout, I was met by a man named Lukas wearing filthy beige overalls over his mud-encrusted boots. Stefan and Helmut bid me a friendly adieu and zoomed away.

"We use the Rhine," Lukas told me, pointing toward the river. "In Kleve you will meet *Luftstreitkrafte* officials who will arrange transport for you to St. Quentin, where the Flying Circus is currently located. Commander Göring will be expecting you."

17
All Clear

Wolfram von Richthofen, a younger 4th cousin of Manfred and Lothar who had joined the Circus shortly before I left, stood statuesque on the boat dock in Kleve. I recognized him immediately, and when we got closer I was surprised to see the now veteran pilot come alive with an energetic wave or his arm. He hadn't been the friendliest of people when he first arrived at *Jasta 11*. Very standoffish he was.

Once docked, I shook Lukus' hand and stepped off the boat to greet Wolfram.

"Hi ya Wolfie! Thought I'd do ya a favor and get you out of combat tonight," I kidded. "You like my baldish look?"

Wolfram chuckled affably as he extended his hand. "You look . . . *evil*."

"Gotta keep them Brits afraid ya know! Can't be too pleasant looking."

"Of course. When will you let your hair grow back?"

"Not sure. Maybe never. I've been shaving it once a week."

"It will take some getting used to," Wolfram admitted. "You're right about the favor. Göring most likely would have sent me out on an evening patrol if I hadn't volunteered to come get you."

"Yeah, I heard Hermann's the chief now."

"Yes, and he's basking in it. He's been strutting around with that *Geschwader* cane like he's king of the world. You should see his airplane. He had his D.VII painted all white, though he hardly flies anymore. - The car is this way. How was the boat ride?"

* * * * *

During the twenty-minute drive to the airfield, a flight of wildly colored Fokker D.VII's came in for a landing flying parallel to the car fifty yards distant. I didn't recognize any of the color schemes of the seven planes. When I'd departed the Flying Circus four months back, the unit was still using rotary engine Fokker Dr I triplanes and a few old Albatros D.Va's and a lone Pfalz D.III. Wolfram informed me that the first Fokker D.VII's had arrived in June. "We were very excited to finally have them," he said. "The early D.VII's were equipped with a Mercedes IIIaü 180 horsepower engine, the same power plant the

Luftstreitkrafte has been using since 1916. Though it's a good and reliable engine, it did not bring out the best qualities of the D.VII. It's only when the BMW IIIa with 185 horsepower was put in them that the aircraft became a supreme fighter. It's easy to fly, fast, and incredibly stable. Very maneuverable, a good climber, diver, and a quick turner."

"That's about got it covered. It's basically the V-11 that I test flew in Aldershof in January, yeah?"

"Correct, with several modifications. The D.VII can reach 13,000 feet in ten minutes. With the Mercedes engine it took over twenty-two minutes. Also, a speed increase of 7 miles per hour to 125, and a service ceiling of 24,200 feet - that's 4,000 feet higher than before."

"Well it was a pretty fine airplane with the Mercedes if you ask me," I said. "It'd be grand to try it out with the BMW."

"I'm sure Göring will let you take one up for a tryout."

"Yeah he will, probably with the condition that I agree to fly a patrol or two."

Wolfram smirked. "I wouldn't put it past him. It still puzzles me that he received the *Pour le Merite* without meeting the standard of twenty victories, which you've surpassed. He didn't get to twenty until June."

"It's gotta be those high placed friends again."

Wolfram turned onto a narrow gravel road that led to the airfield grounds. "Congratulations on your award. It is long overdue."

"Thanks Wolfie. Better get the Blue Max now before they raise the standard to twenty-five." A pair of D.VII's crossed in front of us, heading toward the airstrip. "The Flying Circus without the Red Baron . . . I can't get used to it. It's not right."

Wolfram sighed dejectedly. "You also won't find Lothar, Udet, Reinhard, Lubbert, or Wolff. Eric Löwenhardt, too. He started flying with us soon after you left."

"Say what? Jaysus sakes! I knew about Reinhard, but the others? Please man, tell me they're not dead."

"Lubbert, Wolff and Löwenhardt are dead - all killed in combat. Lothar is out of the war from a leg wound. Udet is currently on leave. He won't be back for another month."

I shook my head. *Stupid war. Udet should ride out the war at home.*

Wolfram von Richthofen drove past a line of identical corrugated iron huts and stopped the vehicle alongside the only one facing east. Of the pilots and ground crew outside, I recognized only Walther Karjus and Richard Wenzl. Their backs were turned as they entered one of the huts.

"Is Fritz still around?"

"He is, and we're all grateful for that," replied Wolfram. "He keeps those engines purring."

The low-hanging evening sun glimmered a brilliant orange-red hue across the curved row of 15 candy-colored aircraft, most of which were Fokker D.VII's save for two red and white Dr I triplanes and a black and white Hannover CL.II reconnaissance two-seater. There wasn't a farmhouse or any type of civilized structure as far as at the eye could see, only flat, drought-ridden fields of clumpy dirt and dry grass. "Not the most comfortable place to live," I commented as we approached the entrance.

The door suddenly opened in a rush.

"A bald Mick Gallagher! How wonderful to see you!" cried the normally reserved *adjutant* Karl Bodenschatz.

"Same here," I replied, double-clutching his hand. "Is the war still going on?"

"Ha! It is, but I doubt for much longer." Bodenschatz led me inside as Wolfram departed. "Göring is in his office. We can catch up there. I will bring you something to drink."

* * * * *

"The Emerald Ace returns to the Circus!" Hermann Göring announced with dramatic flair as he rose from his white cushioned chair. "Welcome back, Mick. - Interesting haircut!"

I shook his hand. "Thanks, Herm. In a way it feels like I never left here, but it also feels so different at the same time."

Göring nodded. "Much has changed over the last several months. All for the worse, I'm afraid. - Please, have a seat."

I planted down in a folding chair while Göring pulled out a small blue box with gold trim from his desk drawer.

"I have something for you."

"Oh Herm, you're not going to propose to me are you? We've known each other for a while now, but let's not rush things."

Göring laughed hard, as did Karl Bodenschatz who had entered the office at that moment carrying a camera. "Don't give me that nonsense," Göring scolded. "All you could talk about was Michelle when you were here. So did you marry her while you were away?"

I didn't want to talk about Michelle.

Switch out of this quick.

"No . . . no wedding for me," I said dourly. "Michelle isn't in the picture anymore."

Göring read my face. "Oh . . . I see. Well, someone else will come along. The heart will heal."

"Yeah, so they say."

Hermann Göring handed me the box. "Richthofen was working hard behind the scenes to get you this before he was killed. I wish he was here to give it to you."

I slowly opened the box.

The Blue Max. The Pour le Merite. I finally got it!

"Congratulations, Mick. Put it on and Karl will take your picture."

* * * * *

"Wolfram told me about all the guys who've been killed," I said a few minutes later. "I hardly recognize anyone here. I did see Wenzl and Karjus."

"We've had a bad run," Göring said. "The war is winding down for us. No hope of winning. The latest Allied offensive has pushed back our 2nd Army from Albert. The Tenth French Army is about to take the town of Noyon, and the First Army will soon overrun Bapaume. We're in the thick of battle here at St. Quentin. The Allies are steadily pushing us back to the Hindenburg Line. I don't know how much longer this can go on."

"It's crazy to continue the war," I said.

"Crazy is not the word for it. - I don't know the right word for it."

Karl Bodenschatz offered me a choice of coffee, tea, or beer. I chose coffee. "Thanks Karl." To Göring, I said, "The D.VII's sure look grand. I was wondering if you might let me take one up for a jaunt."

"Certainly. You can fly mine if you wish. It's the all white one. I wouldn't fly now, though. It's getting too dark. Wait until tomorrow." Göring then gave me a peculiar smile.

"No, no, no," I said, shaking my head. "I know what you're thinking. Don't you dare ask me to fly on a patrol."

"Huh? Why of course not."

"Yeah, you fibber."

"Honesty, Mick. The thought hadn't occurred to me. But now that you mention it . . ."

I rolled my eyes at Bodenschatz. "It's getting deep in here, Karl."

Göring opened one of the beers. "So what have you been doing since you left?"

In fifteen minutes I told of my zeppelin adventure, the Spain trip and shark encounter, the British soldiers in Dublin, the torpedoed ship, the Matterhorn climb, my St. Andrews round, and the shooting in Amsterdam. I left out everything about Michelle and the Spanish flu. Neither man asked about Michelle.

Göring then filled me in with mostly bad news concerning *JG 1* and the details of the Allied push that would later be called the *100 Days Offensive*.

* * * * *

It ended up being a late night.

After our meeting, while I was taking a cold bucket shower in another hut, Göring called for a celebration of my return over the base loudspeaker. He also informed the *jasta* that the morning patrol would be delayed until 10:00.

I got to meet all the new guys and reconnected with Walther Karjus, Richard Wenzl, and Hans Weiss.

"Want to be my wingman tomorrow?" asked Karjus, a little tipsy after draining a couple of large beers. "We'll probably find some of those hot shot Americans again from the 94th - the *Hat in the Ring* squadron. They're flying S.P.A.D. XIII's with a hat in the ring emblem on the fuselage. What these Americans lack in flying skill they make up for it in guts."

"I'll second that," added Weiss. "The squadron does have some good flyers, like Eddie Rickenbacker and Frank Luke. Back in America Rickenbacker was a famous race car driver - so you can see where his guts come from."

"Luke, too," said Karjus. "He's called the Arizona Balloon Buster. The man preys on observation balloons, and is really good at shooting them down."

Richard Wenzl tapped my shoulder with his beer mug, spilling some of the brew on my shirt. "What do you say, Mick? Fly with us one more time for old time's sake?"

"Raise your glass and say 'yes'," Karjus ordered.

"You will fall madly in love with the D.VII," Weiss predicted.

"No doubt about that because we've already met," I said. "In January I flew the prototype of the D.VII at Alderschof. Grand plane she is."

Karjus drained the last of his third beer. "So that's a 'yes' . . . you'll fly with us?"

Several of the other men around our table had been eavesdropping on our conversation. Now their ears really perked up. "Walther, Hans, Richard, and the rest of you brave men of *Jasta 11*," I said with an air of formality, "my fighter pilot days are done. Sorry mates. My mind is made up."

"Hey, we had to try," Wenzl said.

"Good pilots are hard to come by," added Weiss.

Karjus pretended to take an angry bite out of his beer mug. "That's ok, Mick. We understand and respect your decision. We really do. Everyone but me."

I flicked his nose.

* * * * *

Fritz was hard at work on a D.VII engine when I met up with him early the next morning at 0700. "Is it my imagination or have you lost weight?" I asked the plumpish mechanic, known throughout the German Air Service as a workaholic miracle fixer.

Covered in oil and grease, Fritz turned around on his stepladder. "You certainly have lost weight, and it's all from your head. How have you been?"

"Just fine, Fritz. It's nice to be back. I was wondering if you have a spare D.VII that I can take up for a try."

"Sure I do. You can take any of the last three on the west end."

"Göring's plane is good to go then?"

"Yes! It is a good one, except for the color. Paint it green or something for me. Get rid of the white. I don't like it."

"I might have to do that, but it won't be green."

Fritz nodded rather disappointedly. "So it's true then, you're not returning as an active fighter pilot?"

"It's true. I'm retired at 16 and set for life."

Fritz hopped down from the ladder. "I'm sure you are, with your girlfriend's rich daddy."

I nodded. "Yeah."

* * * * *

A key feature of the Fokker D.VII is its thick, cantilever wings. Other than that, to the untrained eye the aircraft looked like a typical WW1 era biplane. It wasn't a sleek design by any means; in fact, the D.VII had a rather box-like appearance.

But man could she fly!

I did choose Göring's plane, but I could have easily gone with Ernst Udet's. It was parked next to the white Fokker, distinctively marked with "LO" on the fuselage in honor of his fiancé Eleanor "Lola" Zink. One unique thing about Göring's plane was that the cockpit rim was cut down to allow easier access. Göring's arthritis had gotten a lot worse since the beginning of the year.

What rust I had from four months off from flying was scrubbed away before I even left the ground. I got a great feel for the airplane while fiddling with her instruments during a long, circuitous taxi route. All the maneuvering controls were tight, but not too tight. There was zero loose play, and the pedals were instantly responsive. The powerful BMW engine was practically begging for me to unleash it. There's no other way to say it, but I was in a veritable hot-rod airplane! Adrenaline surged through me as all the excitement of why I loved airplanes and flying came rushing back.

And I was still on the ground!

Besides Fritz, there were only a few other men who saw me takeoff - all ground crew members.

In the next fifteen minutes that Fokker and I became best friends. It was like I'd flown it for months on end, six hours a day. The machine felt a lot like the V-11 but more refined and smoother in every way. And of course it was far more powerful with the BMW. The experience was positively euphoric. With the D.VII, Anthony Fokker had finally gotten it right. It was fighter plane perfection, for experienced pilots and rookies alike. So easy to fly and so forgiving; so *connected* to the abilities of the pilot. If an enemy plane had suddenly appeared it wouldn't have stood a chance against me. So confident was I that I felt like I could take on the entire *Hat in the Ring* squadron.

* * * * *

As I was coming in for a landing, with darkening skies closing in, I noticed a dark blue car enter the main grounds of the airfield. The open-roofed Mercedes had two occupants, and it was heading in my direction as I touched down. When we passed by each other, I caught a clear glimpse of the blond-haired front seat passenger.
Japers! Is that him? It's gotta be!

* * * * *

It was him.
Ernst Udet.
He stood next to his airplane waiting for me to taxi over. "Don't scratch my plane!" he yelled kiddingly as I approached. My impolite gesture (a reverse 'V' sign) amused him and the ground-crewman heading to grab the D.VII's tail. I shut off the engine and hopped down.
"This can't be a coincidence," I said, grinning ear to ear.
"You're right about that. Göring notified me you were on your way here. I left Frankfurt yesterday."
"Jaysus it's great to see you! I was told you wouldn't be back for another month."
"That's true, but I couldn't let a good friend pass by. How's civilian life treated you?"
"Oh . . . well, I don't know. We can talk inside."
"How did you like Hermann's plane?"

"What's not to like but the color scheme?" I said. "The thing's a jewel. I almost took yours up. How would you have liked to see me coming down in that?"

"You should have. I'd have loved it. The D.VII's a fantastic machine! Allied planes were falling too easily for me. I exhausted myself flying it."

"So is your leave over? Or you gunna go back for more?"

Udet gave me a curious smirk. "We can talk about that inside, too."

* * * * *

We sat down inside an empty Officer's Mess. I got some fresh coffee brewing and grabbed an apple to munch on. Udet wasn't hungry. For breakfast all he needed was a cigarette.

"So many new faces here," I said. "The old guard is mostly gone."

Udet exhaled a long hiss of smoke. "It's that way in all of the *jastas.*"

"How is Lothar? When I left he was still recovering from that bad crash."

"He came back in July as good as ever," Udet said. "He was leading *Jasta 11* until two weeks ago when he took a bullet in the thigh. It was a bad wound. Put him out of the war for good. You can guess the date it happened."

"Don't tell me the 13th?"

"You guessed it. *Again!*"

I slapped the table. "Unbelievable! He shoulda taken the day off."

"I told him too, as did others, but he wouldn't listen. Lothar's still struggling around on crutches. He's hating not being able to hunt."

"It's crazy," I said with a mouthful of apple. "You can't continue to beat the odds when the odds are always stacked against you. Like in the casino, you gotta know when to walk away, yeah?"

Udet stared at his cigarette.

"So - are *you* going to walk away?" I asked. "You've certainly put in enough time."

"It's not that easy for me to walk away, Mick. It's not easy for any dedicated soldier. Already I feel guilty for being away on leave. I wasn't really injured in the conventional sense, but mentally and physically I was exhausted."

"How do you feel now?"

"Much better. I snap back fast - always have. I'm ready to fly again."

"But the war is over for Germany. The Allies are steamrolling over what's left of the army. You guys can't win."

"I know that, and so does everyone else," Udet said. "But I feel it's my duty to soldier on. Until our high command officially surrenders, I must continue to fly. I have to."

"That's not true, is it?"

"It is for me. Think of it this way: I'm sure you've had a football match or one of your Gaelic sports where the score was completely lopsided and your team had no chance to win the game - yes?"

"Too many times."

"Did you ever quit?"

"No."

"And why not?"

"Because . . . look, I know where you're going with this."

Udet took another drag on his cigarette. "Answer me. Why didn't you quit the game?"

"Because you keep on playing until the game is over - yes, yes, I know."

"And if you had quit - what then?"

"Ok, ok . . . I get it."

"You see? Quitting would have let down everyone - first and foremost your teammates. Your coaches and your parents would have been terribly embarrassed. You would have embarrassed and shamed yourself."

"But a lopsided football match and a hopeless war are two different things," I countered. "You're not going to die in a football match." Suddenly grinning, I interjected a bit of humor with, "Hurling, however, is a different story. The stick *and* ball can both kill ya."

Udet got the joke. "But duty is duty," he said. "There's no difference. And that's why I am returning to combat flying. Your return visit has sped up the process for me."

"Jaysus, I should have stayed away."

Udet chuckled. "No, I'm glad you came. The *Pour le Merite* is well-deserved."

"Thanks, mate. I wish the Baron was here, though."

"Me, too."

"What does Lola think of you returning to combat? There's no way she can be happy about it."

"She knows I'm a soldier," Udet replied. "Soldiers do their duty. We will be married after the war - which I predict will end in several weeks. So you see, I won't be flying that much longer anyway. - You should paint one of these D.VII's green and join the *jasta* again, Mick. We can trade off as each other's wingman. You can get your score to 30. What are you at, 23?"

"Yeah. And you?"

"I'm at 56."

"Good god!"

"A month ago I was at 30."

I slapped the table. "Japers, that's almost like one a day!"

"You can do it, too," Udet said. "Seven more is all you need. And in a D.VII no one will touch you. That's a guarantee."

I shook my head. "No . . . there's a different feel now. It's not the same."

Udet stubbed out his cigarette and lit another one. "I'm going to speak freely here, all right?"

"Sure, go ahead."

"Ok - as I see it you don't seem very happy. You're putting on a good front, but I can tell. It's in your eyes and in your voice."

I didn't say anything.

"Could it be that you miss the action in the air? - Tell me, am I right?"

I nibbled at what was left of the apple. "I miss flying, that's for sure. But . . . what I miss most is . . ." I couldn't finish the sentence. "I miss . . ."

And I broke down.

* * * * *

"Mick, I'm not going to pretend that I can understand what you're going through," Udet said a quarter-hour later. "I don't want to think about losing Lo. But as I recall Michelle was a believer in fate.

She knew you and her would be married. And it happened. Tragically, her death cut the marriage short, but she was right. You *did* survive as a fighter pilot. Michelle always wanted you to be happy. She knew flying was a big part of that. If you can honestly sit there and tell me you don't feel an urge to get back in that cockpit and fly with us then I will leave you alone and never mention it again."

Udet paused for a second, twirling his cigarette. "You just told me that you and your friend Paul scaled the Matterhorn and witnessed a murder at the top. You've lined-up other daring adventures around the world. Your life will be put at risk doing them, but you'll do them anyway. I know you will. Risks be damned! You'll be living fully, the way you're supposed to. You have no Michelle to worry about now. There is nothing holding you back. Life is short, so why not get maximum joy from it? Look at all the money you have to spend. And you're sixteen years-old!" Udet threw his hand at me dismissively. "Don't feel sorry for yourself. It's beneath you and it's pathetic given everything you have. - Mick, fly with *Jasta 11* because you want to, not because of what I say or anyone else. – You've heard the expression 'be true to yourself?' Well, you need to be."

I sat motionless, pondering his words.

He's right . . .

Ernst Udet had nailed it! Of course! I couldn't quit on the team. The Red Baron wouldn't have quit. He died for his team. If Lothar von Richthofen could fly he'd be here, too. If Werner Voss were suddenly resurrected, he'd be back in that cockpit in a second. All those killed from *JG 1* would do it, too.

So be it!

My mind was made up. It was time to fly again.

I *wanted* to fly again!

Like Udet said, to hell with the risks! If a lucky shot takes me out, so what? My number was up. Losing Michelle had distorted everything for a while. How could it not? But now, all was clear again. Brilliantly clear. My travel plans would be delayed until after the war. The money would still be there.

I'm a fighter pilot! The Emerald Ace is back!

"Ernst," I said, swishing around the one swallow of cold coffee left in my cup, "thanks a lot, man. You're right. I needed to hear what you said. Thirty minutes ago I never thought I'd be saying this, but I am going to fly with the Circus again. As of this moment, Mick Gallagher is back. All I need is a green Fokker D.VII."

Ernst Udet extinguished his cigarette and gave me a melodramatic salute. "Do you still have the green scarf I gave you?"

Frowning, I said, "Sorry - it's a victim of war."

"We'll find you another." Udet rose from the table. "Before you change your mind, let's go tell Hermann."

18
Back in Action

While heading toward Commander Göring's office, I experienced a momentary flash of second thoughts: *Why am I doing this? Am I crazy? I'll be flying against many French and Americans. My war is with England.*

But then I saw a cadre of pilots dutifully heading for their aircraft for the first patrol of the day. My second thoughts vanished. *Those guys can't walk away from their duty. The game's a stupid lost cause but they have to keep playing. And so will I.*

Göring was elated with my decision. "From the jaws of defeat, Germany will win the war!" he jested after giving me a standing ovation.

His joke wasn't that funny, but I laughed anyway.

Bodenschatz shook my hand. "A proud moment for *Jasta 11*, for Germany, and for Ireland. You are an extraordinary person, Mick."

"Thanks a lot, Karl." To Göring I asked, "When's the second patrol of the day?"

"At 1300, but the weather might cancel it," Göring replied. "Go see Fritz about your aircraft."

* * * * *

Fritz answered my question before I asked it. When he saw me approaching he called out from underneath a propeller: "Yes, I have plenty of emerald green paint for your D.VII."

I laughed. "Japers me, how'd you know already?"

"It was the look you had yesterday. Your words didn't match your face."

"Wow, it was that obvious?"

"To me it was. I'm wondering if it was obvious to you?"

His question gave me pause. "Well, some stuff had happened and I was blind to it. Udet opened my eyes."

"He can do that." Fritz motioned me over to an open crate. "The paint is in there. Brushes and solvent, too. Have you selected a plane?"

"I haven't. Which ones are available?"

"Numbers 3, 5, 6, and 9," Fritz answered. "Try out number 9. It was built by Albatros. They're building the best D.VII's."

"Fokker's rival?"

"Ironic, eh? Albatros is under license from Fokker to build D.VII's in order to keep up with demand. We've got five of them. Göring, Udet, Karjus, and Weiss have one. Number 9 arrived two days ago. I think it's the best of all of them."

"You made it easy for me, Fritz. Nine it is."

* * * * *

The wind and rain were coming on strong by the time I began painting. The airfield soon became a mud bath. The first patrol had returned relatively unscathed, having seen only minor action. One of the pilots, a transfer from *Jasta 29*, Rudi Geschke, achieved ace status (5 victories) by downing a French observation balloon. There was a minor celebration for him in the mess. Göring postponed further patrols until weather permitted. The latest forecast said the low-pressure front wouldn't relent until late into nightfall.

My Albatros-made D.VII was looking magnificent! The emerald green was extremely bright, and it made my airplane shine like a giant lightbulb. On both sides of the fuselage, next to the required German *Iron Cross*, I painted a four-leaf clover in a circle of white - just like I'd done with the Fokker triplane. But this time, directly above the clover, I painted the green, white, and orange flag of the Irish Republic. The airplane was finished by late afternoon but would take some time to dry.

When Göring saw the paint job his reaction surprised me a little. "Your flag emblem is in technical violation of standard protocol, but I will make an exception for you. It does look very good. - I've put you down for the 0700 patrol tomorrow. Yes?"

"Sure thing. You flying, too?"

"Yes I am, along with Udet, Karjus, Weiss, Geschke, Wenzl, and Wolfram. Also with us will be Erwin Vogt, Tillman Wegscheider, and Hubert Lauer. They have seen little experience. I will be keeping a close watch on Vogt. Udet will take Lauer under his wing. Will you keep an eye on Wegscheider?"

"No problem."

* * * * *

After dinner that evening I rummaged through a bag of miscellaneous garments that Bodenschatz had collected. I found a light green scarf that had a few oil stains on it. It would have to suffice until I could find a scarf that matched my airplane.

Udet, Karjus, and I shared a hut with new pilots Vogt, Wegscheider, and Lauer. Vogt was the oldest pilot in the *jasta* at 30. He came from a rich family and had two advanced science degrees from the Humboldt University of Berlin. His personality was rather bland, but he was a walking encyclopedia who didn't mind lecturing to anyone who'd listen - like me. In a few hours over the course of the first two evenings, I must have learned 2 university credits worth of science knowledge.

Longtime friends Wegscheider and Lauer were both 21 and had attended the same schools growing up in Düsseldorf. They were an interesting study in opposites. Hubert Lauer was an unmitigated slob in every way imaginable. His personal hygiene, while expected to be subpar being a fighter pilot at a tent-strewn airfield, was something out of the caveman days. His foul breath reminded me of Colonel Douglas C. McKibbon, the obese commander of the Amiens prisoner of war camp who tried to have Anton Dunkel and me executed (detailed in *Richthofen's Knight*, volume II of these memoirs).

At the other end of the cleanliness spectrum was Tillman Wegscheider. A neat freak to the extreme. I swear he would have married a bathtub! The guy couldn't go two hours without washing his hands, face, and all other exposed skin he deemed contaminated by grime. Filth in all its forms, untucked shirts, soiled shoes, uncombed hair, and clutter were his mortal enemies. His favorite recreational activity, besides keeping the hut looking spic and span, was shaving twice a day - which took him forever and a day because he was so meticulous about it.

Both Düsseldorfians had good-natured personalities that turned everyone they met into a friend. Weggie (the nick-name I gave him) seemed to derive curious amusement from constantly harassing Lauer about his mucky habits - and some of Udet's, Karjus', and mine, too. My stained scarf drove him bonkers. Suffice it to say, we hit it off with Lauer and Weggie big time.

* * * * *

As mentioned in previous volumes, *Jagdgeschwader Nr I* (or *JG I),* dubbed "The Flying Circus" by the Allies, was a permanent grouping of *jastas* 11, 4, 6, and 10. Since its inception in June of 1917 it had been the most important fighter unit in the German Air Service, and now its brave pilots were being pushed to the brink more than ever since the beginning of the latest Allied offensive.

"We're all about defense now," Hermann Göring said as we suited up for the 0700 patrol. "Delaying the inevitable for as long as we can."

"It's a senseless necessity," Walther Karjus quipped reaching for his prosthetic right arm. As an observer, he'd lost the limb after being wounded from a French attack. None deterred by the amputation, and bored with being an observer, Karjus turned himself into a top-notch fighter pilot. His various fighters each had a modified control column and gun-firing lever that could be operated with one hand.

"There is a possibility we could see British in the mix today," Göring continued. "They have a new plane called the Sopwith Snipe. It's supposed to be a replacement for their aging Camels. I've heard it's not much faster than the Camel, but it has a better rate of climb and is slightly more maneuverable. The Snipe is similar in appearance. The French and Americans are flying mostly S.P.A.D. XIII's. They'll be diving on us, so be ready. If numbers are too great, I will not waste our men and aircraft in a suicide dogfight. Our altitude will be low so we stay close to our troops. Use common sense and keep your heads at all times. Help each other, don't waste ammunition, and stick to the fundamentals. Think *Boelcke's Dicta.*"

Udet tossed Göring a flying helmet. "You sound like the Baron."

"It happens when you get this position. You'd be saying the same thing if you were in command."

"In my opinion," said Richard Wenzl, "we have two advantages. One is that the enemy has to come to us and they have to deal with the prevailing wind flying back. The other advantage is our aircraft. The Fokker D.VII is the best fighter in the sky. I don't think there is room for debate. This new Sopwith Snipe does not worry me."

"Their biggest advantage is numbers," mentioned Hans Weiss. "It doesn't matter what type of aircraft they are flying - Camels, S.P.A.D.'s, SE.5's - they're all formidable planes."

"We just need more D.VII's," Udet added.

"And more properly trained pilots," Wolfram said, rubbing stinky whale grease on his face. "The D.VII's will no doubt help, but they won't completely nullify inexperience. An experienced Allied flyer in a slow Sopwith Triplane from two years ago could bring down many of our new pilots." Wolfram turned to the new pilots Vogt, Lauer, and Wegscheider. "I mean you no disrespect with that comment, gentlemen."

Vogt nodded. "Quite all right. You speak the truth."

"We'll keep ya safe," I piped in, fiddling with straps of the Heinecke parachute. The contraption had saved my life during the Johannisthal testing in January. The majority of German pilots had warmed to parachutes despite their extra 30 pounds of weight. It wasn't that way on the Allied side, however. The wearing of parachutes was heavily restricted because it was thought that they would cause pilots to needlessly abandon their aircraft.

* * * * *

Our mission was simple: front line defense and support of troops who were slowly but surely wearing down. Albeit at a snail's pace, the German army was in retreat. Airplanes from all of *JG I* and 11 from *Jasta 29* - 49 aircraft in all - would take part this morning. Such large groupings were necessary to counter Allied aircraft that seemed to be multiplying exponentially by the day.

The morning weather of August 31 was exceptional: clear skies and not a wisp of wind.

Here we go again, I thought, sitting in my spiffy new Fokker. *It's like I've never been gone.*

With the Blue Max draped around my neck, I was raring to go. I had no concerns about the aircraft, the mission, or any dogfighting rust. My confidence was maxed out. However, in all the nervous excitement, there was a strong current of anger surging through me. I was mad, mad at the world. Though it made no logical sense, I wanted to take out the loss of Michelle on the enemy - preferably the British enemy.

Let's put that anger to good use!

"Contact!" I shouted, giving Weggie a thumbs-up. The newbie nervously smiled back and tugged at his black scarf, indicating to me that he did not care for the stained one I was wearing. To my left Ernst Udet and Hermann Göring led the way to the top of the airstrip. Udet's red and white Fokker with 'Lo!' on the fuselage looked deadly. Göring's all white plane reminded me of a giant dove.

Fly smart. Fly for the team. No worries. No Michelle to think about.

* * * * *

We took off with the sun at our backs and quickly met up with the planes from *jastas* 4, 6, and 10. *Jasta 29* caught up to us a minute later. The vast majority of us were flying D.VII's, but there were a few Pfalz D.III's and D.XII's along with two Fokker triplanes in the mix.

There would be zero wait time for action. And the action was instantly intense. No easing into it. The enemy appeared as soon as we reached our front line positions, a mass of 40+ S.P.A.D.'s and Nieuport 28's diving down on us!

They were waiting to pounce! The Buggers!

I pointed behind me, telling Weggie to scram out of here. "Go back! Go Back!" I yelled as though he could hear me. The rookie didn't hesitate. He nosed-up and turned his Fokker around on a dime. I couldn't think about Vogt and Lauer. Göring and Udet had them.

Now it was a free for all.

Everybody scattered.

Bullets zipped by me on both sides, missing by a gee hair. I broke left in a monkey climb to avoid the two diving Nieuports.

Begorrah that was close!

All around me was a crazy twisting mass of mechanical birds! Nearly a 100 aircraft buzzing about! With wingtips so close together, there were bound to be some collisions.

And sure enough it happened.

To my right at 5:00, a diving Nieuport and a banking Fokker clipped wing tips. The Nieuport collapsed like a limp noodle. It fell sideways and twirled earthward out of control. The purple D.VII spun 360 degrees around spraying wing fragments in all directions. The *Jasta 10* pilot tried to exit his doomed airplane, but the gyrations were too intense. His leg got hung up in the cockpit as he attempted to jump out.

Get some distance!

There was a small gap to my right leading to clear blue. A flock of S.P.A.D.'s had just passed by it.

My chance!

I banked toward the opening and sped through. My airplane was performing like a dream. Once free of the congestion, I looped back to get behind the French. Above me at 3:00 I spotted Udet trying to get a bead on a S.P.A.D. that was trying to outrun him. Hubert Lauer was nowhere around so I assumed he'd gone back to the airfield like Weggie. Göring's white Fokker suddenly rolled left on my periphery, but I couldn't tell if he was on the attack or defense. Vogt's yellow-nosed plane passed him going in the opposite direction. It didn't appear that he was breaking for home.

Most of the dogfight was now in front of me, which made it a lot easier to make sense of the melee. The S.P.A.D XIII was faster than the D.VII and was the best diving aircraft of the entire war. I couldn't chase them forever. Fortunately two of them broke off from the group to pursue a couple of *Jasta 29* Fokkers that had become separated.

More newbies, I thought. I had to help them or they were toast.

In a steep climb toward the S.P.A.D.'s I came at them at a perfect firing angle, not quite directly behind. The pilots couldn't see me because I was in their blind spot. For a few moments the prospect of downing two airplanes in one approach caused me some runaway exuberance. But just before I could cut loose with my Spandau machine guns, one of the French banked right and broke off his attack. I'm not sure why he did that. There was no way he could have seen me, and neither of the Fokkers had changed course. Anyway, his action ended my hopes of a two-for one deal.

As for the other S.P.A.D., it couldn't have been positioned for me any better.

Don't blow this one . . .

At a distance of 70 feet, I "hung on my prop" and sent a spot-on burst of tracers into the middle of the fuselage that cut a horizontal line all the way through the engine. The S.P.A.D. XIII twisted left as a cannon-like explosion of black smoke shot out straight into the pilot.

One of the key characteristics of the D.VII was its ability to climb steeply without stalling. In any other fighter, even a dance-about Fokker Dr I triplane, my maneuver would have sent me into a potentially unrecoverable tailspin.

Incredible airplane!

The Frenchman plummeted like a stone past me into the bombed out terrain of no man's land.

I then set off after the other S.P.A.D.

* * * * *

The combat was spreading out. Individual contests were taking place over a two-mile span. It was anyone's guess which side was winning, but something told me we had the edge.

In the distance to my left I saw Erwin Vogt's checkerboard painted D.VII emerge from a cloud. He was flying in my direction straight and steady. Göring was nowhere around.

What you doing? I wondered.

I was currently heading away from our airfield. Was he coming to offer me assistance?

Go home Vogt!

The S.P.A.D. I was after was turning back around, still chasing the newbie German who was making a desperate dash for home.

Ok . . . that's more like it.

The Frenchman realized that he was my prey, so he let the German go and pointed his airplane at me.

We flew head-on toward each other.

Closing in, I began to wonder if my opponent was René Fonck. Fonck was the leading French ace, famous for his mathematically precise method of combat and engineering knowledge. He'd personally modified his S.P.A.D. by installing a 37mm Puteaux cannon into the propeller shaft. Fonck had literally blown half a dozen German's out of the sky.

Is that him?

It was beginning to look like it. And if it was Mr. Fonck, I did not want to be anywhere within the range of that cannon!

I darted right, then dove left, trying to position myself to an advantage. Vogt came into view, clearly bent on assisting me.

You nutball!

By this time the identity of the Frenchman was confirmed: it was René Fonck.

Erwin Vogt began firing, which was a waste of ammo because he was too far away. Fonck banked a hard left and put his airplane into a steep dive. I got off a burst that nipped his tail before turning to pursue. Fonck pulled up and turned his speedy plane to get his nose facing us. The S.P.A.D. was sluggish in maneuverability, so my D.VII had no trouble countering it. While aiming my guns, Vogt fired again. His 3 overly long bursts badly missed high.

Quit wasting your ammo!

As I was beginning a slight bank left, Vogt's airplane suddenly caught fire.

Jaysus - what?

Within seconds the D.VII was engulfed. Vogt stood up in the cockpit with his body aflame. He flayed about as a human torch as his aircraft streaked toward a crop of trees like a meteor.

* * * * *

I was getting dangerously close to Fonck's 37mm. Just in time I nosed down while continuing a left bank.

Boom!

The cannon blast roared by overhead.

Whew!

But Fonck now cut loose with his .303 Vickers.

Rat-a-tat, rat-a-tat, rat-a-tat!

The shots nicked at my top wing, inflicting minimal damage. I climbed briefly and then banked hard into a dive. Another quick turn got me straight on to the side of Fonck.

My turn!

I raked him a good one, but his S.P.A.D. was a tough machine, rugged as all get out. Fonck rolled away, diving again.

On my right, coming into view at 4:00, I saw three *Jasta 11* planes - Udet, Karjus and Geschke. They were about to engage 4 American-flown S.P.A.D XIII's from the 94th *Hat in the Ring* squadron. I let Fonck go (it looked like he was heading home anyway) and raced to make the upcoming battle 4 against 4.

Udet and company had the sun behind them, stair-cased with Karjus slightly out front. The Americans flew in a straight across formation, 30 feet equidistant from each other. I approached adjacently, but that could change in an instant once the two groups engaged.

I was still out of range when both sides unleashed their machine guns. The Circus planes drove a wedge through the Americans, splitting them apart. Udet's first burst hit the mark and buckled one of the S.P.A.D.'s. The airplane shimmied for a moment and then jolted violently upward with smoke jetting out from its engine.

Great shot Ernst!

Another S.P.A.D had separated right toward me. Immediately the pilot realized his predicament with me zeroing in on him on one side and Geschke closing in from behind. I fired a short burst but missed as the American tried to maneuver his way out of the crossfire.

Rat-a-tat, rat-a-tat, rat-a-tat!

Rat-a-tat,rat-a-tat, rat-a-tat!

Geschke was letting him have it. I could have fired as well, but there was some risk that my tracers might hit Geschke's plane.

No matter. The S.P.A.D. was toast.

Our 4 to 2 advantage didn't last for long. Three Nieuport 28's and a S.P.A.D. suddenly joined the fracas diving down from opposite sides. Geschke's D.VII got plastered with lead by the two Nieuports. He tried his best to escape, but there was nothing more he could do. He was going down fast.

The partnering S.P.A.D. started shooting at me but I was too quick for him. The American dove past, making no attempt to circle back to continue the fight.

Scaredy cat!

I searched for Geschke. His Fokker was long gone. Had be bailed out?

* * * * *

As soon as we got back to the airfield, a group of us ventured out to the crash site. Still strapped in his cockpit, Rudi Geschke had made no attempt to save himself. An exam of his smashed corpse revealed fatal bullet wounds to his neck and upper chest.

19
No Quit

But what had caused Erwin Vogt's airplane to suddenly catch fire? It was clear that no one had shot at him. Fritz thought he knew the answer. His hypothesis was proven correct after only a few minutes of examining the burned out wreckage of Vogt's D.VII.

"I never liked how the ammunition was stored in the D.VII's cowling," he said peevishly. "It's too close to the engine. The phosphorous rounds will overheat and explode. Vogt firing his guns didn't make any difference. His plane would have still caught fire. It was a ticking time bomb."

Fritz's solution was simple: he cut ventilating holes in the cowling. The idea quickly caught on at the other *jastas*. By that night every D.VII in *Jasta* 11 had been remedied.

* * * * *

The big dogfight had played out in our favor: 6 victories to the Allies' 3. My score was now 24. Udet upped his to 57. Only René Fonck had a higher total with 60. Hermann Göring exhausted his ammo but came up empty. Weggie and Lauer had gotten back to the airfield unscathed. Feeling guilty about leaving, they vowed to stay and fight next time.

"You won't if I say no," corrected Göring at the post-mission briefing. "Selected engagements only."

"Did anyone see Eddie Rickenbacker?" I asked the group.

"He was in the fight," answered Wenzl. "So was Frank Luke, that balloon-buster fellow. I wasn't able to get shots at either of them."

"Nor I," mumbled Karjus.

"I got off two," a frustrated Weiss said. "One burst got some of Luke's fuselage. That other American, Douglas Campbell, was also there."

"We'll tangle with them again," Göring assured.

* * * * *

I flew full-go over the next sixteen days, usually twice a day. I saw bushels of enemy machines during that span, but the engagement odds were often stacked overwhelmingly against us. Even so, the Flying Circus performed brilliantly, destroying 22 Allied planes and an observation balloon.

Of those 22 victories I took four:

On September 3 I brought down a Nieuport 28 flown by a *Hat in the Ring* American named Roger Mayberry. He survived the crash with only a few minor burns on his back and a broken left leg. Lucky guy.

The next victory came on the 9th, an Airco D.H.9 two-seater bomber that had just been introduced into service. I caught it heading back to its base after a trench bombing mission. Somehow it had gotten separated from its fighter escort. The pilot died from the crash into a tree, but the rear gunner miraculously limped away.

Three days later, Udet and I pounced on a pair of new Sopwith Snipes and sent them down burning. Our attack was textbook. The Brits didn't know what hit them. There were a lot of witnesses on the ground, too.

"That one was a certified legend booster," Udet said afterwards. "For us personally, and for the Flying Circus."

On the 14th I pushed my score to 28 by taking out a Camel during a gnarly dogfight involving 30 planes. The key to that victory was my Fokker D.VII. Being able to 'hang on the propeller' was a godsend.

The return of the Emerald Ace was all over the newspapers. I found it interesting that there wasn't nearly as much outrage and hatred directed at me this time around. It was almost like I'd become a sort of Robin Hood figure, an outlaw who many were rooting for. Don't get me wrong, there was still plenty of nasty print calling me a traitor and other vile names, but there was a detectable shift going on.

Newspapers took care of me having to inform Paul Coburn as to what I'd been doing. I figured he wouldn't be surprised. Gerard, Marci, and Beau would be a little shocked.

Maybe more than a little shocked.

Using an American typewriter that one of the men packed around, I sat down and wrote them a letter. It closed with the following:

The war will certainly be over soon. As you know, the Allies are going to win. Until then I owe my best efforts to my other family - Jasta 11. This healing process will take a long time, perhaps longer than my lifetime allows. I'm doing what I can to cope, just as you are. It is my sincerest hope that you understand and respect my decision to return to combat flying. Being a part of your family is the most important thing in my life. I will see you again as soon as possible. Give my best to Maurice and Gabby, and scratch Sinn Fein behind the ears for me.

All my love,
Mick

* * * * *

I severely twisted my right ankle on September 16 during a game of cabbage-head rugby (our playing field had a million ruts). Luckily it wasn't broken, but the injury sidelined me from flying until the 25th. With little to do and few books to read (there was an English translation of Dostoevsky's *Crime and Punishment* lying about), it was a long ten days. I helped out Fritz and the other pilots where I could.

During that time *JG1* moved to a new location, this time near the town of Metz. On my first day back in the air I made an orientation flight to get my bearings of the area.

On September 26 Ernst Udet, who now had a score of 62, received a bullet wound to his thigh and reluctantly went on a short recuperative leave. "I'll be back in two weeks, probably on the 10th," he told me, hobbling on crutches for the transport lorry. "Don't get yourself killed. No more rugby!"

"Get healed," I said.

"Lo will see to that. She could train nurses for hospitals."

* * * * *

On consecutive days, September 28 - 29, I got into scrapes with the Arizona Balloon Buster: Frank Luke Jr. The 21 year-old blond haired American was on an amazing hot streak. Since September 12 he'd rung up 13 victories - 10 observation balloons, two Fokker D.VII's, and a Halberstadt.

On the 28th, flying on a late day patrol with Walther Karjus, Hans Weiss, and a new pilot named Karl Reimann, we caught up with a group of 5 *Hat in the Ring* squadron S.P.A.D.'s near the village of Mervaux. The Americans were harassing a pair of observation balloons protected by 3 D.VII's from *Jasta 18* and several anti-aircraft guns positioned on top of a hill. The tangle lasted barely two minutes, but during that time the swashbuckling Frank Luke, under a barrage of fire from the air and ground, managed to flame one of the balloons and heavily damage the other. The guy was more reckless than the great Canadian ace Billy Bishop! What's more, I got off some fine shots at his plane, seemingly enough to bring it down. His S.P.A.D. must have been coated in bulletproof shellac.

Him, too.

Crazy!

Like I said, it was a brief scuffle. From the west a big group of Sopwith Camels showed up, forcing us to bolt for home.

The next morning I led a patrol that duplicated the previous day's route to a T. Wolfram von Richthofen, Richard Wenzl, and a now experienced Tillman 'Weggie' Wegscheider accompanied me. Approaching Mervaux we saw the ashen remains of two observation balloons a mile apart from each other. A couple miles ahead of us, another balloon was about to be attacked, ostensibly by the same group of 4 S.P.A.D.'s that had attacked the other balloons. Three Fokker D.VII's were circling the balloon ready to defend it. There were also several heavy machine gun crews positioned on a steep ridge.

Frank Luke's plane was easy to spot. He was going after the balloon, leaving his group to take on the Fokkers.

All right, I'll get you this time, I thought.

My three flying partners headed for the dogfight while I broke away and took after Luke. The American had already made one pass at the balloon. He was in the process of circling back by the time I got there.

He passed my gun sights at extremely long range, but I took a chance and fired anyway.

No luck.

I climbed steeply for a few seconds and then banked a hard left, trying to get on Luke's tail. By this time Luke had lined himself up for another run at the balloon. The balloon's machine gunner blasted away at him as he swooped in.

But the balloon didn't have a chance. Its hydrogen filled bag burst into a fiery cloud of orange and black. Fortunately both crew members managed to safely bail out.

The guy did it again!

* * * * *

I wasn't going to let him get away with it!

Captain Frank Luke Jr. flew at top speed to escape my guns. I had a good angle on him, and was steadily closing the distance. My trigger finger danced around the firing button.

You're mine mate! Hope you've got a parachute.

As I was counting down from 3 preparing to fire, something went wrong with Luke's S.P.A.D. It suddenly slipped to the right and entered a shallow descent toward a large patch of flat ground that contained a small cemetery. I didn't think he was going to be able to get down in one piece but he did, though the landing qualified as a crash. Flying past the wreck, I saw Luke emerge from the cockpit. He limped away and made for some trees with a gun in his hand. It looked like he'd been hit in the shoulder.

Circling around, heading to rejoin the other fight, I saw a squad of German soldiers reach his S.P.A.D. They hit the deck and a shoot-out began. Frank Luke made a mad dash for a stream that had lots of underbrush, firing his .45 automatic pistol at his pursuers.

Then he collapsed.

Thus ended the life of the Arizona Balloon Buster.

The fatal wound was a single bullet from one of the hillside machine guns. It had entered his right shoulder and exited through the left side of his body.

* * * * *

The month of October began with a spell of rotten weather. I didn't fly at all from the 1st through the 4th. The next day I got back into the air on three patrols but nothing much happened. Day after day the Flying Circus saw little enemy action.

JG1 moved yet again on October 9 - to Marville, close to the Argonne Front. The move didn't bring out the enemy the way we'd hoped. It was lots of long patrols with no results.

Ernst Udet returned on October 10, eager to boost his victory total over 70. "The number of scoring opportunities has dwindled to almost nothing," Göring informed him inside the mess. "Flying 24 hours a day is your only hope to surpass Richthofen."

"I don't care about that. But I do want to get ahead of Fonck. He's at 69. His bragging ways do not sit well with me."

"The door is open for you," Göring said. "Reports tell us he is currently on leave until the end of the month."

I slapped his back. "Let's go out and see what we can get. There's enough light left."

"Hermann, yes?" Udet asked.

* * * * *

An hour later eight of us returned empty-handed.

It's been like that," I said. "The war isn't what it used to be. I guess we'll have to start another one."

Udet's frustrated face cracked a bemused grin. "Let's wait a while before we do that."

* * * * *

I finally got number 29 on October 20. Taking a page out of Frank Luke's book, I went after a British observation balloon during a skirmish with French Nieuport 28's. Once again, I hung on my propeller and sent one long tracer burst into the wooden carriage, killing the machine gunner. The balloon operator dropped the tether and hopped over the side right as the balloon's gasbag ignited. His parachute worked flawlessly.

At this point I thought 30 kills was a cinch for sure. All I needed was one more. Three days later I got a prime chance.

20
October 23

The first two flights on this cloudy cold day turned out like so many before: no enemy encounters worth mentioning. I expected the same result going into the late afternoon third flight.

For most of the patrol it played out that way.

Returning to base, just south of Tellancourt, I spotted a lone airplane far off in the distance. I assumed it to be an Allied plane, but I wanted to find out for sure. Our 5 D.VII's were getting low on fuel, so I ordered the others in the group - Wenzl, Reimann, Weiss, and Lauer - to stay on course for home while I investigated.

I banked right and flew straight at the mystery plane. Twenty seconds later my hunch was confirmed: it was an S.E.5a with blue streamers on the wings, indicating the flight leader. His machine appeared to be experiencing engine trouble. It was steadily losing altitude and flying erratically.

A gift number 30 you are, I thought. *Fell smack into my lap.*

The pilot didn't have a chance. He was toast with jam on top.

Jaysus, it's like shooting a bear cub out of a tree! Another Teddy Roosevelt. There's no sport in that! Bugger! What if that guy was me? Oh man . . .

I came right up on his tail, no more than 40 feet away, pondering what to do. The S.E.5 had been through the ringer, and then some. It was chocked full of bullet holes. Sections of fabric had torn from its top wing. Sputters of oil were spraying from the smoke-puffing engine. Given the dire situation, the Brit seemed quite cool and collected. He nonchalantly turned around and stared at me for a few moments.

That did it.

Forget number 30.

I wasn't going to shoot him down.

No parachute, of course. You're expecting to die. Well, I'm not gunna be the one who kills ya.

The Brit slowly lifted his hand and held it out to me.

A helping hand? Is that what you want from me? Well now, let's see . . .

I flew up alongside on his left.

Hi ya. Don't you be pulling out a pistol!

The Brit saluted me.

I saluted him back.

At the rate his airplane was descending he had maybe a minute left of flying time, perhaps a little more if he could keep his nose up. The biggest problem was maintaining control. The herky-jerky machine was behaving like a two year-old throwing a tantrum. If the engine conked out he'd fall like a rock.

Gotta find him a flat spot . . . but where?

The S.E.5 was losing altitude more rapidly now. I stayed with the Brit, following his inconsistent descent while scanning about.

There!

Dead left, through an opportune break in the clouds, I located a narrow dirt road (it was actually more of a glorified trail) bordering a field of grazing sheep. It was his only option. The rest of the surrounding area was too hilly and uneven. There were fences, a curvy ditch, and other small obstacles all over the place, too.

But could he turn his crippled machine toward the road? I pointed at the destination and got a nodding thumbs-up from the Brit.

I climbed over his plane to the other side. The highly skilled Brit fought tooth and nail to turn right. Several times he came within a whisker of stalling out when his machine twisted while dropping suddenly - each time about 10 feet.

A little more . . . come on, keep that nose up!

His altitude hit 300 feet. The S.E.5 was fluttering like a wounded pheasant.

You can make it!

200 feet.

You're almost there! Stay with it, turn a little more.

100 feet . . . 75 . . . 50 . . .

Suddenly his engine died.

Oh no!

The S.E.5 dipped to near vertical and nosedived to the ground.

* * * * *

I zoomed past the wreck and quickly circled back, hoping that it wasn't as god awful as it initially looked.

Wishful thinking. It was far worse. The S.E.5 was a crumpled, twisted mass of junk. It had crashed 50 feet in front of the road on top of an irrigation ditch. I couldn't see the cockpit.

Could the Brit have survived the impact?

Doubtful, but maybe. If he was alive, he might not be for long.

I circled around again. All I saw this time was a tiny glimpse of his head pinned under the collapsed top wing.

You're in a bad way . . .

And that's when I made up mind to help. I could easily get down on that road, no problem there. The D.VII didn't need much landing distance. If I could just extricate him from the cockpit and offer some basic first aid.

Maneuvering in, I touched down on the flat, bumpy road. One particular bump caused my left wingtip to scrape the ground, but nothing serious. I shut off my engine and, once stopped, rushed over to the Brit.

All of the sudden visions of Kurt Hoffenmüller's crashed Albatros in Aunt Patti's field flashed before my eyes.

It had been over a year ago.

Thirteen months!

So much had happened! Unbelievable!

* * * * *

This crash wasn't at all like Kurt's, however. His was a tea party in comparison. Right away I knew fire was imminent. There was petrol leaking all over the place.   Speed was of the essence!

"Hey - hey - can you hear me?" I hollered. "Gotta get you out of there! Can you speak? Talk to me!"

Digging through splintered wood and canvas, I lifted off a section of wing to expose a part of the cockpit. Now I could see him. There were trickles of blood on the side of his face and lips. Smartly, he'd taken his goggles off before impact

I ducked through the gap and nudged his shoulder.

"Hey man! You alive, yeah?"

A faint, painfully strained grunt sounded.

"Ye - yes . . ." uttered the Brit.

"A fire's coming any second. Can you move?"

"A little I think. Can you - can you pull me out?"

"I'm gunna have to. Are you still strapped in?"

"Yes. I think I can detach. - Just a sec . . ."

I couldn't see his arm move, but I heard a click.

"Got it," the Brit said weakly.

"This won't feel good. Bear with me."

I grabbed underneath his left shoulder and pulled. The pilot winced, trying to hold back a scream. He was dead weight because I first had to lift his upper body out of the cockpit before I could drag him. When he'd moved far enough, I grasped onto his other armpit.

"Come on mate, were gettin' it. Wail like a banshee if you need to. No shame in that."

"My legs are broken. Shinbones."

"Anything else?"

"Not sure. Ribs and chest hurt. My neck, too."

I kept pulling, now with lots more force.

* * * *

We were almost through the wing gap when a searing blast of fire suddenly shot out at us. The flames stuck to the back of the Brit's flight suit.

He was burning.

I yelled the mother of all curses and pulled hard enough to throw the Brit a hundred feet.

The effort got him out onto the ditch bank.

I immediately rolled him over and madly hurled handfuls of dirt on his back to douse the fire. Once the flames were out I dragged the Brit along the ditch away from the S.E.5 wreckage, which by now was totally engulfed in flames.

"Holy schmykees," I said, trying to catch my breath. "You can't get any closer than that!"

The Brit lay flat on his stomach, arms under his head. He began to cough, amplifying all the pains in his battered body.

"Take it easy there," I said. "Good thing that flight suit is thick. Your back would be cooked to a crisp if not." I took a closer look at the burn marks on the suit. "It doesn't look like the fire got to your skin."

The pilot groaned, turning his head at me. Blood covered his face and thin mustache. He coughed again, spraying more blood.

I took off my scarf and wiped most of the blood away.

"Sorry about that," the man said.

"No worries. - You said your ribs hurt. My guess is you got a break in there, and it's cut into something."

The Brit nodded, coughing some more. "Collapsed lung, possibly."

I used the scarf again. "You need a doctor. Those shins need to be set quick. I don't want to think about how much that must hurt."

"Could use some water."

"Coming up," I said. "There's ditch right here. Lots of water. It may not be the cleanest, but it's all we got."

There was a siphon tube within arms reach, so I plugged the bottom with the palm of my hand and filled it to the top. I gently placed the opening on his mouth and helped him to raise his head.

"Here ya go. Drink up."

Most of the water spilled over his chin, and his bloody coughing complicated the process. Three refills later the Brit signaled that he'd had enough.

"No more water. You should go. I know who you are."

"Figured you probably did."

"Wouldn't have expected this," the Brit said. "Our newspapers don't like the Emerald Ace."

"Traitors to the Crown aren't high on the popularity chart," I said.

"I'm Captain Thomas Palmer, Commanding Officer of R.A.F. 48."

"Pleased to meet you. Your airplane was pretty shot up. Were you alone?"

"I left my flight to help a new pilot who got separated. He didn't make it, and I got into a pickle with 3 Fokkers. Managed to get away . . . well, almost."

"You're a grand pilot," I complimented. "That plane couldn't have been easy to handle."

"Very tricky. When you appeared, I thought it was curtains for sure."

"You'd have been my 30th, but I couldn't do that to ya. Turn the situation around – then what? Would you have shot me down?"

Palmer coughed again, but no blood this time. "Very doubtful. Fair play, human decency, you know."

I scanned the surrounding area. "There's nothing around here but sheep."

"We have some soldiers around - I know that. Get in your airplane and go now. I will manage."

"Yeah . . . I better do that. As soon as I get back I'll send word about you. You'll be rescued by Allied soldiers, not German. I promise you."

"I appreciate that Mr. Gallagher. Thanks for your assistance."

"Anytime. See ya later, Captain. It will be interesting if we meet again in the air."

Palmer chuckled silently. "Yes, quite."

* * * * *

It didn't feel right leaving him like that, but I couldn't hang around forever. Sooner or later Allied planes would spot my green D.VII. Palmer said British troops were somewhere in the area. It would take me 15 minutes to get back to base. Once I sent word out about Palmer's whereabouts, he could be picked up and in a doctor's hands within an hour or so.

I stepped up to the cockpit and primed the choke. As I was reaching high to crank the propeller, a rifle shot hit smack between the lower blades. Wood splinters stung my chin.

Good god!

Then came another shot, this one hit straight into the airplane's nose.

I dashed for cover underneath the fuselage behind the wheels and hit the deck. Looking up, I scanned in the direction of the rifle shots while drawing my Webley revolver.

He's in those shrubs by the trees.

"Stop shoo-!" Captain Palmer tried to yell, his weakened voice interrupted by coughing.

The shooter fired again, sending another bullet into the heart of the engine. Seconds later a fourth shot cut the jugular. The BMW hissed as if the last of its air was being squeezed out. A few feet in front of me coolant began to leak out in a stream.

He's killed my engine, I thought. *The gobshite!*

"Stop shooting!" Palmer yelled again, this time with considerable more power and volume.

"*Les main en l'air!*" the shooter shouted - (Hands in the air!).

It would be daft to make a break for it. There was too much open ground. The shooter obviously was a spot-on marksman, positioned 70 yards away. If I took off through the sheep field, he'd probably nail me dead to rights before I could run 200 yards to the nearest shelter - a small open barn. I'd also have to get over (or through?) a wire fence. And if I somehow did make it to the barn, then what? There wasn't anywhere to go after that.

But I had to move. The D.VII didn't provide me enough cover. My only option was the ditch. It was only 20 yards to the rear the airplane.

I crawled backwards as flat as possible and got directly behind the tail.

A bullet ricocheted off the landing gear.

"*Rends-toi! Vous ne pouvez pas me échapper!*" - (Give yourself up! You can't escape me!)

One, two, three!

I sprinted.

A shot sailed past my left ear as I dove into the ditch bank.

* * * * *

What we had now was a stalemate.

There was nowhere for the shooter to go except to leave the scene in a straight line behind the 40-yard patch of trees. Fat chance of that! If he emerged from his position I could maybe get him with the Webley. It would be a brilliant pistol shot with the short barreled Bulldog, but not impossible.

As for me, I was literally stuck in the mud. In both directions the ditch curved closer to the shooter before straightening out. Captain Palmer's pleas weren't doing me any good, and he certainly couldn't move himself over to the shooter for a conversation.

The ditch was between 3 and 4 feet deep with half a foot of water. I decided to crawl a few yards in Palmer's direction and check on him.

I poked my head up for only a split second.

Palmer was either dead or unconscious. He lay facedown on folded arms.

Great . . . No help from him.

I pounded my fist into the bank.

You sympathetic idiot! Why did I land? I'd be halfway back to the airfield by now.

My only hope was for Germans to spot my plane. They had to be coming sooner or later. Udet would grab some pilots and be in the air the second Wenzle and the others landed. He just needed to get here before the Brits - or the French, or the Americans.

Believe it or not I started to laugh. "Ah geez - what a day."

* * * * *

5 minutes crept by.

Nothing moved, nothing stirred; no shots, no sounds other than the squawking of some crows.

I crawled 15 yards the other way and peeped my eyes at the trees.

Still the same.

Palmer was still out.

Another 5 minutes . . .

Then another.

This time when I risked a peek, a shot nearly blew my head off. The bullet hit the dirt a foot in front of me.

Yeah, you're still there . . .

Near my feet a frog jumped out of the water.

* * * * *

Perhaps 10 minutes later I detected a faint humming sound coming from above.

Ah, finally!

But whose airplanes were they? The ditch limited my view of the sky.

Come on Ernst. Get me out of this.

The planes were getting closer, but I still couldn't see them.

"Mick, where are you?"

It was Palmer.

"Over here, Thomas. Care to join me?"

"You've got the RAF overhead. I'm afraid there's no getting away."

"What a pisser. - Is that sniper still out there?"

"Keep talking Mr. Gallagher, I'm almost there. - Not sure about the sniper. I came-to only a minute ago."

"He's a dead-eye shot. - How ya feelin'?"

"Pained and weak. Gammy legs feel like someone's stuck branding irons inside them. On the bright side I don't think my lung has collapsed. Not yet anyway."

Palmer's head poked over the bank.

"Hi ya Captain."

"I hope you don't mind if I stay up here," Palmer said. "That sniper, if he is still out there, doesn't seem interested in me."

S.E.5's soared by overhead.

"Are those your guys?" I asked.

"Indeed they are. It looks like two of them are going to land. - Yes, that's Lang and Barnaby."

"Well Thomas, I'm still hoping that the Flying Circus shows up and fights them off."

"Sorry to disappoint you, but I don't see any German planes on the horizon."

Another motorized sound entered the mix. It wasn't from above.

"What's that?"

"Let me see . . . ah, yes - it's British soldiers. Drat for you. I'm officially rescued and you're officially captured."

"Don't suppose you could tell those guys to let me go, yeah?"

Palmer smiled. "If it was only my boys, then yes, I would. The soldiers coming will not be so cooperative."

I heard voices now.

They got me.

"You know Thomas," I said, "the last time you Brits captured me I had just rescued a drowning boy. - I gotta quit the rescue business."

21
Gaol Time

There would be no miracle escape for me this time.

The rifleman turned out to be a fifty-something local French farmer named Benoît. He came out of his sniper's nest when I gave myself up. He'd honed his marksmanship while serving in the army back in the 1880's. Before the British let him go, he spat at my feet. *"Traître qirlandais! J'espére quails vows trident!"* (Irish traitor! I hope they shoot you!)

When I handed over the Webley Bulldog I said to the frisking soldier, "I'll give you a million pounds if you let me keep that."

"Sure you would," replied the young private.

Funny that I really could, I thought.

"You might want to check and see if it's loaded. I'm not sure."

The soldier actually looked!

"That's funny, Private," I said.

Breaking the ice with my captors that way worked out well. Surprisingly, the Brits were pretty nice to me. No name-calling, no threats of execution or abusive punishment; there was no Sergeant Thurber punching me in the face or kicking me in the stomach (recounted in *Richthofen's Knight*).

The infantry squad leader, Major Sam Nellsbridge, listened to Palmer's account of what happened with a considerate ear. So did his 7 men, all of whom were only a few years older than me. Captain Palmer relayed his story while pilots Barnaby and Lang carried him on a stretcher to the transport lorry. He even went as far to say, "Though this man has been serving with the enemy as a fighter pilot, in my opinion he deserves our highest award for valor."

"Japers Thomas," I said. "Victoria Cross? That's a bit much, yeah?"

"No it's not. You saved my life at extraordinary risk to your own. I'm not sure exactly why you did it when, according to everything I've heard and read, you harbor a profound dislike of our empire."

"I do at that. Eight hundred years of subjugation is why I fight. Put England in Ireland's position and you'd be fighting the occupier, too. My father was killed during the Easter Rising, and that was the kicker for me."

"I heard that your aunt was killed by British soldiers," Barnaby said. "Is that true?"

"It is. They barged into her home and murdered her."

"If that is true, it was a despicable act," Nellsbridge said angrily. "The perpetrators must be found and punished." He then let me augment Palmer's account with my own details - wittily delivered I might add.

"Remarkable story, but I have to take you in," Nellsbridge said with an air of apology. "I will leave a few men here to secure your airplane from any potential souvenir hunters. My commander, Colonel Fosbeck, is a fair man. You will receive no ill treatment."

"Maybe you and Thomas can put in a good word for me, yeah?"

"I will. So will my men."

"Same with me," Palmer called out from inside the lorry.

I shook Nellsbridge's hand. "Thanks Major. I don't know if any of that's going to help keep the firing squad away, but thanks. And thanks for guarding my plane. Isn't she a beauty? I'm gunna miss her."

"Germans!" hollered Lang, pointing at the sky. "Captain Palmer!"

"Get going!" Palmer ordered.

There were still seven S.E.5's circling overhead, but to the South eight Fokker D.VII's were approaching in a stepped-V formation.

"It's the Circus," I said. "Ernst Udet and company."

You guys are too late.

* * * * *

I didn't get to see much of the ensuing dogfight. We left the scene posthaste in the lorry. I sat in back with Palmer and the other men. The journey took twenty minutes.

Nellsbridge was spot-on about his commanding officer. Colonel Tyler Fosbeck treated me with fair-minded respect and kindness. So did his staff and most of the soldiers I interacted with in the camp. During his questioning I asked him, "Colonel, I'm sensing that you Brits have changed your tune about me. You guys seem to like me more now. Everyone's being all chummy with me. - What's going on? This isn't the way it used to be."

"All I can say is that time often grows legends, Mr. Gallagher," Fosbeck replied. "Irish sympathies have also grown in many British people since the Rising, especially in the past six months. His Majesty's government has taken notice, though they are still adhering to a hardline position on Ireland with the war still going on. However, I predict that once the war ends - which will be soon - you'll see the Home Rule vote come up again in parliament."

"Home Rule's a start, but full independence the goal."

"I believe you will achieve that someday, but not anytime soon."

"Do you think I'll be shot?"

Fosbeck had a natural frumpish look about him, so it was difficult to read his thickly mustached face. He looked down at his tidy desk and then piercingly at the calendar hanging on the wall next to him. "British military code is severe regarding treasonous activity, Mr. Gallagher," he stated matter-of-factly. "However, I do believe there are mitigating circumstances in your case. Your actions earlier today should weigh heavily on any decision concerning your fate. Major Nellsbridge's report confirmed what Captain Palmer told me. The account left me speechless."

"How is Palmer doing?"

"The colonel is currently receiving the best medical attention. His injuries are not life threatening."

"Grand. Palmer's a star fellow."

"That can also be said about you. You're the biggest hero nationalist Ireland has going. The executions of the Rising's leaders have proven to be an egregious mistake on the part of the British government. I doubt they would want to repeat the mistake by shooting you. That would be adding fuel to the flame. However, I could be wrong. Of late I've been wrong about many things."

"I hope you're not wrong on this one, Colonel."

* * * * *

The next day I was taken to a military base on the outskirts of Paris. There, inside a large, two level red brick complex, I was interrogated by one fancy-titled official after another - some of them cordial, some not so. For I don't know how many endless hours, I told and retold, and re-retold again most of my story, all the way from Kurt

Hoffenmüller's crash landing in Aunt Patti's field to my recent capture. Nothing was held back: I talked about Michelle, Beau, and the Guerintaux family, the Red Baron and every other pilot at *Jasta 11*, and my dogfights and crashes; my adventures with a night train assassin, Russian Cossacks, and a wacky film director; shoot outs in the snow, my sabotage of the Sky Devil's base, and the zeppelin raid; my shark battle in the Balearic Islands, the torpedoed boat, and fight with Dublin soldiers; the Matterhorn climb, golf in Scotland, and spy gun-play in Amsterdam.

The one story I did *not* mention was my avenging the murdered woman I'd found in the cave near the Sky Devil's base.

* * * * *

My gaol cell was a 13 x 13 foot solid concrete room equipped with a cot, sink, flush toilet, and a small table. One book-sized window and a naked bulb provided light.

I asked if family could come visit me. My request was denied, but I was allowed a telephone call late in the morning of October 25.

"Hi Marci. Greetings from a prison near you."

"Mick!" Marci cried. "Mick, we've been so worried! The sergeant who called said you are in Paris."

"Yeah, on the edge of the city somewhere. I don't know how long they'll keep me here. Who knows, I may never get out. Or if I do get out, it may be in a wooden box."

"Mick, don't say such things!"

"It's all up in the air, Marci. There's not much I can do. My life is in the hands of a military tribunal."

"They will be lenient."

"That's what I'm hoping for."

"It's so good to hear your voice. I've read everything in the newspapers. Some of it hurts me."

"Don't buy into the propaganda. Listen, I can't talk long. I love you and Gerard, and all the family."

"We love you too."

"Is Gerard there?"

"Yes, he's right here. Goodbye Mick. Please take care and come home soon to us. Here is Gerard."

"Hello - Mick?"

"Hi Gerard. How are you at gaol breaks?"

"I don't know. I've never organized one. Did you crash?"

"No, nothing like that. Believe it or not, I was trying to help a British pilot on the ground and got captured in the process. I'm not sure what will happen to me. Could be firing squad, could be years in prison."

"They won't shoot you. I guarantee it. You're too popular in Ireland. Even in France your name is admired by many people."

"Well that's nice. All I need is a statue. - Gerard, I was wondering if maybe you could help me by using your connections – you know, your British connections to some parliament members? You've got some, yeah?"

"Yes I do, several prominent ones in fact. I have already spoken to one of them today. He told me he would speak with Winston Churchill."

"Churchill has a soft heart for me. Or that's what I've read."

"I've read that too. It will be a long day on the telephone speaking with my other contacts."

"Grand, at least I got that going for me. - Hey, I told Marci not to believe any negative propaganda about me. Nothing but honor on my end - *always*. Ok?"

"Yes, Mick. I know. Sons of mine never lose their honor."

"But sometimes they do lose their temper."

"Ha - yes. Beau."

"Thanks Gerard. - They're telling me to get off the phone. I don't know when or if I will get another chance to call."

"All right, you do what you have to do. I will, too."

* * * * *

Over the course of the next two weeks I lived pretty much in a cement cocoon. The only people I talked to were those same officials who kept filling my head with bags of military court stuff. One day I'd think things were looking up, and then the next day someone was telling me that things were not so optimistic.

Into the second week of this bollocks routine I started to wonder if something else was going on. It felt like I was in a limbo state. There were fewer visits from officials, and when they did come to my cell the chats were shorter and more conversational in tone, joking even in a few instances. The tribunal court talk was mostly downplayed or ignored completely. I played along because either my goose was cooked and the execution countdown had begun or maybe some positive intervention on my behalf was at work. Maybe Gerard had got the wheels turning with some sympathetic parliament members? That could lead to some good news for me - hopefully.

Or could be that the war was *very* close to being over, perhaps in only a matter of weeks or days? I did hear from a friendly guard named Darren (who had a big interest in Gaelic sports, and always wanted to talk shop about Hurling and Irish football when he delivered my dinner every evening) that armistice talks had been in the works. If true, maybe punishing the world famous Emerald Ace didn't qualify as necessary anymore. My so-called treasonous actions might now be seen as acts of valor by a freedom fighter in the name of Irish independence.

I had little to do in that cell but think and exercise. Michelle Guerintaux was on my mind a lot, sometimes overwhelmingly so. I did throw a few nighttime pity parties for myself that didn't do me any good.

Keeping up my fitness regimen, always a priority with me, involved thousands of push-ups, sit-ups, deep knee bends, lunges, jumping jacks, wall-sits, stretching, running in place, standing jumps, and upside down shoulder presses. Doing all this physical exertion was invaluable in maintaining my mental balance.

Overall I was treated pretty well. Conditions were far better than expected. The well-lit complex was clean and the interior walls had been freshly painted. There weren't any bad smells.

Three times a day they let me go out to the rectangular prison yard for a half hour at a time. There was a smooth metal rod sticking out of the wall that I used as a pull-up bar to give my back and biceps muscles a workout. A sturdy wooden bench served as a perfect step-up platform. Often times I took little catnaps on the soft sand. The yard reminded me of the one at Kilmainham Gaol in Dublin where the leaders of the 1916 Rising were executed. If the same fate befell me, I assumed this is where it would take place. Morbidly, I pictured myself blindfolded with hands tied, standing up against the far wall facing a line of riflemen.

Every day, usually in the morning, I was allowed five minutes to take an ice cold shower. In water like that, five minutes was plenty of time. My bald look was long gone by this time. I hadn't cut my hair in almost two months.

Strangely, I didn't ever see any other prisoners, inside or out. Having my own private prison inspired me to dub it with a new name. Using a coin, I scratched *Gallagher Gaol* into the cement wall of my cell.

22
The Minister of Munitions

An entire week passed with no contact from court officials. "Hey Darren, do you have any idea what's going on?" I asked on the evening of November 9 when he brought me a dinner of meatloaf and mashed potatoes. "Is there anyone at home here?"

The towering guard took an extra hard roll out of his uniform pocket - which he'd done for every dinner save the first two - and handed it to me. "All I know is that something big is happening. Marshal Foch's private train is at Compiégne to receive a German delegation. That's all I know for sure. I don't think that would be happening for any old thing. This may be the end of it."

"Are you talking about the war or for me?" I half-kidded.

Darren gave me a quizzical look. "The war, you jokester. Sorry, but I don't know anything new regarding you. This place has been very quite lately."

"Tell me about it. - All right, well the meatloaf smells tolerable. Any Gaelic sports scores?"

"No, I haven't been able to check."

"You Brits have gotta be football starved. It's been over three years now without it."

"It'll be back next year. My Arsenal will win it all."

* * * * *

Two days later, while I was out in the courtyard doing pull-ups, Darren burst out hollering, "It's over, Mick! The war's over! They signed an armistice!"

"You serious?"

"Don't I look it? Yes! At eleven o'clock it went into effect. No more shooting. It's over! Bloody hell, the war is finally over!"

I leaned against the wall shaking my head. "Janey mack. Incredible news, Darren. Stunning, man."

The guard spun around and did a little shuffle dance. "Honey, I'm coming home! Coming home to you! Wahoo!"

But what was in store for me?

* * * * *

When Darren delivered me dinner that evening he said, "I'm almost out of here, Mick. Tomorrow morning at eight I leave for Normandy. If all goes smoothly, I should be back to my Margie in a couple weeks." He tossed me the extra hard roll. "I doubt I'll be seeing you again. - Don't take that the wrong way."

I mockingly scowled at him. "Yeah . . . you wanker. You want me full of holes, don't ya?"

"Rubbish. If I could, I'd escort you out the front door. I mean that."

"Thanks, Darren. You've been good to me. Tell Margie hi for me. Oh, do you think you can tell the next guy about the extra hard rolls, yeah?"

"Sure will. Consider it done. It's been nice talking with you, Mick. I'll be sure to keep up on those Gaelic sports."

"You better. If I make it out of here, you might see my name in a hurley match score. And I'll be following Arsenal. Go Gunners!"

* * * * *

At around the same time the next day an anonymous guard unlocked my door. He wasn't carrying any food. "You have visitors," he announced.

In walked a beaming Gerard Guerintaux.

I popped off the cot. "Gerard! Japers!"

A big bear-hug followed. I didn't see the other visitor enter the cell for a good many seconds.

"Mick," Gerard said, "let me introduce to you Winston Churchill, the Minister of Munitions for His Majesty's Government."

"Hi ya Mr. Churchill," I greeted, extending my hand. "Back in the government, yeah?"

"Hello to you, Mr. Gallagher. Lloyd George saw fit to correct Asquith's mistake of sacking me over the Dardanelles." Churchill removed his black top hat, revealing a balding head over a fleshy, almost baby-like face. He handed his fashionable walking stick to the guard. "How have you been fairing?"

"Oh, I'm . . . fairing. Three weeks in here now. Would you like a tour of my room?"

Churchill lit a broad, genuine smile. "No, that won't be necessary. I did a self-guided tour while you and Gerard embraced. - Do mind if we have a chat?"

"Not at all. Haven't had much chatting of late. It's been a ghost gaol around here. Now I hear that the war is over."

"It's over," the minister said, taking a seat at the table. Gerard sat on the edge of the cot, as did I. "Hostilities have ceased. The armistice went into effect yesterday on the eleventh day of the eleventh month at the eleventh hour."

"Catchy."

"The agreement was signed earlier at five in the morning stipulating that the guns would fall silent six hours later. Sadly, and most regrettably, the killing went on until the very last minute."

"So daft, just like the entire war," I commented.

"I agree with your statement in many ways," Churchill said. "You've played a uniquely enigmatic part in this dubious war to say the least. Your brave escapades have made front-page news for a year. Since you first appeared on the scene, there has been a tidal wave of divisive debate about you."

"Yeah, fighting you guys with the Germans will do that."

"Indeed it did. You certainly fought well, young man. Extremely well, I should say. Your rescue of Captain Palmer in an extraordinary story. You have a strong, honor-bound sense of justice, on the battlefield and off. - I'm a long time soldier myself and have a profound degree of admiration for brave men, friend or foe, fighting for what they believe in."

"I believe that my country should be free from you. Eight-hundred years of subjugation is enough."

Churchill sat up straight. "The matter of Ireland is a highly volatile one. The Rising in '16 was most incendiary. Similar to how I felt about the Boer War, I am sympathetic to arguments on both sides of the Irish debate, and it's a major reason for my visit here today."

I looked at Gerard. "Those telephone calls must have worked."

Gerard smiled but didn't say anything.

"Gerard did play a catalytic role," Winston Churchill confirmed. "He accelerated the process to bring your recent situation to my direct attention. His efforts may have saved you a week or more having to stay here."

"Sorry, I don't follow. What do you mean by that? I'm moving to some other place?"

"You will be soon, any time from this point forward in fact. You will be moving to wherever you want."

My heart began to pound. "Huh? - You mean I'm getting out of here?"

Churchill nodded. "My government is offering you a full, unconditional pardon for your activities in the war. This pardon comes directly from the prime minister. I have a copy of it with me if you would like to see it."

"Holy schmykees!" With my jaw agape, I stared at Gerard for a few seconds. "A full pardon?"

Churchill pulled out a folded piece of paper from his suit breast pocket. "It's right here. You're a free man, Mr. Gallagher. It did take some persuasion from me to convince Lloyd George to drop his one condition. In return for the pardon, the prime minister wanted you to sign a pledged agreement that you would never again take up arms against the United Kingdom." Churchill paused, studying my face. "Yes, your contemptuous expression is what I expected. I told the prime minister you would never sign such a pledge."

"You're right about that. I'd never sign it. I couldn't."

"If I was in your shoes, carrying your intense passions for your homeland, I wouldn't either - nor would any true patriot."

"So there's nothing required of me to get out of here?"

"No," Churchill said. "But if England and Germany ever go to war again - and I believe there is a significant chance of that within a generation - if not sooner - I hope we will not find you in their armed forces fighting against us."

"Doing that in one war was enough, thank you," I said. "But you could very well see me in an Irish military uniform in the not so distant future."

"You have the right to do so. I cannot keep you from doing that. But could I by chance interest you in a job with the RAF?" Winston Churchill chuckled at his own joke. "You are dandy fighter pilot."

"If Ireland was free and independent, and I had nothing better to do - and if England was at war to protect freedom - then maybe I would."

Churchill seemed pleased with my answer. "The Red Baron's Flying Circus was a fascinating outfit. Richthofen intrigued me. I would love to hear more about your experiences with the squadron."

"I've got plenty of stories for ya."

"You haven't had dinner, have you?"

"No. I thought the guard here was bringing it."

"Then you must be hungry." Churchill rose from the table. "Once we are out of here, I would be honored if the two of you would accompany me to dinner at the *Hôtel de Crillon*. It's my favorite hotel and restaurant in Paris. There we can dine while conversing over our war stories. Like you Mr. Gallagher, I have many."

I nodded at Gerard.

"We gladly accept your invitation," Gerard said.

"This prison garb won't cut it for the *de Crillon*," I said. "Neither will my flight outfit."

"Spare yourself the worry," Churchill replied. "My assistant will take care of the matter."

* * * * *

Five minutes later two guards escorted the three of us to a counter window where I was handed a large canvas bag containing my personals. The unloaded Webley Bulldog revolver was in there buried under the flight suit; its bullets were inside a small box.

"Proper attire will be there for you at the *de Crillon*," Churchill announced. "My assistant has already telephoned the hotel and given them your general measurements. The clothes should fit you most adequately."

Once outside we climbed into Churchill's roomy Vauxhall D-Type and headed for Paris.

Good-bye Gaol.

Good-bye Great War.

* * * * *

Constructed in 1758 during the reign of Louis XV, the *Hôtel de Crillon* was, and still is, located in the heart of Paris at the *Palace de la Concorde*.

"This is quite the place," I said as we were being seated. "What's happened has me shaking my head. Talk about two extremes. I go from prison an hour ago to this."

"It's like when I went from the mud of the Somme trenches to a bed with silk sheets," Churchill said, holding an unlit cigar. "I hope you enjoy the meal. The *de Crillon* is all about atmosphere - the golden opulence, crystal chandeliers, mirrors everywhere, the great service. I could dine here every day for the rest of my life and never grow tired of it."

As you surely know, Sir Winston Leonard Spencer Churchill is one of the most famous people in history, the man who saved Western Civilization from Adolf Hitler and the Axis Powers. In 1918, at the age of 44, he was already a prominent world figure. For years I hadn't liked the guy and much what he stood for. But on this evening my feelings about him changed (though not *all* of my feelings; some of his politics still rubbed me the wrong way). The gregarious man was a brilliant conversationalist, incredibly knowledgeable on a diverse array of subjects. His quick wit could rival that of Oscar Wilde's; his laughter was infectious. There was a showy arrogance about him that, though off-putting for some, I found amusing. In short, Winston Churchill and I hit it off. Within fifteen minutes we were bantering on like old friends, trading stories back and forth, cracking off-colored jokes left and right.

I mention the above because Winston Churchill would go on to be a key figure in my life for the next forty years.

A Brief Introduction To The Next Chapter

The next phase of my life was about to begin. The Great War was over. Michelle Guerintaux was gone. I would be 17 in a few days, with access to enough money to last me a dozen lifetimes. With my best friend Paul Coburn, I'd already dabbled in some traveling adventure. I could do that for the rest of my life. I could also play golf every day and try and qualify for the Open Championship in 1919. But was traveling around the world like Philias Fogg and spending ten hours a day on the golf course what I wanted to do *right now*? A few months back I'd thought so; in fact, I was hell-bent on the idea of changing my 'universe'.

Now I felt differently.

Oh I was still going to bring change to my life. I had to! But the best, and most necessary, way to do that was by helping Ireland change.

And this time I would help *directly*.

I would go back and live in my hometown of Dublin.
I would join the Irish Republican Brotherhood, be active in nationalist politics, and continue my schooling.

Golf? I'd play when I could, maybe even some rugby and hurling, too.

It is in Dublin, dear reader, where my life would be centered for the next four and a half years. There I would meet the man who would become not only a great friend but also my commander, teacher, and hero; a man who would lead the Irish Republic through a new kind of war; a man who would become the most wanted outlaw in the British Empire with 10,000 pounds on his head, who could pedal around the streets of Dublin on his bicycle in broad daylight, smiling and waving at his pursuers, untouchable to all of them.

The man who kicked the British out.

The man who won the war.

The man who brought freedom to Ireland.

His name was Michael Collins.

END OF BOOK